THE DEAD MAN
Volume 3

LEE GOLDBERG & WILLIAM RABKIN

THE DEAD MAN VOLUME 3:

James Daniels, Jude Hardin & Bill Crider

THE BEAST WITHIN

FIRE AND ICE

CARNIVAL OF DEATH

Cover Design by Jeroen Ten Berge

Published by 47North
P.O. Box 400818
Las Vegas, NV 89140

ISBN-13: 9781612183794
ISBN-10: 1612183794

TABLE OF CONTENTS

THE DEAD MAN:
THE BEAST WITHIN

By James Daniels

CHAPTER ONE

"Sorry, ma'am—we don't take checks."

"You don't, ah, take...?" The young woman looked up, worried, pen poised in her hand.

"No." The smirking clerk behind the grocery store counter jabbed her fat finger at a scrap of paper taped to her cash register. "See the sign? Right there. *No Checks.* Plain English."

Matt Cahill, standing in the back of the checkout line, frowned. The clerk's comment was out of line. First of all, the handwritten sign (which actually said *No Check's*) was practically buried under a blizzard of Post-its, memos, notices, and fliers. Second, a good ol' boy with oiled hair and a bolo tie had been allowed to pay by check only moments before. But most of all, the "plain English" comment seemed intended to embarrass the young woman with the caramel-colored skin and soft foreign accent.

"So no check...," she said nervously, patting the checkbook. "But I hev, ah, no credit card?"

The cashier folded her arms over her chest. "Guess you'll just have to pay with cash, then."

"Kesh. Yah." Her accent seemed almost Russian. Matt couldn't place it. He watched with interest as the woman took out a wallet and began pulling out crumpled bills, which she flattened and set on the stack of coupons already in front of her. "Here is...some kesh? But I don't think..." Desperately, she snapped open her wallet's change pocket and poured out some quarters and dimes, which she set on top of the cash. It wasn't nearly enough.

"Looks like you better put some a' that stuff back where you got it, huh?" the clerk said with satisfaction.

"But I..." She threw a panicky look at the pile of milk, eggs, fruit, and baby formula that had gathered at the end of the counter. Bit her lip. Hesitated, then reluctantly picked up a bag of apples.

"No need," Matt said, and laid down a fifty-dollar bill.

The young woman stared at it in surprise, then looked up at him. She shook her head vigorously. "No, I kennot accept..."

"Sure you can." Matt touched her elbow. "It's OK." Actually, the fifty was supposed to last him 'til the following week—but what the hell?

Something in his voice must have reassured her. Her voice softened. "You are sure?" she asked.

Looking at her, Matt realized for the first time that she had large moss-green eyes flecked with amber. They were so rich and warm that he began to feel tongue-tied. She looked, he decided, like the wide-eyed Afghan war refugee who had graced the cover of a famous *National Geographic* when he was a kid. He'd cut that photo out, kept it on his bedroom wall for years—mesmerized by her wide-eyed beauty. "Yeah, really," he said, finding his voice, "it's fine."

The woman sucked her full lips in, thought about it for a moment, then gave a short, grateful nod. "I will beckpay you?" she asked under her breath.

Matt smiled. "If you like."

"Yah. I thenk you so much, ah..."

"Matt."

"Matthew." She swallowed, did a quick calculation. Said quietly, "You are not from here, Matthew."

"No."

"You will give me your address, then? Matthew?" The effect of her green eyes, and the way she repeated his name, made Matt's blood rise.

"Sure. I've got a card. It's outside, with my bike."

"I will wait for you outside, then, Matthew. And so you know?" She touched his wrist lightly. "My name? Is Roma."

Quickly, she picked up her bags and walked out the door. Her every move was lithe, graceful. Catlike.

Feeling a telltale prickle at the base of his neck, he turned to see the cashier glaring at him.

"Do you have a purchase, sir?" she demanded.

Matt looked down at his red plastic basket, which was filled with hamburger meat, frozen pizzas, and a dozen other items that were supposed to get him through the week. Then he looked at the four bucks he'd gotten back in change.

Not gonna happen.

He took out of the basket a single can of Hormel chili and a twenty-four-ounce Bud Light. "That'll do it for today," he said, and watched her turn as red as a chameleon. He laid down the cash, bagged the beer, and picked up the can of chili.

"You know," the clerk said, jabbing her finger at another handwritten Post-it, "we've got a policy about leaving unpurchased items at the register."

"Well, make an exception for me," Matt said. "Just like you made an exception to your check-writing policy for that old fart with the bolo."

The cashier's jaw dropped. "That was *Judge* Thompson, for your information. He's lived in this town for fifty years!"

"And he *still* can't read?"

The cashier slapped her big hands on the counter and had just begun educating Matt when she was cut off by a loud shriek.

Matt shoved through the glass door. There, in front of him, the girl with the accent was sprawled on the pavement. She gave an agonized cry. Her groceries were spilled everywhere. Her right ankle was twisted upward, and Matt saw that it was entwined by one end of a thin chain about nine feet long.

The other end of the chain was in the fist of a goateed young guy in camouflage army fatigues and jacket. He wore a black knit cap embroidered with a Confederate flag, and he was grinning wildly.

"Lookit here, boys, I just caught me a raghead trout!"

Approving laughter from his three friends. Matt took them in at a glance: All three were dressed in camo as well—not the crisp fatigues of the newly enlisted, but the worn-out army surplus gear that was the preferred uniform of deer hunters in small Michigan towns like the one Matt was in. The biggest guy was bald, wore white-and-black winter camo, sunglasses, and a dark neoprene face mask. He sat watching from behind the wheel of a big black ATV.

The other two were skinny, with patchy red beards, and had a yellowish smoker's tinge to their skin. They looked like twins. They were both playing kick the can with a container of green beans that had fallen from the woman's bags.

"Reel her in, Keith!" one shouted.

"I'm tryin'," the Goatee said, laughing, giving the chain a tug, "but she's a fighter! Must weigh a hundred twenty at the—"

The rest of his sentence was lost when a can of Hormel chili, going about seventy miles an hour, hit him square in the mouth. Keith let out a muffled grunt, dropped the chain, and fell back onto his butt.

"What the fuck...?"

"Look what that bastard done to Keith!"

Matt wasn't listening. He was at the woman's side, helping her up. She was terrified, gasping in pain. When he lifted her, he saw that her palms were bloodied from her fall.

"Got to get you to a hospital," he said.

Her green eyes were huge with fear. She yelled something in a language he didn't understand, then, pulling away, cried out, "Behind—behind you!"

Matt spun just in time to see something metal flashing at his face. He raised an arm defensively and a steel ball bearing the size of a golf ball whipped around his wrist, trailing a thin chain that led to the hand of one of the red-bearded twins.

What the hell?

A split second later, he was yanked off balance by the twin, who was a lot stronger than he looked.

A fierce humming sound—Matt twisted his head to see the second twin slinging a similar chain in a glinting wheel above his head. He released it—there was a flash of steel and a metallic whisper as the links shot forward like a striking snake—and Matt felt the ball bearing slam into his thigh with the force of a hammer.

Matt stumbled, and the first twin gave the chain on his wrist a sharp jerk, slinging him to the ground, where he rolled once and came to rest at the wheel of a motorcycle.

Which was lucky. The motorcycle was Matt's: an old Yamaha bought with money he'd earned from chopping eight cords of wood. Attached to its seat were two saddle-bags and a three-foot-long object wrapped in bound canvas. In a single movement, Matt unbuckled a leather strap and pulled the canvas package off the bike.

And not a moment too soon. The first twin immediately started dragging Matt away from the bike, while the second, giving a rebel yell, spun and flung his humming chain a second time.

A second before the ball bearing would have punched a hole in his skull, Matt raised the long canvas package up, gripping the wooden handle that extended a few inches from one end. The chain wrapped around the object with an insectile whine, and when the second twin gave it a jerk, the chain slithered free, ripping the canvas wrapping off.

Revealing an ax.

The ax was beautiful: Its head was more than seventy years old, had been forged by Matt's grandfather from the iron of a meteorite that had ripped through his barn one Christmas Eve. The handle was a perfectly balanced slant of blond oak that Matt had cut himself. The head and handle fit together in a lucky-number-seven shape that fit his grip perfectly. It was his livelihood, his one heirloom, and the only work of art he would ever own.

And it came in handy in situations like this.

In a heartbeat, Matt slapped his bound wrist to the ground and swung the ax with his free hand. The blade chopped effortlessly through the thin chain and bit deeply into the macadam. Matt stood. When the second twin slung his chain again, a strange calmness came over Matt, and it seemed to him he could see the ball bearing snaking toward him in slow motion.

He swung the ax like it was a Louisville Slugger. His aim was true: the ax head sliced the bearing off, and the thin chain rattled harmlessly past.

Painfully—his leg hurt like hell—Matt limped toward his two assailants, holding the ax. "All right," he panted, "can we end this? Or do you two bastards still want to dance?"

The yellow-skinned twins backed away from him, their eyes wide with hate and fear. "Keith," they yelled. "Keith!"

Matt had no idea why they'd called out their goat-eed friend's name until he heard a *whunk* to his right. He glanced over and saw a perfectly round, inch-wide hole that had been punched into an El Dorado's silver door. He turned back toward the grocery store and saw why.

Keith was standing behind the retreating twins, grinning. His lip was split from the Hormel can, and his teeth and chin were slick with blood. In his hands, he held a slingshot. It wasn't a wooden, whittled, Tom Sawyer sort of slingshot, either, but a deadly tactical deal with a grooved pistol grip and fluorescent yellow, tubular latex bands. These bands were, at that moment, being stretched back by Keith's right hand, which clasped the next ball bearing within a leather release pouch.

Matt's gut clenched. He held up a hand. "Don't," he said.

"Kiss off, bitch." Keith pulled the leather pouch all the way back to his squinting right eye and released.

But not before Roma—with a loud shout—had thrown herself against his shoulder.

There was a wet crunch, and the twin to Matt's left jerked forward and spat out all his teeth. He stared down at them in confusion and dropped to his knees, as if to pick them up. He swayed there for a second, then flopped face forward onto the street—revealing a bloody hole at the base of his skull.

Everything started happening at once.

The still-standing twin shrieked out his brother's name and ran to him. The big bald guy in the winter camo and sunglasses gunned the ATV. It lurched forward and swung right up next to Keith and the remaining twin. Baldy ripped down his neoprene face mask and shouted, *"Load him up now, load him the fuck up."* The two followed his instructions, screaming that they were *"gonna revenge us on that motherfucker."*

In the meantime, Roma ran across the street to where Matt stood frozen in his tracks and grabbed his hand. "We have to go!" she cried.

Matt's head was spinning. "I think…I think we need to wait for the police…fill out a report or—"

"No! We have to go *now.*"

Matt was about to argue about the legality of leaving the scene when he caught a better look at Baldy. He was still wearing the sunglasses, but now that he had ripped down his face mask—and turned his way—Matt could see that his white skin was laced with hundreds of inflamed red veins that pulsed across his face like the interlocking grooves of a jigsaw puzzle.

Matt knew what that meant: *time to get gone.*

"C'mon," he said, and pulled her back to the Yamaha. He quickly strapped the ax to the back, got on, keyed in, and gunned it.

"Climb on," he said.

She hesitated, looked back over her shoulder at the huge black ATV. Matt noticed for the first time that it had an armored grill studded on top with a row of steel spikes the size and shape of rhino horns. Its tires were massive, with a three-inch-deep slanting tread. Painted over its grill were evil-looking slit eyes above jagged fangs. And below that, in red letters, was the word RAHOWA.

What the hell did that *mean?*

He didn't have time to figure it out. Everyone had climbed into the ATV, and Baldy twisted the wheel and hit the gas. It shot forward—straight for Matt and Roma.

Roma didn't hesitate. She leapt onto the Yamaha's backseat and wrapped her arms around Matt's chest. As she did, he wrenched the handlebar to the right and slewed onto the sidewalk. He let the throttle out, pealing forward in a cloud of scorched rubber just as the ATV rammed into the rusty Buick Century he'd put between them. It hit the Buick so hard that it knocked the front half up onto the sidewalk, crashing into the storefront where Matt and Roma had been only a moment before. The store's display window shattered into long blades of glass and clashed to the pavement.

Matt roared down the sidewalk, heading for the intersection. As he approached it, he heard a screeching sound behind him and glanced back. Baldy had wrenched the ATV in reverse, to little effect. Matt saw that the stainless steel spikes lining its hood had gouged deeply into the Buick's frame, and when the ATV tried to pull back out onto the street, it had pulled the Buick with it. Baldy, Keith, and the upright twin were all screaming and trying to pry the vehicles apart.

Good luck with that, Matt thought, seeing how deeply the spikes were embedded. And then, with a chill that prickled the hairs on his neck, *That could have been us.*

At the intersection, he took a right and pulled away from the fray. Thought of something. Turning back to Roma, he asked, "Where exactly are we going?"

"My home, please."

"Sure. And where's that?"

"It has no address. But if you listen? I will take you there."

He nodded, let the throttle out. Her arms tightened around his chest, and they were off.

CHAPTER TWO

Matt followed Roma's directions, and together, they sped through the small town. It didn't take long. The town of Wittman had a population of only four thousand.

Matt had arrived that morning, looked around a bit. Every other storefront in the downtown was closed. The ones that were open consisted of the Jewelry Loan, the VCR Repair Shop, the Pro-Life Bookstore, a grocery/gas station, an antique store that specialized in bladeless pocketknives and Ku Klux Klan memorabilia, and a dingy diner called the Cosmopolitan. There were also, directly across from each other, a liquor store that sold guns and a gun store that sold liquor. The town's main function, Matt guessed, was to ensure that every fall hunter and winter snowmobiler was fully equipped with ammo, antifreeze, a Bible, a bottle, a Hot Pocket, and a Glock.

Halfway out of town, Matt asked Roma over the Yamaha's roar who the thugs had been and why they'd attacked her. But she didn't respond.

Matt let it go—for now. Christ, she'd basically killed one of them, saving Matt's life in the process. He thought back to the red-bearded twin's look of bewilderment as he saw his ivories take flight. Thought of the brother's rage and Keith's *Kiss off, bitch*. These were not people who would forgive and forget. Once he returned Roma to her home, he was going to have to get out of the county by nightfall. Especially considering what he'd seen in the face of the big guy, Baldy.

The irregular grid of red veins pulsing across the thug's face had put Matt on high alert, but it hadn't horrified him. He was too used to it by now. In fact, he'd been seeing such sights regularly for the past nine months.

Almost a year before, while skiing with a friend, Matt had been buried in an avalanche. He was given up for dead, but his body was eventually recovered three months later— frozen solid beneath a bank of snow. It wasn't until the coroner made the first cut for his autopsy that the truth came to light: *Matt was alive.*

He had survived a three-month deep freeze!

Matt's doctors couldn't explain his complete recovery, although they tried, as did psychics, celebrities, scientists, and talk show hosts. For a few news cycles, Matt was the man of the hour: He'd turned down endless invitations for interviews, special appearances, guest slots on late-night talk shows. He'd even had *Ripley's Believe It or Not!* banging on his door.

And yet, not one of the millions who read the newspapers or watched the reports on TV knew the strangest fact about Matt's miraculous resurrection. Once he was out of the hospital, he began to see things that no one else did: Certain people seemed to be afflicted with rot, decay, disease, and disintegration. People who looked perfectly healthy to everyone else looked like lepers to Matt. And worst of all, the rot he saw (and smelled) proved time and again to be only a harbinger of evil things to come. Every decomposing person he had seen had gone on to commit some act of destruction: mass murder, mindless mayhem, arson, robbery, rape.

After his season on ice, Matt had received forewarning of all kinds of human carnage—often in connection with a shadowy jokester who identified himself only as Mr. Dark. Half the time, Matt suspected that he'd been given a second chance at life to discover and prevent evil disasters from destroying innocent lives.

The other half, Matt suspected that he was just bat-shit crazy.

Which theory was right? Only time would tell. But until it did, Matt had learned to steer clear of infected souls when he had the chance—and fight like hell when he didn't.

But in this case, retreat seemed the best possible option, and he had no trouble committing to it. Especially with the strange young woman sitting behind him, her thighs pressing against his, her arms locked around his chest, her chin resting on his shoulder.

Left, here, she told him. *Now right. And right again. Now we drive for long time.*

He liked the sound of her voice in his ear, the low, mysterious accent purring instructions over the throb of the Yamaha's cylinders. Following her directions, they left the outskirts of Wittman behind and passed a scattering of seed stores, shuttered farmers' markets, and dilapidated antique "shoppes." The low cloud cover made evening come early, and a misty rain began to fall. Matt slowed down a little, concerned about the roads.

Roma might have been concerned too, because she edged closer, put her chin against the back of his jaw, and for the first time in ten minutes, spoke to him.

"I am sorry for this…this trouble I have caused to you."

He shook his head. "You saved my life back there, Roma."

"Yah, after you save mine."

For a few moments there was only the thrum of the motor and the hiss of rubber on wet blacktop. The mist slid down Matt's neck and pooled in the hollows of his throat.

"Can I ask, Matthew, why you come to this place?"

"To meet someone."

A slight pause. Her chin settled on his shoulder. Then: "A friend?"

"No. I've never met him. But I read a book he wrote."

"Aha. And he knew you were coming?"

"No."

"You live near here? From nearby?"

"No. My home's on the West Coast."

"Ah. West Coast." Thought about that. "So you..."

"Traveled three thousand miles to meet him."

"I see." Even though she didn't. "It must have been a good book he wrote, this man."

Not quite, Matt thought. But he didn't say it. The book had been, hands down, the worst piece of shit he'd ever read.

"You should leave tonight, Matthew. For you to stay here? It would not be safe."

"I know." If her lips brushed his earlobe one more time, he was probably going to drive off the road. He had to do something, anything, to get his mind off her. "About those guys who attacked us—" he began.

"Go left here," she said immediately.

Matt slowed. The two-lane road through the woods was intersected by a gravel path that wound up a steep hill. An old wooden sign by the side of the road indicated that the path led to the WITTMAN SKI RESORT, but the paint was peeling and the words were badly faded. Nailed to the signpost, a much newer, diamond-shaped, hazard-red sign had been posted:

PRIVATE PROPERTY
KEEP OFF
TRESPASSERS WILL BE SHOT
By order of Owner,
Charles Kingman

Matt came to a stop, staring at the sign.

"It is all right, Matthew. You can go. This is my home."

"Charles Kingman," Matt said, staring at the sign as the engine idled. "You know him?"

"Of course."

"How?"

She leaned forward, trying to catch his gaze with her green eyes. "We are married, Charles and myself. For the last six months. Why?"

He finally turned toward her. Gave her a long look. "The author I mentioned? The one I came all this way to meet?"

"Yah?"

"Is your husband."

CHAPTER THREE

The narrow gravel road was about a quarter of a mile long, and they had to stop a few hundred yards in. Roma had patted him sharply on the back and told him to pull over. When he did, she slipped off the bike and walked cautiously forward, her hands outstretched before her like a sleepwalker. Suddenly, she stopped and rested her hands on something invisible, midair. She walked sideways to the nearest tree and unhooked whatever it was with a great deal of effort. Then there was a whisper in the leaves that lay scattered on the road, and she waved him through. He walked the bike forward, looking down. As he passed her, he caught sight of a thin black wire lying on the ground, extending to a second tree on the opposite side. Then she lifted it behind him and reattached it to the first tree. It hung invisibly in the air, exactly neck height.

A trip wire.

If she hadn't stopped him in time, it would have easily taken his head off.

Jesus.

A few seconds later, she came back to the bike.

"Is OK now."

"Why do you keep a line strung over the path like that?"

She slung a long leg over the leather seat behind him, scooted forward until the insides of her thighs pressed against his buttocks. Locked her arms around his chest.

"Is not much farther."

Ignoring his question.

He let the throttle out. They eased carefully over a bridge that spanned a creek, the old boards *whump-whump-whumping* beneath the wheels. "I bet it's been *ages* since someone tried to sell you Amway," he said.

"Am...way?"

"You know, like door-to-door salesmen, selling... Actually, I have no idea what Amway is." If the joke could have fallen flatter, he didn't know how. "I just mean, the sign, the trip wire, the long driveway...It probably cuts down on your visitors, right?"

"We don't, ah, get out so much."

"Homebodies, huh? You and Charles?" Glanced back at her. If he were married to this woman, he wouldn't get out much, either.

"Y...yes." A strange hesitation. "Charles and myself." Carelessly: "And the rest."

The rest? He was curious. "You two have kids?" Curious because he'd seen the photo of Charles Kingman on the dustcover to his book. And the idea of *that* man with this beauty...

"Kids? No." She pressed her cheek into his shoulder. "Go on, Matthew. Is not far now."

The woods thinned as they followed the path. They rounded a corner, and all of a sudden, Matt could see the east face of the big hill and how the trees had been cleared away to make two decent ski runs. At the top of the hill he could see what looked to be an old-style lodge, and an honest-to-God ski lift went from it to the bottom of the hill, where it led to three ramshackle buildings that looked like places where you could get skis, rent lockers, and maybe buy lunch. It looked like a nice little setup.

Three things struck Matt as odd, though. The first was that, up at the top of the hill, a ten-foot chain-link fence had been erected to surround the lodge. It cut right across the top face of the ski runs, making them pretty much unusable.

Second, even though there was no snow on the ground and the ski runs were wrecked by the fence, the parking lot they now were passing was full of old beat-up pickups, and there were dozens of tents erected around the ramshackle buildings at the base of the hill. Matt saw a few dozen men, all in camo, many of them carrying branches toward a big bonfire woodpile. All of them stopped to stare as Matt drove past.

The third thing was that, as they passed the men and the bonfire pile, Roma leaned into him again, pressed her cheek against his jaw, and said, "Drive faster, please."

So he did.

"Problem?" he asked. But again, she didn't answer, which didn't surprise him a bit by now. As the path wove back into the woods, he glimpsed at his rearview mirror and saw one of the men drop his load of wood and point in their direction. Then the pines swallowed them up, and he was gone.

A few minutes of steep zigzagging and they reached the fence. Matt pulled up in front of it and stared at in surprise. It had looked kind of thrown together from the bottom of the hill, but up close, he could see that it was actually a double fence, both of them chain link, fifteen feet tall, with barbed wire at the top. There was about five feet of space between the two fences, and it was filled with three large coils of razor ribbon. A red triangular sign on the fence said HIGH VOLTAGE HAZARD and had a pictogram of a stick figure being blown backward by a lightning bolt.

"Wait here, Matthew."

The center of the fence had a sliding entry gate, also of chain link. Next to it was a touch pad and speaker that emitted a red light that blinked at steady intervals. Roma approached it and tapped its keypad. There was a pause, and then the gate slid sideways with a grinding sound.

Roma stepped in and waved him onward.

Again, Matt walked the bike forward, looking around as he did.

On either side of the gate were twin towers of scaffolding, topped with camouflaged deer blinds. The deer blinds were covered with branches and brush. As he looked at the one to his left, he saw a large hunk of brushy debris separate itself from the rest and lean over to watch him pass. It appeared to have two brushy arms. Which appeared to be holding a brushy AK-47.

Matt let his gaze drop from the guy in the gillie suit and glanced ahead. The entire property—about two acres—was ringed with the electric double fence, and every thirty feet or so a large halogen lamp crowned a fifteen-foot fence post. Strangely, all the halogen lights were facing outward. And each of them was accompanied by a thin black box that also faced outward.

Surveillance cameras.

The property itself was filled with a mishmash of tin sheds and construction materials. Everywhere you looked there were pallets of bricks, bundles of tin sheets, troughs of plaster, buckets of screws, and great stacked rafts of ply-wood and particleboard.

And then there was the lodge.

Clearly, it had once been nice. Built in a seventies retro style, it had a steep, peaked roof and a large second-story wooden deck where skiers could sip hot chocolate and take in a view of the slopes. On the left side of the deck was an angular turret with a peaked roof, and on the right the ski lift was anchored to a large concrete base that snugged right up against the deck. Below the deck was the first-floor entrance, which was flanked by stone pillars and dark wooden beams to give the place an alpine accent. It looked like it had once been a fun place to spend a snowy Saturday afternoon.

But those days were long gone.

The front entrance was now screened by hanging plas-tic camo curtains. The second-floor deck's guardrail had been buttressed by large interlocking sheets of tin, with slits cut into them just wide enough to allow for a sight line—or the muzzle of an AK-47. The windows were likewise covered with tin sheets. The turret bristled with outward-facing flood lamps, a red-blinking security box, and two satellite dishes. The peaked roof of the turret had been cut away and replaced with a circular row of six-foot-high white PVC piping, over which hung a thick canopy of camo netting. A shadow moved within it—there seemed to be someone up there.

Squinting to get a better look, one of Matt's eyes was momentarily blinded in a red flash. It was gone as soon as it had arrived. Matt put a hand to his eye, and when he drew it away, just for a second, he saw the crimson dot of a laser sight play along his thumb. Then it slid off into nothingness and was gone.

Matt's jaw locked as he looked around at the compound. Anyone else would be amazed at what had been done to such a good piece of property. But not Matt. He had read Charles Kingman's god-awful book. So he was not surprised in the least.

"Nice little place," Matt said, getting off the bike.

Roma gave him a lopsided smile. "But too much, ah, construction, yes? Please, Matthew, follow me. My husband and brothers, they will be so pleased to meet you."

Matt followed her up on the porch. It creaked, sagging beneath his step. "Did you say 'brothers'?" he asked, looking around. The camo netting darkened the front entryway, but Matt could see that the original wooden door had been replaced by a steel double-wide portal. Tin sheets had been hammered into the wall around it, as if to make the entryway fireproof. A small intercom box was screwed into one of them.

"Two brothers, yes," she said, pushing the intercom button. "Half brothers, really. Jasha and Arkady. They are visiting from Russia."

"Can't wait to meet them."

"So don't wait, Matthew." Again, the mysterious smile, the gold-flecked eyes that glinted even in the darkness. "See, to your right? This is Jasha."

Matt turned his head and was startled to see a huge guy about eighteen inches away from his elbow. How had he missed him?

Jasha was enormous. His arms were the size of Matt's thighs. His thighs were the size of Matt's torso. His head wasn't that much smaller than a basketball and was crowned with a perfectly round bowl cut that hung in front of his eyes. He was sitting on a two-foot section of a tree trunk, slowly dismantling an Uzi.

He didn't look up at them.

"Jasha, my big teddy bear." Roma stepped lightly over to him and gave him a kiss on the cheek. She didn't even have to bend down to do it. He leaned into the kiss but kept his eyes on his work.

Then Roma whispered something in his big ear in a language Matt didn't understand.

Jasha paused momentarily and then began reassembling the Uzi.

"Nice to meet you," Matt said. "I'm Matt."

No response. Jasha's eyes never flicked up from beneath the shaggy-dog bowl cut, and his banana-sized fingers never stopped their business of deftly rotating screws the size of cloves.

Roma walked back to the door.

"Jasha does not, ah, talk English so well? And is very shy. But such a *big* heart. But my brother Arkady, he speak English very well now. So well is hard to understand him sometimes."

That made no sense to Matt. "Why would it be hard—"

"You will see." And she reached for the handle of the steel door.

Before she could turn the latch, it rotated on its own and the door slid open.

The hallway beyond was dim, but Matt took in the figure beyond in an instant.

White face.

Black lips.

Big nose.

Evil clown eyes.

Mr. Dark.

CHAPTER FOUR

Matt lunged at the deranged clown in the doorway. Throwing himself in front of Roma, he grabbed the apparition by the collar of its surprisingly solid T-shirt and slammed him against the steel door.

"Matthew, no!" Roma shrieked from behind him.

"Roma—run!" Matt pulled the squawking figure off the door and slammed him right back. "He's dangerous! Get back!"

"Matthew, is not dangerous—is my brother Arkady!"

Matt paused, and then three things happened that convinced him to let go. First, he noticed that, aside from the clown makeup, the guy he'd grabbed was a lot shorter and pudgier—not to mention more solid—than past apparitions of Mr. Dark. Second, the black-and-white clown makeup was smearing where Matt's knuckles had grazed his chin and lip. Third, with no warning whatsoever, Jasha had silently crossed the porch, driven his shoulder into Matt's rib cage, and crushed him against the wall.

Pinned, Matt gasped for breath like a beached whale.

"Matthew..." Over Jasha's shoulder, Roma looked at him in amazement. "Why...?"

Sucking air, Matt looked from her face to Jasha's, to the outraged figure in the doorway. He swallowed. "Sorry," he said. No way to explain what he'd just done—so he said the first thing that popped into his head. "*So* sorry. I…I've just got this *thing* about clowns."

"Well, is that not being the shizit?" the guy in whiteface said in a thick Russian accent. He stepped out of the doorway toward Matt, glaring at him.

Matt squinted. "What?"

"Player-hating fool come to flex on myself?" The guy took a wide stance. His hands flew into gang signs. "Clown Loco G give as good as he get, yes? Be looking close, bitch." He hoisted his crotch. "I am a world-class melon smuggla, titty juggla, and not hesitating to bust a cap in your ass, *whoop whoop*."

Matt stared at him. Then at Roma.

"My brother Arkady," she said, rolling her eyes, "is bigtime juggalo. You know, fan of ICP? The musical band—"

"Insane Clown Posse," Matt finished. "Yeah. I know about 'em." Thinking, *Jesus Christ, what next?*

As it turned out, what was next was a brief tour of the lodge. Roma told Matt that her husband was always in his study before dinner and that she'd introduce him. So Matt followed as she led him through the entryway, past what would have originally been a visiting area with a large fireplace, then up a large staircase and down a hallway to the turreted study.

Everywhere he looked, Matt felt the carpenter in him cringe. The crown molding that had lined the entryway had been ripped off so that thick twists of electrical cord and cable could be stapled into the walls. They roped through the visiting area and wove between the maple banisters of the stairway like black snakes. The visiting area had been converted from a cozy common room to a makeshift armory. A display cabinet with mullioned windows was loaded with boxes of ammo. A row of tenpenny nails had been pounded into one wall, and from each one hung a semiautomatic rifle. Two large wooden crates lay on the floor, overflowing with pink packing foam. On the lids, in red block letters, were the words WARNING: EXPLOSIVES: HANDLE WITH CARE. From a hat rack hung three black rubber-snouted gas masks, looking for all the world like S and M gear for pigs. Leaning in a corner were two completely illegal pump-action sawed-off shotguns. And lying in a long inset in the far wall—which had probably been built to hold a row of crystal or china—was what appeared to be a *bazooka*.

From one end of it, hanging by a nylon strap, was a Dora the Explorer car seat.

My God, Matt thought, *where am I?*

As they crossed the parlor, Matt asked Roma if he'd entered into a war zone without knowing it. She didn't turn, just smiled tightly. Of course, she may not have heard him, what with the whine of a Skilsaw coming from the kitchen, and Arkady following close on his heels, rapping the lyrics to ICP's "Santa's a Fat Bitch."

Walking up the stairs, Matt stumbled. Each step was littered with brass ammo casings, shotgun shells, pacifiers, and a squeaky rubber teething giraffe.

At the top of the steps, they turned down a hallway and were passed by two young guys with crew cuts. Both wore black cargo pants with Glocks strapped to their waists. Both had shield-shaped badges on their chests embroidered with a white fist; both had black armbands split with the insignia of a red lightning bolt.

And yet, they were still practically kids—had acne and nervous eyes. One had a fauxhawk and was attempting to grow a mustache. The other was bare armed under his bulletproof vest. Tattooed along his big triceps in two-inch letters was the word RAHOWA.

Both said hi to Roma as they approached, but when they saw Matt, their eyes widened and they grew silent.

Roma stopped at a door at the end of the hall. She rapped on it lightly.

"Yes?" came the muffled voice.

She turned to Matt shyly and whispered, "Wait here, Matthew." She stepped inside and shut the door behind her.

Matt heard low voices, but he couldn't make out what was being said. He looked back down the hall and saw that the two guys they'd passed were still watching him. Fauxhawk acknowledged him with the slightest upward tilt of his chin. The other guy had folded his tattooed guns across his chest and was openly glaring at Matt.

Have to remember to give him a low score on the hospitality survey, Matt thought. Then the door creaked open, and Roma gestured for Matt to follow her.

He did.

The turret room had clearly been intended to be an office, and it still was. Its rounded walls were lined with built-in shelves. A dark cherry wood desk was in front of the window, and a lean old man stood behind it, extending his gnarled fingers in Matt's direction.

"Young man, allow me to shake your hand. Roma told me of the service you performed today, and I am honored—honored!—to make your acquaintance. I am Charles Kingman."

"Matt Cahill."

As Matt shook Kingman's hand, he got a close-up look at the guy he'd traveled three thousand miles to meet.

He wasn't exactly impressed.

Charles Kingman looked like a de-shelled turtle. He was scrawny and bald, with a beak-like nose and thin lips. Between them was a small gray postage-stamp mustache that had gone out of style around 1939. He was about thirty years older than his beautiful wife, and a wattle of loose skin hung beneath his chin. He wore a faded corduroy jacket with suede on the elbows, which was probably supposed to make him look professorial. His eyes were gray and sharp and searching behind thin wire-rim glasses. Matt couldn't shake the sense that Kingman bore a strong resemblance to someone he'd seen recently.

The old guy was still pumping his hand. "Clearly, Mr. Cahill, I owe you more than I can ever repay! Apparently, Roma's escort abandoned her when she needed them most. If not for your timely intervention…"

"No problem," Matt said, wondering when he'd get his hand back. "I just did what anyone would have done."

"Not so, not so!" Kingman's grip was like iron for a guy his age. "True valor is a rare commodity these days, very rare! Though not surprising in your case, considering your, ah, features…" He finally released Matt's hand. But now his eyes were flicking compulsively from Matt's forehead to his ears and chin and back again.

"My—"

"Features, yes, yes, yes." He spun around, picked something off his table that looked like a medieval torture device. It consisted of a metal hoop about nine inches across. Attached to the hoop by big bolts were four connected metal bands, which crossed each other in a dome shape above the hoop. Kingman carried it around the desk, toward Matt. "Surely you won't mind if I—"

"Uh, what's that?" Matt asked, taking a step backward.

"Won't take a second." And before Matt could register what had just happened, Kingman had slipped the device over his head. The metal hoop was cool against Matt's brow. Biting his tongue in concentration, the old man turned the bolts until it was snug.

"Aha...yes, of course..." While Kingman's left hand held the caliper in place, his right stroked the top of Matt's head.

Matt pulled back immediately, freaked out by the device, the stroking. But Kingman didn't seem to notice. The old man was beaming. "All twenty-seven brain organs in fine fettle, and my caliper registers a brow-to-nose ratio of one to one-point-seven percent!"

"What a relief," Matt said, barely able to contain his irritation.

"Isn't it?" Smiling, Kingman set the device back on his desk. "I'm sure you were confident in your phrenology, but the fact is, you never know. I had a fellow worked for me for years, always claiming that he came from one hundred percent Austrian stock. I finally took his measurements, and what do you know? His brow-to-nose ratio was *one-point-eight to point-nine.* And this is someone that I had entrusted with the keys to my heavy equipment!"

"You don't say."

Kingman's wattle swayed as he shook his head in amazement. "One just never knows, until scientific principles are applied." His gray eyes flicked brightly back to Matt's. "But never fear, your measurements are well within the acceptable margins—clearly, you have nothing to worry about."

"Clearly. Thanks for the, uh"—Matt barely avoided saying *load of horseshit*—"for the analysis, Mr. Kingman. But, now, if you'll give me a few minutes of your time, I've got some questions for you. You see, I'm familiar with your work."

"Oh, really?" Kingman was clearly delighted. He gestured for Matt to sit in a worn leather chair, and he returned to his seat on the other side of the desk, giving Roma a quick look as he did. "Some tea, my dear?"

"Of course."

Matt sat, watching Roma sway out the door. She had a feline grace that was mesmerizing.

"Lovely woman, your wife," he said quietly.

"She should be. She has cost me much, yes, *much*."

Matt looked back to Kingman, confused by the strange response.

But he had moved on. "So tell me—to what do I owe the pleasure?"

"Oh, right." Matt pressed the palms of his hands together. This was going to take some explaining. "It started, I guess, when I read your book."

"Aha!" Kingman crowed, clapping his hands and settling back in his seat. "Of course! Nine hundred forty-seven copies sold since the first printing, as of January of this year! Not bad, eh?"

"Uh…no," Matt said, resisting the urge to point out that the book's cover page had showed the first printing to be in the mid-eighties. "Anyway, a month ago I came across a reference to your book. Once I found a copy and read it, there was one chapter in particular that I couldn't put down. It… it really intrigued me, you see, this one chapter, intrigued me so much that I knew a letter wouldn't do it. I knew I'd have to come out here in person and ask you to explain—"

"Stop."

He stopped. Kingman's eyes had closed, and he smilingly held up an open palm toward Matt. "Stop, stop, stop. Say no more. I know *exactly* the chapter you're talking about, and I have *no* problem whatso*ever* justifying my conclusions. It's the most controversial one in the book—'Chapter Eleven: The Jewish Conspiracy Unveiled.'"

"That's actually not—"

"True, the Rothschilds are no longer the force they were, but—"

"That's not—"

"But the very *idea* that the International Money Fund is not a cat's-paw for a global consortium of Semitic bankers…"

And he was off. Matt looked away, biting his tongue hard to keep from telling Kingman to shut the fuck up, that he was an idiot, that Matt hadn't come three thousand miles to hear him spew racist bullshit.

Not that he hadn't expected it. Kingman's book, *The Aryan's Lament,* was a crazy quilt of contradictory conspiracy theories about how various non-Aryan racial groups had orchestrated just about every war, recession, depression, assassination, and natural disaster on record. It also included a supposed history of the Aryan race, which gave serious consideration to the Nazi theory that Aryans alone were not descended from apes, but had fallen, fully formed, into ancient Norway, frozen like TV dinners in the heart of an icy meteor. And of course there had been a thick, *thick* chapter on phrenology, with lots of comparisons of brow ridges and nose/chin ratios, accompanied by many a helpful diagram.

In short, it was full of shit.

And not *new* shit, either. Growing up, Matt had been exposed to plenty of prejudices and petty hatreds. When two Vietnamese boys started attending his junior high, there had been a lot of kids who'd called them *gooks* behind their backs and said that they should get the hell beat out of them "for what they did to our guys in 'Nam."

Matt hadn't really known what to think. They *did* look different from anyone else in the school. But as for these two teens being responsible for fifty thousand American dead, the idea didn't really resonate. Not to mention that the only vet he knew personally was his buddy's uncle Dwayne, a grizzled, tobacco-spitting jackass who had lost both legs in 'Nam while trying to take a drunken crap down his own mortar tube. It was hard to see how Nguyen and Tran were responsible for *that*.

Still, Matt had been tempted to side with his friends just to fit in, and might have done so, when by total chance, his dad—to console him for failing to get tickets to the sold-out opening night of *Jurassic Park*—had spent seventy-five cents to buy him a secondhand copy of *Mack Bolan: The Executioner #38* at a newsstand.

At the time, Matt thought this was a pretty sorry consolation prize, but he'd taken it home anyway, gone to his room, flopped onto his bed, opened the front cover—and fell into a world he never knew existed.

To a twelve-year-old, Mack Bolan was the consummate badass. He had done it all. A sniper with ninety-seven confirmed kills in various Vietnam battle theaters? *Check.* Master sergeant with lethal proficiency with a .460 Weatherby? *Check.* Scourge of Mafiosi who had killed his dad and whoreified his sister? *Double* check.

Matt began hunting down other *Executioner* books and discovered that Mack Bolan had another side too. He liked kids. He even liked Vietnamese kids, and in one issue, he took a couple of them under his wing and treated them kindly—when he wasn't ventilating the baddies. *He* didn't call them *gook, chink,* or *slant*—and he had fought in 'Nam! So why should Matt not give Tran and Nguyen the benefit of the doubt? He couldn't think of one good reason. So he decided that, given a choice between siding with the Dwaynes of the world or the Mack Bolans, he'd choose the Executioner.

Eighteen years had passed since then, and he still felt the same way—in fact, he still had his well-thumbed copy of *The Executioner #38* tucked away in his rucksack—one of the very few personal items he'd allowed himself when he packed. It meant something to him, that book...It reminded him of his dad, for one. And just holding it brought him back to spending rainy Sunday afternoons reading in his tree house and living on a strict diet of BBQ potato chips while he washed down each page with a swallow of Schweppes ginger ale. *Bliss.*

"...wealth that the Jews had amassed from *stealing* the mighty treasure of the Knights Templar!"

Matt blinked, returning to Earth. He'd forgotten that Kingman was still raving.

"This theory—though widely accepted now, of course—was met with disbelief when I first published it in *Aryan's Lament*. My critics claimed that—"

"Actually," Matt interjected quickly, "that's not the chapter I meant."

Kingman paused. "It isn't?" He seemed bewildered. "Well, it...it can't have been the phrenology chapter—those standards are long established..."

Among dipshits worldwide, Matt thought. But he didn't say it. What he said was, "No, it wasn't that one, either. It was actually the epilogue that I wanted to talk to you about."

"Ah, yes. The epilogue." Kingman drummed his fingers on the desk. His face had gone neutral, but his eyes burned with a crafty light. "That epilogue doesn't appear in any edition but the first, you know."

"I didn't know that," Matt said.

"Yes. It was excised in the second and third editions, at my editor's request. Just didn't seem...ah...*of a piece* with the rest of the book."

"Well, it does sort of...stand out," Matt said, choosing his words carefully.

"In what way?" The tone of the interview had changed. Kingman was no longer blathering joyfully about eight-hundred-year-old conspiracies. Now he was watchful, alert. Matt could feel Kingman's sharp gray eyes burrowing into his own, and for the first time, he realized how much he'd put himself in this nut job's power—surrounded by his black-clad crew, his electric fence. Bazookas on shelves and all that. He might be in great danger, Matt realized. But he had come all this way. He couldn't back down.

"If I can explain, Mr. Kingman?" He settled back into his chair, pressed the palms of his hands together. "The way I read your epilogue in *Aryan's Lament* is that it's a...well, like a parable of sorts."

Kingman stroked his bristly gray postage stamp. "Proceed."

"Well, as you know, in this epilogue, this parable, a young guy—you call him Charles—is buried alive in a crypt. The black kids in his high school don't appreciate his...his original ideas, and so they find a way to lock him in a crypt on Halloween."

"Yes."

"And he eventually escapes the following morning, but after he's been buried, he can see things that no one else sees: He sees scabs and boils on the faces of those who want to hurt him. He smells rot on those who are plotting against him."

"That's right."

"In fact, Charles realizes that ever since he left the tomb, he's had a *second shadow* following him wherever he goes, only it doesn't always do what he does. He names it Shadewell, and after a while, he starts to talk to it."

"Yes."

"And then, after a while, it starts to talk back."

Kingman was nodding, his arms crossed, his gray eyes bright and watchful.

"Shadewell tells him to do all kinds of terrible things—to start rumors that destroy people's reputations, to steal from those who trust him, things like that.

And he does these things. But then, at the end of the parable, Shadewell whispers to him that he should kill his girlfriend, that he should burn her alive. And all of a sudden, Charles realizes that it's gone too far, that he has to get rid of the shadow. And he does. But there's no description of how he does it in the parable. All it says is something like, 'Making use of a dark rite found in an ancient book, Charles gained control over the malicious spirit that had sought to control him.' But in the book, you never describe the rite he uses!" Matt settled back, put his hands flat on his thighs. "Mr. Kingman, I've wanted to know for a long time now *what that rite was.* I was hoping you could tell me."

Finished, he looked at Kingman expectantly.

"Well, well." The old turtle settled back in his seat, closed his eyes, and picked at a melanoma forming on his mottled scalp. "Of all the reasons that people have sought me out, this is the first time it's been for literary criticism." The eyes opened, locked on Matt. Kingman's thin lips hinged upward at the ends in an enigmatic smile.

"I'm not *criticizing* the story you wrote," Matt said quickly. "I'm just..." He paused. "I'm just curious about the rite."

"Any particular reason?"

Matt sighed. Kingman was cornering him. He was going to have to take a chance with him and tell the truth. "I had this idea that the parable maybe wasn't entirely fictional. That maybe it—or something like it—had actually happened."

"Aha." The gray postage stamp twitched. "And what would lead you to that conclusion?"

Matt stared at him, thinking, *You have to be kidding.* "Well, the parable does end by saying that 'Charles' uses this mysterious rite a number of times to make the shadow do his bidding, right? He makes the shadow bring him money and fame. Ultimately, the shadow helps him assemble a big militia of over a hundred soldiers called the White Aryan Caucasian Fist of God. Over time, this militia is strengthened and empowered by regular applications of this rite."

"And...?"

"And White Aryan Caucasian Fist of God was, I think, the name of the militia which you claim to have started. At least, it was, according to the author's profile on the book's back flap. "

A flash of teeth. "Was and is. And until recently, we were still nearly one hundred strong!"

"Right." Thinking, *What does "until recently" mean?* Matt decided not to ask. There was only one thing he needed from Kingman, and that was information on Mr. Dark—*if* he had any. Which was a big *if.*

Matt gave Kingman an open look. "So you tell me...Am I on to something? Or did I just drive three thousand miles for nothing?"

The old guy held his unblinking gaze for two, three, four seconds and then let out a short, rasping laugh. "You didn't come all this way for nothing," he said reassuringly. "Roma's tea is famous in these parts. Come in, my dear, come in!"

The wild hope that had briefly flared in Matt's chest was quickly extinguished. He turned around impatiently. Roma had entered the room, bearing a tray that held two china cups and what looked to be an old-fashioned pewter samovar. The steam rising from its spout obscured her features—all but the slanted green eyes, which cut briefly toward Matt as she passed him. As she crossed to Kingman's desk and leaned over to set down the heavy tray, Matt's pulse started to beat like a drum at the base of his throat.

"Remarkable, isn't she?"

Embarrassed, Matt glanced quickly back to Kingman, who he now realized had been watching his reaction. He began stammering out something, but Kingman held up his hand, palm out. "No need to apologize," he laughed. "Roma is beautiful, is she not? You said so yourself earlier."

Mortified, Matt clenched his jaw and glanced guiltily at Roma. But she was just standing at the corner of Kingman's desk, impossibly at ease, hands clasped modestly before her and eyes demurely downcast. The faint smile on her lips was unreadable, could have been shyness, satisfaction, shame— or contempt. Or all four.

"How much"—and here Kingman walked from behind his desk over to Roma—"how much would you pay for such a woman, Matt?"

"Pay?" Matt couldn't believe what he'd just heard.

"Yes, pay. How much would you pay?" Kingman stood right next to Roma, arms crossed, giving her a satisfactory look-over, like a coin collector inspecting a buffalo nickel with a valuable defect. "You'd be surprised what Roma has cost me. Two thousand dollars I paid to a marriage broker to winnow down the field of potential brides, then three thousand more to cover the introductory visit, another thousand for the visa, two and a half for various bribes to Kamchatkan officials, then four more to pay for the plane tickets for her *and* her two brothers, whom she refused to leave behind. So, twelve thousand five hundred dollars, all in all." With a rasping chuckle, he ran a liver-spotted finger along her biceps. "What do you think, Matt? Was she worth it?"

"Worth it?" Matt's throat felt dry. He still couldn't believe Kingman was talking about his wife like she was a second-hand camera he'd bought on eBay. But he had to respond. "*Hell* yes," he said. "Mr. Kingman, I'd say, all things considered, you got the deal of the century."

Roma's enigmatic smile didn't change at his words, but her eyes, which had been downcast to the floor, rose slightly. Not enough to meet Matt's gaze, but just enough to claim the middle distance between them. The barometric pressure in the room shifted. As did Matt's pulse.

"The deal of the century, eh?" Kingman, agitated, had begun to pace. "But you haven't yet heard how much she actually cost me, have you? The twelve thousand dollars, yes? But that is *nothing*. That's just money. I could care less about the *money*." He gave a short, barking laugh. "No, Roma was far more expensive than that, weren't you, my love? Ultimately, she cost me my army, which has jeopardized the entire Rahowa."

That word again. "You'll have to explain that last part," Matt said.

Kingman looked at him in disbelief. "Don't tell me that you are unfamiliar with the works of Ben Klassen?"

Matt raised his eyebrows and turned up the palms of his hands, as if to say, *Sorry.*

Kingman sighed. "*Rahowa* is a made-up word for a very real concept. And that concept is that we are heading inexorably toward a world-wide *racial holy war*, or Rahowa."

Matt stared at him. Kingman didn't blink. Apparently, he was serious.

"Aha." It was either that or *You must be fucking kidding me.* *Aha* won out, but not by much. "And how," Matt said, trying to connect the dots, "and how did Roma jeopardize your winning this...war?"

Now it was Kingman's turn to look at Matt like he was an idiot. "Well, look at her, Matt," he said, as if speaking to a five-year-old. "What's the first thing you see?"

So Matt had to look at her again, like she was a piece of meat. And he really couldn't tell what he saw first: he was overwhelmed by the immediacy of her full lips, high brow, tigerish eyes, long neck, and the harp-shaped hips that joined a slim waist to endless legs.

"Well," Matt said, "she's beautiful, I guess."

Kingman rolled his eyes and made a *gah* of exasperation. "Her skin, Matt, her *skin.* Do you *notice* anything about it?"

This was getting unbearable. "It's...ah...smooth?"

"Of course it's smooth, but what about its color?"

Matt closed his eyes and focused on not choking Kingman. "What about it?"

"Well, isn't it obvious?" Kingman had stepped into Matt's space, raising his voice. "You've opined that Roma is beautiful. But in your learned opinion, is she *Aryan?*"

Matt opened his mouth, then closed it. Tried to massage away the approaching migraine. "I have no idea."

"Of course you don't! And neither do any of the seventy-eight fools who believe that I spent twenty years assembling the most formidable militia in Michigan only to *miscegenate.*"

He spat the word out like a live coal. "She"—he jabbed a finger at Roma—"has cost me my army!"

Roma just stared at the floor. She could have been carved in wax.

Matt struggled to find something to say to this nut job. "Your, uh, numbers still seem pretty strong to me." He pointed out the window. "We passed a few dozen of your guys on the way up the forest path."

"Of course you did. But do you see them now? Of course you don't. And why is that?" Kingman's eyes nearly crossed in fury. "Because they have quit the White Aryan Caucasian Fist of God! They are AWOL! They are deserters! All because of *her*, seventy-eight of the best militia in Michigan have turned *traitor*!"

He flung his teacup at the wall, where it shattered in a brown spray.

A stunned silence from everyone in the room. *Jesus, this guy is unhinged.* Matt felt the need to calm the old guy down before he popped a vein.

"Well, 'traitor' seems a little strong," Matt said. "I mean, you're clearly still...ah...coexisting, right? You and the prodigal seventy-eight?"

Now it was Kingman's turn to look amazed. "Didn't you see the fence?"

Matt stared at him. For a second, he didn't understand. Then he did. And when he did, the skin on his arms lifted into goose bumps and the hair at the base of his neck prickled.

Holy fuck.

"Wait a minute. Mr. Kingman..." Matt struggled to keep his voice even. "Are you saying that that electric fence is...is the only thing keeping those seventy-eight 'deserters' out? That you and her and the handful of people in here are... are..." He groped for the right phrase.

"Under siege?" Kingman smiled grimly. "That is exactly what I'm telling you, Matt."

CHAPTER FIVE

Footsteps behind him, coming fast.

Matt turned to see the militiaman with the fauxhawk stride past him, holding an open laptop. He was followed by Jasha and the guy with the RAHOWA tat.

"Sir, Alastair wants to talk to you."

"Later, Walton."

"Sir? You're going to want to hear this."

A pause. The old man's crafty eyes shuttled back and forth between the soldier and Matt. He wiped a line of spittle from the corner of his mouth with the pad of his thumb.

"Well, by all means, then." Kingman pointed to his desk. The soldier crossed to it, set the laptop down, and stepped back.

Matt took a sharp breath, felt his heart lunge within his chest. The laptop's screen showed the red-fissured face of Baldy.

"Well, Alastair." Kingman stood imperiously in front of the screen, his hands clenched behind his back. "You've been busy this morning. I hear you had your army of deserters attack my wife."

Baldy gave a nasty smile. "You should thank us, old man. We were just upholding the law. Doesn't your wife know that public displays of affection are illegal here in the US of A?"

Kingman tensed. "What are you talking about?"

"Didn't she tell you?" Enjoying this. "That sweet brown thing musta came down with one bad case of jungle fever. She had her tongue about halfway down a guy's throat when we caught sight of them."

"What...what guy?"

"The guy standing right next to you."

Kingman's mottled face snapped toward Matt.

"Lying," Roma hissed, crossing quickly to Kingman. "He is lying to you, my love, I swear."

"And that buck had his hand so far up her skirt we all thought he was givin' her a free exam, so naturally we had to—"

Kingman slapped his hand down onto the keyboard with a clatter, and the connection was broken. He stood there, staring at the *Call Disconnected* message, his chest rising and falling, his breath whistling harshly in his beak.

Suddenly, an IM notification appeared at the bottom of the screen.

"Charles," Roma whispered, "don't—"

He hit a button. Five words appeared on the screen:

BY MIDNIGHT
TONIGHT
OR ELSE

Kingman slammed down the laptop lid. He stared at it for a minute, then looked up at Matt. His eyes a little too wide. His smile a little too tight. Said, "You must be awfully tired from your trip, Mr. Cahill."

Matt didn't like the paranoid light in his eyes. He also didn't like the red fissures that were spreading across

Kingman's face, dividing and subdividing it into a red grid. "Well, actually, I'm feeling pretty rested. Should be, ah, getting on my way."

"Nonsense. It's getting dark out. Likely to rain again. You'll spend the night with us! I *insist*."

From behind, Matt felt a big hand grab his arm just above the elbow and another slap heavily onto his shoulder.

Matt had never taken a martial arts class, but he'd seen this predicament play out dozens of times on TV, and the hero's response was always the same: with his free arm, he'd reach behind himself, grab his attacker by the scruff of the neck, and then bend forward, flinging the thug over his shoulder onto the floor. So Matt tried doing that.

Unfortunately, he quickly discovered that what worked for Shatner, Selleck, Norris, and Hasselhoff didn't necessarily transfer to reality.

In short, TV had lied to him.

While Matt did manage to reach back and grab a hunk of Jasha's hair, all Jasha had to do then was grab Matt's wrist and wrench it back even farther, while knocking the back of Matt's knee with the front of his own. In less than a second, Matt was kneeling helplessly on the floor, his hands pinned behind him, praying that Jasha didn't exert the single pound of pressure it would take to dislocate both arms at the socket.

He didn't. But he did twist them sharply, switching Matt's gaze from Roma's horrified face to Kingman's reptilian, red-veined mask.

"Kingman, I never touched her—I swear."

"I'm sure you do." His tortoisey head bobbed up and down. "And I have no qualms about relying on the words of a man of honor. So all that's left, at this point, is for me to confirm that you *are* a man of honor. Walton?"

The militiaman with the fauxhawk stepped behind Matt and pulled Matt's wallet out of his back pocket.

"Got it, sir."

"Good. A background check, immediately."

"Yes, sir."

"And what happens 'til then?" Matt panted, humiliated. "We all just stay here? Or do you have a dungeon where you can conveniently dump me?"

"Dungeon?" Kingman's eyes crinkled shut and he gave a snort of laughter. "Perish the thought. You're our guest. You'll keep your bag, your ax. And while we do our due diligence, you'll be escorted by Jasha, Walton, and Sig to the White Aryan Caucasian Fist of God's *penthouse suite.*"

CHAPTER SIX

Matt had guessed that "penthouse suite" meant the attic. But he realized he was wrong when Jasha firmly guided him back into the hall and then out onto the second-story deck. Just how wrong he'd been didn't become clear to him until Jasha led him to the ski lift and pushed him firmly into a sky chair.

"Gotta be honest, guys," Matt said, "I totally forgot to bring my snowboard."

"Not gonna need no snowboard where you're goin'," said the militiaman with the RAHOWA tat—whose name was Sig, apparently. He tossed the ax and backpack to Matt, then opened the ski lift's control box. "Now, a parachute? That's another matter." And he flipped a switch.

Immediately, the sky chair jerked away, pulled down the hill by a steel cable that fed into the rusting carousel wheel grinding to life above the militiamen's heads.

As the sky chair pulled away from the wooden deck, the ground dropped steeply away beneath it. In three seconds, he was ten feet above the slope. In five seconds, he was fifteen feet above the slope. In ten, there was nothing between him and the muddy slope but twenty feet of air.

And that's when Sig flipped the switch again.

The rusty carousel wheel stopped grinding.

The cable stopped sliding.

The sky chair stopped moving. Or rather, it stopped traveling down the hill. It was still moving plenty, rocking back and forth like a pendulum as Matt clung to it for dear life.

"Yeah, that'll about do 'er," Sig said with satisfaction. "Guess I better run that background check, like Mr. Kingman said. In the meantime, Mr. Cahill? *Enjoy the view.*"

And he walked back into the house, followed by Jasha.

Which left Walton. The kid settled into a wooden Adirondack chair with a grunt. He set a high-powered rifle over his knees and glared down the hill toward the dozens of men who, in the late evening light, were building a bonfire.

"So how's the dental and vision plan here?" Matt asked.

Walton didn't say anything.

"Measured any craniums lately?"

Nothing.

"I've got an idea," Matt said. "How 'bout we compare lists of our favorite chapters in *The Aryan's Lament.*"

Beneath the shades, Walton's jaw began to work. "Seein' as you're a prisoner of the White Aryan Caucasian Fist of God? I'd shut the hell up, if I were you."

Matt snorted with derision.

Walton hopped out of his seat. "Something funny, Cahill? Spit it out!"

Matt held up a hand. "Look, I was just trying to get a handle on your group's name, is all. Kind of a mouthful."

"Our name, huh? Well, laugh it up, bud." Walton, pacing, ran a hand over his fauxhawk. "White Aryan Caucasian Fist of God. I bet you think it's a triple redundancy, right? But it's not. It's a matter of necessity, our name is."

"It is, huh?"

"Damn straight. We came by it gradual. At first we was just the Aryan Fist of God. Nice and simple. Looked good on the web page, and people liked it. We was pleased as hell when our Internet membership went up to seven hundred. And them was dues-payin' members, every one of 'em! Then we took a closer look, saw that more 'n half of them fuckers listed their home country as *India and Pakistan*. Scroll down the list, and every other goddamn name on our roster was Rama-Lama-Ding-Dong. Turns out you don't have to be white to be Aryan! Who the hell knew, right? So then we changed it to *White* Aryan Fist of God. That about did it for most of them snake charmers, but there was still a dozen or so was albino—it's commoner than you'd think—and them twelve ragheads, they kept orderin' shirts and hats, and goin' on our website, postin' photos of their mutant asses and givin' opinions on magic carpet ridin' or whatever the fuck else they wanted to talk about, and well, as you can imagine, it just did *shit* for morale around here. So finally, we named it White Aryan *Caucasian* Fist of God. That there was the nail in the coffin for the yoga brigade. Only it was right about then when *he*"—and here his voice dropped to a belligerent whisper—"he went on that *trip*, and came back...came back with, you know, *her*." He sat back down, crossed his arms. "I got the lecture—we all did—about her hometown bein' from where all white people come from and all that. I ain't no PhD, but all I can say is, things ain't been the same since. And now I gotta sit here and babysit *your* sorry ass."

"Sorry about that," Matt said, confused by that last part but not caring enough to ask for clarification. "It wasn't exactly my idea. You should've brought something to read."

Walton snorted. "Ain't never read a book in my life."

Matt smirked. "Right."

"No joke."

Matt looked at him more closely. Twilight shadowed his features, but the kid seemed dead serious. "That a fact?"

Shrugging. "Dropped out of school when I was fifteen. Wasn't no good at it. Got my letters mixed up every time I tried to read." Staring at his feet. "Worked a bunch of shitty jobs, slept in the back of my truck for a year. Then Mr. Kingman, he took me in. Gave me a job, three squares a day, a gun, training. Taught me all about my Aryan heritage. Gave me the only gift I ever got from anyone. See this here?"

Matt squinted. Walton had turned the back of his right hand to Matt. He was pointing to a large, chunky ring on his right index finger.

"A ring?"

"Not just any ring. Got a skull on it, with garnets for eyes. And it says RAHOWA on the side. Worth a lot of money, this is."

I bet, Matt thought. He'd seen junk like that in head shops on sale for twelve bucks. The word *garnet* always had two *T*s and was followed by a copyright sign. "So that ring's why you're here?"

"No." Walton slapped his hands down on the Adirondack armrests. "I'm here because for the first time in my life *I'm worth something to somebody.*"

Matt stared at him, then looked down at the ground swaying gently far beneath his feet. He felt a little seasick. A few comebacks came to mind, but what was the point? Suddenly, his contempt for the kid dissolved into pity. Matt came from a small town too, but his home was like Seattle compared to Wittman. Matt thought of the rusted-out trailer parks he'd passed on the way in, tried to imagine what it would have been like growing up in a home where you were never given a single thing, going to a school where shame over your disability made you drop out. Then, when you're rootless, without hope, living out of a truck, some published "author" comes along and tells you there's a secret about you that no one knows: that you're not only as good as everyone else, you're *superior...special...chosen.* And all you have to do to embrace your destiny is put on a ring, get a gun, move in, eat up, and get ready for the racial holy war.

Hell, Matt thought, *when you've got nothing else going for you...*

"Hey, Walt." Sig had appeared. "I can't get the Internet to work. Would you take a look?"

"Yeah, OK." Walton got up, walked passed Sig. "Keep an eye on him, though," he said, jabbing his thumb at Matt. "I don't wanna be the one to tell Mr. Kingman that he busted his head tryin' to climb down."

"Sure, sure," Sig said, watching him leave. When the deck door shut, Sig watched it for a second and then slowly, slowly turned to Matt.

And just like that, Matt knew he was in trouble.

"Havin' a good time, bud?"

"Absolutely." Matt noticed that Sig was carrying a duffel bag. For some reason, he knew this was bad news.

"You givin' my buddy Walt flack?" Sig swaggered up to the control console and leaned against it with a deliberate casualness.

"Nope."

"Hope not. You two get your panties in a twist, and I'll have to separate you. Put you to bed. Sing you a lullaby." He looked over his shoulder. Seeing no one, he put his hand casually on the control panel. He gave Matt a weird, lopsided grin. "Do you *want* me to sing you a lullaby?"

Matt stared at him. "Not...really."

"Well, too goddamn bad. I gotta do something to keep myself awake. So here goes." And he made an *ah-ah-ah-ahem* sound, like an opera singer getting ready for rehearsal.

Matt wasn't liking any of this. And that was before he heard the song.

> *Rock-a-bye baby, on the treetop,*
> *When the wind blows, the cradle will rock*

When he sang the word *rock*, Sig flicked the switch on and off, and Matt's sky chair lurched forward and then jerked backward, nearly spilling him off the wooden-slatted seat.

"Hey!" Matt yelled. "Cut it out!"
But Sig just kept singing.

> *When the bough breaks, the cradle will fall,*
> *And down will come Cahill, cradle and all.*

On the final word, Sig quickly flipped the switch on and off again three times. The still-rocking chair snapped back and forth so wildly that Matt fell out—and the only thing keeping him from the muddy slope twenty feet below was the fact that his left hand snagged the cold aluminum bar that served as the sky chair's footrest. He clung to it, feet sweeping the air, clutching his ax in his free hand.

Matt's heart pounded like a trip-hammer. "What the hell are you doing?" he yelled.

"What's it look like, Matt?" Sig drawled as he flipped the Airlift switch back into the *on* position and climbed into the first available sky chair. "I'm switching sides. I'm gonna join the winning team. And you're gonna be my peace offerin', just to make sure I get a warm welcome."

Matt watched in horror as their sky chairs creaked away from the lodge and over the electric fence that protected Kingman's camp from the rebel militia. His right arm ached painfully as he twisted in the cold night breeze. He attempted a one-armed pull-up and gave up immediately with a gasp. *Not gonna happen.*

"Hot damn!" Sig crowed from the sky chair swaying fifteen feet behind Matt's. "That didn't take long! Lookit them swarm! And they even brought their puppy dogs with 'em!"

Matt craned his neck to look down the slope. His heart nearly stopped as he saw the headlamps of a big ATV come to life. With a roar, the vehicle began climbing the steep slope toward them, followed by four barking pit bulls.

"I hear they only feed them pits every three days, Matt," Sig cackled. "How long you think it takes for them to strip a fella to the bone?"

A fury released in Matt, white hot at its core.

"Let's find out," he said, and switched hands so that his left gripped the cold footrest bar, freeing his right.

Sig shook his head, grinning. "Can't say's I see much of an improvement there, Cahill. After all, your right hand's probably the strongest."

"It is," Matt gasped, picking up the ax with his free hand. "See?"

And he flung the ax.

With a shout, Sig recoiled from the humming disk of wood and iron that slashed toward him through the darkness.

The moon glinted off the spinning blade as it sailed harmlessly over the militiaman's head.

But Matt hadn't been aiming for Sig.

CHANK!

The blade bit deeply into the thin aluminum brace that connected the sky chair to its cable.

Chopped it in half.

With a loud squeal, the sky chair seat went from horizontal to vertical.

With a *louder* squeal, Sig toppled off and fell shrieking to the muddy slope twenty feet below them.

He didn't go alone. Agitated by his fall, the cable joggled wildly—too wildly for Matt's sweat-slick hand. Seconds later, his fingers slid free of the footrest bar, and he, too, plummeted toward the hill below.

CHAPTER SEVEN

Ka-THUNK.

The bad news was that Matt fell twenty feet onto a mud-slick slope.

The *good* news was that the ski slope was rated "black diamond" and was so steep that, instead of breaking Matt's back, it merely knocked the wind out of him.

The *bad* news was that as soon as he hit its steep, slushy surface, Matt began to slide helplessly toward the blazing eyes of the ATV below, which lit the backs of the four charging, snarling pit bulls.

Gasping, Matt clawed helplessly for purchase, to no avail. The barking was getting closer.

Come on, come on!

Flipping onto his stomach, Matt jammed his fingers into the ground, digging ten furrows in the soft, slick earth. He began to slow.

Thank God. He groaned in relief.

But the groan morphed into a shout of surprise as Sig, sliding past him, snagged his ankle, dragging Matt down faster toward the brightening glare of the ATV.

"Sig, what the hell are you doing?"

"Thought that was obvious." Sig laughed over the rabid barking, his free right hand lifting up a familiar slant of blond wood, topped with an iron blade. "I'm gonna chop you into Kibbles 'n Bits."

He had Matt's ax!

"Wrong answer." As Sig slammed the blade down, Matt jerked his leg back. With a wet *kutch* sound, the blade missed Matt's ankle by six inches—and chopped off Sig's left hand at the wrist.

Sig's eyes bugged and he let out a scream as Matt grabbed the ax handle and pounded the sole of his Carhartt against Sig's forehead, driving him down the slope and into the snarling shadows of the four pits.

Matt struggled awkwardly to his feet. The ATV headlights nearly blinded him, but he could see enough to tell that two of the pit bulls had begun dismantling Sig, whose screams were swiftly devolving into wet gurgles.

But the other two dogs had taken a pass on the one-handed militiaman.

Were midair.

Were on him.

Massive jaws clamped onto Matt's elbow. He kicked the beast in the gut and it released with a grunt. Pulling the ax free, he lifted it just in time for the second dog's jaws to snap onto the wooden handle. The dog's face was so close to Matt's that its wet nose brushed his own. Matt slung the ax to the side, flinging the dog back down the slope.

Crunch.

Followed by panicked yelps.

He whipped around. The ATV had ploughed over both Sig and the dogs that fed on him and was now just twenty feet away and closing fast.

Matt tried to run, but he could barely stand. The slope was too steep, too muddy.

Fifteen feet.

Ten.

Five.

The roar was ungodly. The blaze of its lights was like looking into the sun.

But suddenly, that bright blaze silhouetted a thin black strip that seemed to drop down out of nowhere. Matt stared at it stupidly as the ATV bore down on him. And only when he heard the words "Be grabbing on, bee-otch" did he realize what it was (a chain) and what to do (*grab it—now*).

He did.

Immediately, he was hauled off his feet. He looked down to see the black, spiked, RAHOWA'd hood of the ATV roar harmlessly beneath him. Baldy's jigsaw face gaped in amazement to see Matt levitate out of harm's way. As he passed above, Matt drove the steel toe of his Carhartt into the guy's brow and watched his head snap backward. The ATV slewed off to the side and began the long sideways slide down the black-diamond slope.

Matt looked up. He was rising swiftly toward the sky chair, in which two shadows awaited, one small and one huge. The huge one silently pulled on the slim chain that Matt clutched, hand over hand, lifting Matt up with no more effort than a fisherman reeling in a small perch.

Squatting next to him, his painted black lips peeled back in delight, Arkady, the smaller shadow, let out a woodpecker laugh and chanted, "Busting rhymes like a chef break eggs, I am having mad skills like a frat got kegs. Yo, G, be speaking truth—Jasha and me, we saved ya like a savior, right?"

"Word," Matt said, grinning, as he rose toward the stars.

As the sky chair was pulled by the squealing cable back toward the lodge, Matt's eyes left the welcome sight of the half dozen militiamen gathered around the control box, their sniper scopes scouring the hillside, and turned to his two companions.

Jasha, the silent giant, took up the entire sky chair, and the cable groaned beneath his weight. Matt, panting with fatigue, sat on one of his huge thighs like a kid in Santa's lap.

Arkady perched on the sky chair's armrest, his eyes bright with chaos, his grin a white, maniacal slit separating the black-painted lips. His thick blond dreads gave off a funky cocktail of greasepaint, ganja, and something brown.

"I want to...thank you guys," Matt panted. "Wish I had something to give you, but I'm broke as a joke." *Jeez*, he thought, *he's even got me rhyming now.*

"No need, my brutha in arms. 'Cause we just paying you back for playing it straight up for our little sis, right, Jasha?"

Jasha, his eyes covered by his bowl cut, said nothing. Then he did. Or rather, his lips moved, though no sound came out.

But Arkady didn't have any trouble understanding him. He nodded and rattled off something in Russian. Jasha then pulled a necklace off his neck and held it toward Matt.

"My bro, he be wishing to give you something."

Matt looked closer. It was a long loop of leather with a three-inch bear claw hanging from it. He took it, felt the tip of the claw. Razor sharp. "Thanks," he said. "But why the gift?"

"Is not a gift, yo? Is being like a trade."

Matt looked from Arkady to Jasha. "A trade? For what?"

"My brother, he is wanting your ankle bracelet."

"Ankle bracelet?" Matt stared at him blankly. "I don't wear a…" He looked down.

And almost threw up.

Wrapped tightly around his ankle, ragged and red, was Sig's *hand.*

CHAPTER EIGHT

"It seems I owe you an apology, Matt."

"Please." Matt held up a still-shaking hand, blocking out Charles Kingman's face, which he couldn't bear to look at. "No apologies necessary." His voice was thick with sarcasm. He winced as Roma, who was sitting next to him on the bed, wiped the blood off his brow with a wet towel.

"If it's any consolation, Sig's defection was completely unforeseeable. He was one of my most trusted—"

"Oh, give me a break." Matt lowered his hand, glared at Kingman. "It *isn't* a consolation. I'm not *consoled*, Chuck. I talked to that freak for five minutes, and I wouldn't have trusted him to take out my *garbage.* You want to give me consolation? Pick up the fucking phone, call 911, and get some police out here so I can get the hell out without getting shot or run over or eaten alive. Or is that too much to ask?"

"Unfortunately"—Kingman pursed his pointy lips and steepled his fingers—"it is."

Matt stared at him in disbelief. *"What?"*

Kingman sighed heavily. "You see, as of fifteen minutes ago, Alastair activated a scrambler, so we have lost the ability to access the Internet or make cell phone calls."

Matt couldn't think of anything to say. He just sat there, feeling his heart start to pound like he was still back on the hill with the ATV bearing down on him. "So what's the game plan?"

"I'm glad you asked." Kingman sat down next to Matt, setting an open laptop on his knee. "This is the game plan."

The laptop screen was split into four quadrants, each of which contained a live video feed. In the upper right-hand corner of each was an all-caps digital identifier. THOR's quadrant showed a dim, grainy view of branches being slowly pushed aside by a gloved hand. LOKI's quadrant showed a worm's-eye view of a sun-bleached deadfall being crawled over by someone with Mylar boots. ODIN's showed a night-vision view from halfway up a tree. And FREYA's showed the muzzle of an AK-47 brushing aside prickly loops of wild raspberry brambles.

"Four of our best remaining militia," Kingman said proudly, gesturing to the screen. "Each one a master of invisible reconnaissance. All of them sent out by me through a secret opening in the electric barrier to steal covertly past Alastair's forces, make their way into town, and alert the authorities. I expect them to fulfill their directive by dawn."

"Sure. Great." Matt kneaded his temples with one hand. *What a fucking nightmare.* Then something occurred to him. A separate set of words he'd seen on that very laptop, just before everything went to hell.

He looked up. "So, Charles, you said 'by dawn,' right? How's that jibe with the message that Alastair sent you an hour ago—the one that said, 'BY MIDNIGHT TONIGHT OR ELSE'?"

Matt had seen footage before of sharks, how before they went in for the first bite, a nictitating membrane slid over their eyes to protect them from blood and viscera.

Something weirdly similar happened to Kingman as his eyes glazed over. His reassuring smile became tight, became fake. Slowly, his ancient head rotated 'til it faced Roma.

"Roma, my dear, I'd like to speak to Mr. Cahill privately now."

Without a word, she stood up and strode lithely out of the room, shutting the door behind her. Matt stared wistfully after her, already missing her gentle touch, her humanizing presence.

Once the door had closed, Kingman set the laptop on the bed, rose to his feet, and began to pace.

"Alastair's message, Mr. Cahill, is simply a bluff. My forces may have deserted, but they would not dare attack the compound. They simply need time to process the fact that Roma's presence here is not a rejection of my life's work, but its *fulfillment*. Which is obvious, when you understand her actual ancestry." He paused and gestured toward Matt with a professorial gesture. "Let me ask you this: Do you remember the section in my book where I explained the origin of the Aryan race?"

"I think I may have skipped that chapter."

"Pity. In it, I clarify a common misconception; namely, that all Aryans are merely 'white people.' In fact, Aryans are those who are directly descended from the Ob-Ugrians, the Uralic branch of the Indo-European family tree. The Ob-Ugrians migrated to Europe from northeastern Siberia. They conquered wherever they went, going as far west as Ireland and Iceland and as far south as Iran, Afghanistan, Pakistan, and northern India. In all these places, they subjugated the lesser races and created great works of art and architecture and mighty civilizations."

"Is that a fact?" Matt's head was beginning to pound. *Keep him talking.* "So you're saying that all the people from Dublin to Tehran are Aryan?"

"*Were* Aryan, Matt—*were*, until they intermingled with the blood of Picts, Huns, Semites, and subcontinentals, and so bastardized their pure bloodline through miscegenation. A process that *I*, in choosing my bride, have chosen to *reverse*."

Matt just stared at him. "And how do you reverse—"

"Would it surprise you to know that lovely Roma is not only Aryan, but a princess of the proto-Aryan Nivkh tribe? That she was born in the northeastern tip of Russia, on Sakhalin Island at the mouth of the Amur River, the very *cradle* of Aryanism? That she herself, at the age of seventeen, on May Day, like her mother, grandmother, and great-grandmother before her, was ritually married to Ursus Major, the Great Bear god? Making her, in essence, a *goddess of Aryanism?*" Behind his rimless glasses, Kingman's eyes gleamed with madness, and spittle had collected in the corner of his mouth. The red, wormlike fissures beneath his skin squirmed and darkened with every word.

But the word *ritual* stuck in Matt's head. "Wait a minute," he said, a terrible idea dawning in his mind. "Does this marry-the-bear ceremony you're talking about have anything to do with the last chapter in your book? The one I asked you about earlier?"

The terrapin head bobbed eagerly. "Of course. Where else should an Aryan soul seek purification, other than in the very crucible of Aryanism...*which is nothing less than the body of an Aryan goddess?*" His face was fissured like a jigsaw.

Matt's head was spinning. Was Kingman saying what he *thought* he was saying? "So you're saying...that the way

'Charles' got Shadewell to stop haunting him...was to... ah...hook up with a white chick?"

Kingman snorted, shook his head in dismissal. "Oh, Mr. Cahill, I'm disappointed. You're as dense as the rest. I did not say 'hook up.' I said, 'He purified his spirit in the crucible of her Aryanism.'"

"Right." *Whatever that meant.* "So that's what Alastair wants? To do a little purifying in her crucible himself?"

Kingman's features hardened with a fury alloyed with panic. "That traitor," he spat, "does not understand...does not appreciate...He would take the godhead herself—she who was *married to Ursus Major*—and...and..." He paused. Seemed to notice that Matt was still there, was listening closely. "Well, anyway." His thin lips clamped shut. He crossed to the bed, snatched up the laptop. "I don't expect you'd understand. Some truths can only be grasped by the select few—those who have studied a lifetime, have sought, have *suffered* for such secret knowledge—the true believers, in other words. And I don't think you're a member of that club, Mr. Cahill."

"I'm afraid not," Matt said. *Thank God.*

Kingman went to the door. "As I said, I fully expect the authorities to be here by morning, at which point you're welcome to go. But until then, I'm going to have to ask that you remain in your room. In a militarized zone such as this, it's not safe for a civilian to wander around unattended. I'm sure you understand."

"Of course," Matt said.

"Well then, good night."

"Good night." *You demented shithead.*

CHAPTER NINE

Matt lay on the bed in the darkness for a long time, aching, missing Roma's cool touch. Wondering what it'd be like to kiss those full lips, to run his hands through her thick black hair. To see those gold-flecked, moss-green eyes staring up at him...

Aroused, he shifted his position only to have the fantasy dissolve as a dozen new bruises revealed themselves. The bone of his hip. The ball of his heel. The pad of his left thumb. His left collarbone. His right ring finger. His tailbone. His sternum. His skull.

Jesus...so fucked up.

He put his face in his hands. His palms grew hot, then wet.

His lust—mixed with pain, guilt, and fear—had somehow transformed into a cocktail of regret for his lost life, his lost love.

How he missed his wife!

Janey.

It took him by surprise, the overwhelming surge of sorrow. How incomplete he felt without her. Since she had died, he had been haunted by the idea that not only had he lost her, but he had lost a huge part of himself, had somehow erased every moment that the two of them had shared. They had gone to San Francisco together on their honeymoon, had wandered Fisherman's Wharf in the rain, taking photos of Alcatraz, fending off the seafood sellers, tearing off steaming pieces of a sourdough from Boudin's. They had ridden (and swiftly abandoned) a trolley car, laughing all the way back to the hotel over what a god-awful grinding, screeching, jerking, slow, surly, expensive, and tourist-swamped ride it had been. They'd stood on the beach, holding hands and watching the waves lift into a mist that rose above the lush ferns while the seals barked.

All these things were gone now. Sure, they still existed in his head...But so did Yoda. So did Zorro. So did E.T., and the Na'vi, and every other unreal, made-up thing he'd ever heard of. And now she was just like them, permanently demoted from a person to a memory, and forced to share ranks with the Fonz and Limp Bizkit and Ewoks and whatever the fuck else was in his head, slowly receding and distorting with time, until the real Janey was lost forever, and all he was left with was the faded, faulty outline of what once had been his only love. And in the meantime, he was left with the unshakeable sense that *he* was becoming less real too: going from a normal guy with a normal job and normal relationships to a nightmare-haunted loner who rode the highways with an unexplainable psychic power and a bloody ax. Sometimes he looked into the mirror and was terrified at the face looking back at him. If he were to bump into Janey tomorrow, would she even recognize him? He couldn't say for sure. And that uncertainty sickened him.

Ahhhhhhhhhhhh...

Matt sat up (*ouch*). Listened.

Ahhhhhhhhhhhh...

There it was again. The unmistakable sound of moaning...coming from somewhere *above* him.

He stood up. Was there actually another floor to the lodge, above the second? He didn't think so. But there probably was an attic.

Matt walked softly over to the door and turned the handle. It wasn't locked. The door opened with a soft squeal.

He poked his head out. The hallway was deserted. But there, at the far end, a trapdoor in the ceiling had been opened, and a retractable ladder extended from the trap to within a foot of the floor. A dim, flickering light came from above.

Ahhhhhhhhhhh...

Matt slipped out of his room and crept silently down the hall. He stood at the base of the ladder, listening to soft grunts coming from above. He really, *really* didn't want to go up there. But what if someone were in trouble? He wouldn't put anything past Kingman and his brain-dead troops. What if they'd kidnapped some woman? Some *kid*?

That did it. He put his foot on the lowest rung, grabbed the sides of the ladder, and cautiously climbed up.

When he got to the top, his head slowly lifted above the attic floor. Rafters, cobwebs, and cardboard boxes blocked his view. A weird green-and-blue light played against the slanted beams of the ceiling. He now could hear a strange metallic creaking noise as well.

Ahhhhhhhhhhh...

His heart pounding, Matt hoisted his knees (*ouch*) onto the planked floor, then rose to his feet. A rack of old clothes was in his way. He walked around it, toward the green light.

Stopped.

What the hell?

An old bed on a metal frame was set up against the far wall. And someone *was* tied down to it—but not the damsel in distress that he'd pictured. No damsel he knew had arms as big as his thighs and a basketball-sized head...

But Jasha did.

Matt stared in bewilderment at the huge Russian, whose face was flushed and whose eyes were clenched shut. Sweat beaded his brow. His arms and legs were handcuffed to the iron bed frame, and he tossed and turned feverishly, groaning in his sleep.

Matt looked for the light source, found it, and wished he hadn't. On a small table next to the bed frame, five greenish-blue flames flickered from the tops of a weird black candle. It had a misshapen base and five curved tapers, one thicker and shorter than the rest.

Matt's eyes got big. Could that be...?

He took a step closer.

Yep. No doubt about it.

Sig's hand. It had been dipped in pitch, laid in a ceramic bowl, and set on fire. The greenish witch flames that rose from it bathed Jasha's writhing in a sick, unsteady light.

CHAPTER TEN

"Matthew?"

Matt jumped about a foot off the ground and spun around to see Roma standing by the clothing rack, a plate of food in her hand.

"Roma! What...?"

"So sorry." With eyes downcast and the faintest of smiles on her lips, she eased past Matt and sat herself on a crate between Jasha and the slow-burning hand. "Did Jasha wake you?"

Matt said no but that he'd come up to investigate the noises he'd heard. Roma didn't seem to be paying attention. She leaned over the huge man and whispered softly in a language Matt didn't recognize. Then she took a damp napkin and wiped Jasha's eyes, his brow.

Matt felt a tinge of jealousy. Maybe more than a tinge. "Some candle you've got there," he said. "Not sure if your lighting system's exactly up to code."

She didn't acknowledge the joke. Which made it seem all the lamer.

"Is difficult time for him," she said. "For Jasha. Every autumn is so, like you see. But it passes." She lifted his head with effort and put a glass of water to his lips. He drank a little, coughed, and drank some more. His eyes never opened.

Matt stepped closer. "So, if he's this sick, why isn't he at a hospital?"

She flexed her lower lip in a way that was at once a shrug, an acknowledgment, and a deferral. "Because he is not sick, Matthew."

"Not sick? Look at him! He's fighting something."

"His nature," she said. And took some blueberries off the plate and pressed them between his thick lips. He ate them greedily, gnashing them between his oversized teeth.

Matt couldn't figure out what she was talking about, but for some reason, it reminded him of his conversation with Kingman.

"I had a talk with your husband," Matt said.

"Oh?" She didn't seem interested.

"He's fond of you, all right, but half the time I can't tell what he's talking about. He seems quite taken with the fact that you were married to a bear at some point."

"Ah. Yes." A smile flicked across her full lips, and her eyes edged in his direction, almost—but not quite—making contact. "An old custom in our village. Every May. A young girl, picked by—how do you say—lottery? Wearing a crown of flowers? And given to Urso, the spirit of the woods. To wed the Great Bear. For to bring luck and good crops to the village, you see?"

"Sure. But what's the bear get out of it?"

"Someone to love," she said, again ignoring the joke.

"So what, do they have a trained bear?"

She laughed. "No, Matthew. Is a boy *pretending* to be a bear."

"Aha. Sweet. Though I guess it's proof that magical marriages don't last much longer than real ones nowadays."

She looked at him, raised an eyebrow.

"I mean, you're obviously not still with him. The boy, whoever he was."

"But"—placing the last blueberry between his sharp teeth—"it was Jasha."

Matt felt a little light-headed. He felt like there was something going on that he should be catching but wasn't. His mind wanted to tell him something, but his brain kept getting in the way.

He shook his head. He couldn't think of anything clever to say, so he just said what he'd been wanting to ask for the past hour. "Roma, why are you with these people?"

A pause. Now she slid a chunk of something silver and shiny between Jasha's lips. "Have you ever been to Kamchatka, Matthew?"

"No."

She nodded, easing another slick piece into the big guy's maw. "Then you would, I think, not understand." She gave him a third.

Matt looked closer. "Are you feeding him *raw fish?*"

She flashed him a nervous smile. "Is a delicacy where we come from." She wiped her hands quickly, as if to hide the evidence. "But to answer your question? Jasha and Arkady were in trouble with…some people. People of influence. Coming here as I did, through the matchmaking service? It was the only way to protect them, to provide a new life for them. And for my child." And here she placed her hand on her belly.

Matt hadn't realized. Then he remembered the baby formula that she had been buying earlier. He had to ask: "Is Charles the father?"

She gave him a look that needed no interpretation: *No.*

Chewed on that.

She gestured around them, seemed eager to change the subject. "This room we are now in? Will be the baby's nursery. Charles gave me a little money to decorate it and buy some toys."

"Nice." Matt looked around. It wasn't nice. Kingman could apparently pay three thousand dollars for a bazooka, but when it came to providing for his child, it looked like he'd given Roma whatever change he'd found between the cushions of his White Aryan Caucasian couch.

Still, she had obviously tried to do the best she could. She'd gotten a third- or fourth-hand crib with white spots on the headboard where stickers had been applied and pealed off by the previous owners. It was also missing vertical slats in two separate places, and she'd replaced these with what looked to be pieces cut from a plastic broom handle. On the wall above the crib she'd taped pages from a parenting magazine that showed letters from the alphabet, a smiling baby's face, and a picture of Winnie the Pooh.

A faded Detroit Tigers comforter lay on the floor, next to a cardboard box of plastic toys so old that they could have been hand-me-downs when Matt was a baby. For lack of anything better to do, he fished around in the box, lifting a few pieces out as he did. There was an old Fisher-Price garage and a wood-and-plastic vacuum cleaner that would make a popping sound when pushed. There were several plastic dolls with blank eyes and no clothes, and a threadbare sock monkey. Then he pulled out what looked like an orange clock with a drawstring. It had a ring of animal pictures on its face instead of numbers.

"That one, I don't know what it does," Roma confessed.

"This?" Matt looked closer at it. "This is a Mattel See 'n Say. I haven't seen one of these since I was really little—like four, maybe—and it would have been old then. Who knows? It might actually be worth something. Maybe you could sell it on eBay." *And use the profits to leave this shithole for good*, Matt thought.

"Yes, eBay, sure." Roma looked away from Matt as if she'd read his mind. "But how does it, ah, work?"

"Oh, right. I'll show you." He pulled back the drawstring. With a *click-click-click-click*, the plastic central arrow swung around until it pointed to a picture of a horse. A warped recorded voice from within said, *"This is the sound a horse makes: Neigh! Neigh! Neigh!"* He pulled the string again. *Click-click-click-click.* Again, the arrow spun, until it pointed to another picture. *"This is the sound a dog makes: Rarf! Rarf! Rarf!"*

"Yes, I see," Roma said.

"You could do shadow puppets to go along with the See 'n Say using this." Matt pointed to a dusty 1970s slide-show carousel that was sitting on a box. He took the plug, found an outlet.

"Shadow puppets?"

"Yeah, like, with your hands. But you need a projector." Matt hit the *on* button. The carousel clattered and came to life.

Clack. Its bright eye projected a slide on the wall above the crib: it showed the lodge in happier times—three pit bulls sunning themselves and chasing their tails in the grass.

"I didn't realize there were slides in here," Matt said.

Roma clapped her hands together, said that her child might like the picture and to leave it there.

Matt nodded, moved by her simplicity. "Sure." He sat down across from her, at the foot of Jasha's bed. He had to take action to protect this woman, her unborn child, and himself. "Roma, I need your help. I want to leave this place tonight. Charles told me there was a secret opening in the electric fence. Do you know where it is?"

She hesitated, then gave a short nod.

"I want you to show it to me. And I want my ax back, and my backpack. I'm not sure who took them when I was reeled back onto the deck, but someone did. I can't leave this place without them—especially my ax. Can you help me?"

A moment of indecision, in which the carousel again *clacked* and showed more pictures of romping dogs under a darkening sky.

"Roma! Roma, where are you?" Charles Kingman's quavering voice came wafting up from below and shattered the stillness.

Roma stood immediately, gathered the plate and the glass. "Of course, Matthew, I will help you. I know where they took your ax, your bag. After I attend to Charles, I will get them for you and put them in your room."

"Good. Thanks."

"Let me go down the stairs first, to make sure no one is there."

"No problem."

She moved past him, around the clothes rack, to the trapdoor. He caught her scent as she passed: sweet and strange and somehow feral, like lavender mingled with the faint musk of the wet earth in spring...

Clack.

He turned. The slide show had changed again, showing the pit bulls playing in the grass from a different angle. From the new angle, Matt could see picnic tables set up and militiamen and their fat girlfriends sitting at them, drinking beer and eating off paper plates while smoke wafted lazily through the darkening evening air.

Jasha groaned and twisted fitfully. The black hand sputtered in its bowl, making shadows bend. Downstairs, Matt could hear Kingman's quaking agitation and the low sound of Roma's soothing response. Matt wondered if it was too soon to get out of the creepy attic.

Clack.

The slide-show carousel clicked again, this time showing a scene at nightfall. No more plastic plates, but plenty of beer in evidence as dozens of militiamen stood laughing in front of a bonfire at full blaze, lifting their cans in salute. The fire was at least twelve feet high and so bright that the white-hot heart of it caused the picture to overexpose, reducing the fire image to a blinding patch of white with a few indistinct shadows at its center.

Matt looked away from the photo. Something about it made him uneasy. Roma's newborn could probably do without that slide projected over the crib.

His hand itched for his ax. Downstairs, he could no longer hear any voices. Roma had probably retrieved his stuff by now. Definitely time to head down.

Clack.

Keep going, a voice in his head said, but Matt couldn't help but glimpse back.

The latest slide showed laughing men gathered around the fire and one sloshing an arc of gasoline from a square red gas can toward the blaze, which had died down to half strength—enough so that it was no longer an overexposed blur and the darkness at its heart was no longer shapeless.

Matt froze in his tracks, staring at the projection. Felt the back of his throat close. His palms flash with the damp ache of horror.

The dark shape within the fire...

It was a *log* of some kind.

A weirdly shaped log.

It *had* to be.

It—

Clack.

Matt gasped.

The shape was not a log.

The shape was a *woman.*

The shape was a woman with blackened skin and blazing hair, a woman who strained against the steel pole to which she'd been tied, her mouth open in mid-cry, her eyes rolling white and as mad as a mare's, her clothes incandescent, her head haloed in yellow points of flame.

Click-click-click-click.

Matt's gaze snapped down. For no reason whatsoever, the See 'n Say on the crate had rattled to life, the plastic arrow whirling around in a circle until it came to rest on a pig picture. The warped, distorted voice that warbled out of it in half time was barely recognizable as human.

"This...is the sound...a hog makes," it said.

But what followed was not the grunt of a pig. It was the ear-shattering shriek of a woman being burned alive, and it went on, and on, and *on*...

Matt clamped his hands to his ears, bounded to the crate, grabbed the possessed toy, and flung it against the wall, where it shattered into a hundred pieces. As soon as it did, the oily green flame rising off the blackened hand flared up with a tearing sound. It rose three, four, five feet above the bowl in a roaring tongue of fire, then split into a Y-shaped blaze that morphed into the slant-eyed visage of a hook-nosed clown, jaws agape in laughter.

Matt staggered backward, his mind reeling.

Where else should an Aryan soul seek purification than in the very crucible of Aryanism?

The tongue of flame grew thinner, grew blacker, and resolved itself into a helix of smoke with a sudden w*hoof.*

Ahhhhhhhhh...

From the bed, Jasha groaned, blindly lunging against his bonds, eyes rolled back into his skull.

But Matt wasn't there to hear it. Matt was already past the clothes rack, was down the ladder, was in the hall. He dropped to the floor gasping, nearly broke his ankle. Rose unsteadily, expecting chaos, but didn't get it.

The hall was strangely silent.

Well, *almost* silent. From Kingman's study at the opposite end of the hall came the hiss of urgent whispers.

Could Roma still be talking to Kingman? Wouldn't he have heard the shrieking upstairs? Wouldn't she?

None of it made sense to Matt. No surprise there: his brain felt as useless as a blown fuse.

What had he just seen? Had it even happened?

As he crept down the hall, Matt was dimly aware that he was probably in shock. People who see a photo of a woman being burned alive should not be walking silently down halls. They should be weeping or freaking out or shouting at the top of their lungs. But he couldn't do any of those things. Because he now knew what the purpose was of the pyre being built at the base of the hill.

He knew what "BY MIDNIGHT TONIGHT OR ELSE" meant.

He knew what was in store for Roma if he didn't find a way to save her.

And he knew he'd have only one shot at doing so, and if he failed, they would both be ashes by morning.

CHAPTER ELEVEN

Closer now to Kingman's study, Matt could begin to make out snatches of the old man's hoarse whispers.

"...not much time left, but listen! *Listen to me...*"

Was he still talking to Roma? Clenching his fists, Matt positioned himself by the cracked door and peered in. He saw Kingman from behind, his scabby scalp hovering above a tatty red robe.

"...'course I know what the alternative is! But she's... proto-Aryan princess!...of the Bear...how can we just..."

Matt's fists unclenched slightly. Kingman was talking *about* Roma, not to her. Unless she was in the room, listening silently?

A pause. Matt waited. Matt couldn't hear another voice, but clearly there had been one, because Kingman strode agitatedly out of view, saying, "You think I don't know that? You think I don't want my army back? My beautiful, magnificent, army...*Fist of God...*" He almost sobbed the last few words.

Matt eased the door open an inch to get a better view. He could see Kingman again. The old man was leaning against a strip of wall between two bookshelves; his palms and forehead were pressed into the wallpaper as if it were the only thing keeping him upright. He looked exhausted.

Another silence.

Then: "Don't...don't you *dare* patronize me!" Kingman jerked his face back from the wall, staring at his shadow, which the lamp behind him cast upon it. "I'm fully aware..."

Matt eased the door open another two inches. He could now see more than half of the room. No one was standing near Kingman.

Who the fuck is he speaking to?

"Oh, go ahead. Yes, you think you're so smart," Kingman sputtered, backing up, jabbing a finger at his shadow. "But I'm not lost yet! She gives me strength! Power! She renews me! Shares my *bed!*" Hunched over, Kingman pounded his chest with his fist, shouting at the wall and the black shape on it.

Matt cracked the door open another two inches. He now could see the far window, which reflected the entire room.

There was no one else in it.

Kingman was alone.

"Laugh all you want, you bastard! But I cannot...*I will not burn her!*" Kingman grabbed a book off his desk and flung it against the wall before him. "She's not like the rest. She's not! And I will not be bullied...I will not..." He covered his ears with his hands, shook his head fiercely. "Oh, god*damn* you...!" Kingman staggered backward, as if standing in a gale, and then threw himself against the wall before him. His clawlike fingers grabbed a scrolling tip of wallpaper and ripped it off in one long sheet. He flung it to the floor. Now nothing remained on the drywall before him but his shadow.

"You can't make me..." The old man wheezed, backing up, clutching his chest with one hand while he jabbed a finger at the wall with the other. "You can*not* make me..."

The skin on Matt's arms lifted into gooseflesh. *Jesus Christ. He's talking to his shadow!* Matt took a careful step backward. *Guy is fucking nuts.*

And then something happened that shocked Matt so completely he couldn't process it at first. It was a simple thing. Kingman spun away from the wall, his face haggard, his eyes glazed, and staggered over to a low mantel to grab a half-filled decanter of amber liquid, which he shakily poured into a shot glass.

There was nothing unusual about what Kingman did.

What was unusual was that even though he'd walked away, *his shadow remained on the wall.*

Matt stared, wide-eyed, feeling his chest tighten 'til he couldn't draw a breath.

The shadow didn't move.

And yet, it did. Because it wasn't completely motionless. It swayed slightly. Very near the shadow, the drywall had a long, diagonal crack. The shadow's shoulder wasn't touching the crack. But then it was. But then it wasn't.

Matt forced himself to breathe, to take a step backward. He fought off a creeping, dreamlike paralysis that threatened to freeze him in his tracks like a headlight-blinded deer.

Got to get out of here, he thought, stepping away from the cracked door—but not before he saw the shadow slide down the drywall, spill onto the carpet, and glide, like an oil slick, toward Kingman.

Got to get out of here—now.

Even if it meant leaving his backpack, his ax.

But wait, hadn't Roma said she'd put those things in his room?

She had.

Moving fast now, he backtracked down the hall toward the room they'd left him in. He pushed open the door—and there, on his bed, waiting for him like two old friends, were his backpack and ax.

Bingo.

Matt slung the backpack over his shoulder and grabbed the ax. He felt better immediately. The smooth grain of the handle was warm and dry in his palm, and the panic in his breast vanished.

Then he noticed something else: Roma had set Kingman's open laptop on his bed as well. But why? Had she wanted him to know where to find her?

He picked it up to take a look. The screen was still split into four quadrants, each showing a separate live video feed from the cameras carried by Thor, Loki, Odin, and Freya.

But none of the feeds showed Roma's location. Two were dark, while the other two just showed...

Matt blinked. Could that be...?

He peered closer. Snorted in disbelief.

Yep, it was.

Bare breasts, that is.

The lucky bearer of the Loki camera was clearly lying on his back somewhere. His video cam was pointed upward at the interlocking branches of overhead pine trees. The pines, however, were for the most part obscured by the half-naked commando bouncing up and down above him. Her camo jacket was open, and her baby-doll T-shirt was rucked up to her collarbone. The feed showed his hands rising up and massaging her full breasts, plucking at the dark nipples. Her eyes were closed, and she was breathing hard. As

Matt watched, she threw her head back, brow furrowed, and said, "Fuck *yes.*"

Meanwhile, Freya's feed showed the flushed face of a supine militiaman, his bristly jaw slack with pleasure.

Despite the horror of the past few minutes, the sheer innocence of the cam-recorded tryst almost made him laugh. He was glad someone in this godforsaken place had something better to do than commit murder, practice black magic, and measure craniums. The transported look on the young woman's face reminded him of better days that he'd once enjoyed, and might again—if he could find Roma and get her to guide him out of this compound to wherever these lovers frolicked. He gazed enviously at the image of the healthy young woman astride her companion, her face lifted against the night, with a full moon above her shoulder.

Full moon? Matt did a double take. When he'd been in the sky chair, he'd seen the moon, and it was a crescent.

Looked closer.

That full moon wasn't a moon.

It was a face.

"Oh my God," he said.

Baldy's white, vein-laced face loomed out of the darkness above Freya's shoulder. She didn't notice. But Loki did: Matt saw the soldier's eyes get big. He gave a muffled yell of panic at the same time that Baldy's huge fists slipped a black wire around Freya's neck and lifted her up, up, gagging—revealing the full breasts, the pale belly, the triangular thatch, the thrashing thighs, the kicking black combat boots.

Suddenly, Thor and Odin's feeds flashed to life, showing dozens of bodies in motion, swiftly approaching the compound's electric fence.

He glanced down at the laptop's clock: midnight.

Time's up.

Matt threw down the laptop, raced into the hallway, and at the top of his lungs, yelled, "Here they come!"

CHAPTER TWELVE

In two minutes, the entire compound was roused, and its staff—which by now included nine militiamen, Kingman, Arkady, and Roma—had assembled in the downstairs armory. And in that two minutes, every single halogen light along the compound's perimeter had been blown out with rifle fire.

In five minutes, the Fist of God's members were armed, armored, ammo'd up, and reporting to battle stations throughout the first floor. From outside came the ominous snarl of chainsaws biting into tree trunks beyond the fence.

And in eight minutes, a booming, amped-up voice came thundering from the direction of the front gate.

"WE'RE HERE, OLD MAN. COME OUT, COME OUT, WHEREVER YOU ARE!"

Charles Kingman stepped out onto the lodge's porch with Arkady and three other militiamen. Matt followed, his heart pounding. He'd tossed aside his backpack and slipped a bulletproof vest over his denim shirt. In his left hand he held a Glock. In his right was the ax.

So bright: Matt blinked, squinted against the harsh glare that bathed the porch.

As his eyes adjusted, he saw that, thirty feet beyond the electric fence's main gate, the huge headlights of a familiar ATV were focused on them like the eyes of a giant predator.

The ambient light from the halogens picked up the gleaming row of steel spikes on the ATV's hood, the fanged maw, RAHOWA.

Clutching a rifle, Kingman walked stiffly up to the camo-covered chain link that screened in the porch and peered out.

"What do you want, Alastair?" he shouted.

"YOU KNOW WHAT I WANT, OLD MAN. WE GOT THE PYRE. WE GOT THE GAS. ALL WE NEED NOW IS THE GIRL."

A sharp intake of breath behind Matt. He glanced around. Roma was standing behind him, her hands pressed to her belly, her eyes wide with fear.

"Never," Kingman croaked, his voice shaking with rage. "Not this one. I will not give her up. How many times have I told you? She is proto-Aryan, married in May to the Ursus—"

Alastair didn't wait for him to finish.

"I DIDN'T COME EMPTY-HANDED, OLD MAN. I'M PREPARED TO TRADE PRISONERS."

"Trade…?" Kingman seemed at a loss. Then he understood, and his voice rose to a hysterical pitch. "You release my scouts immediately! They are your brothers-in-arms, Alastair! I forbid you to harm them!"

This drew ragged laughter from the rank of traitors in the darkness beyond the fence. *Christ*, thought Matt, *sounds like a lot of them.*

"Hmm." Alastair was no longer using the bullhorn. He seemed to be mulling it over. "Well, now that you say it like that—all authoritative-like—goddamn, but it's awful hard to say no. You sure can be convincing when ya wanna be.

God knows I spent my entire life bein' convinced of all *kinds* of shit you said...*Dad.*"

Oh my God, Matt thought. *That's all that was missing.* He gripped his ax more tightly. Alastair's last sentence was spoken with a deep fury. Clearly these two had major issues with each other.

Alastair cleared his throat. "Anyway. I'm more'n willin' to let bygones be bygones. So here's your weak-ass foot soldiers. Don't never say I didn't give you nothin'."

There was movement out beyond the fence's main gate. Matt peered through the camouflaged chain link.

Slowly, the silhouettes of four figures staggered single file in front of the ATV. Their hands were bound, and they were all linked together by a long strap, like prisoners on a chain gang.

Kingman gave a sharp intake of breath when he saw them. "If you've hurt them, Alastair..."

"Naw, old man, see for yourself. They're just a little soggy, is all."

The figures staggered away from the ATV and toward the gate, each linked to the others by a six-foot cord. They appeared to be gagged. As they approached the fence, Matt could see that they were indeed soaked. While their features were still shadowed, their clothes were clearly black and stuck to their skin, which gleamed. Their hair was plastered to their heads. They looked like they'd been dragged through a creek. And probably had been.

"Get a move on, you four," Alastair said. "G'won home like the ass-whipped bitches you are."

Walter stepped up nervously behind Kingman. "Sir, the fence is live! If they touch it...!"

Another kid next to him said, "Sir, they're gonna want us to turn off the juice. That's why they're doin' this."

Kingman nodded. "The electricity stays on. But we will open the gate to let those four enter."

"Sir!"

"We *will* open the gate," Kingman hissed, turning on him. "But as soon as they're through, close it up. And shoot anyone who tries to follow them."

"Yes, sir."

Walter flicked open the control panel and tapped in a code.

There was a hum.

A loud click.

And then the electrified gate began to rattle back on its steel track.

The four prisoners stumbled forward, muffled groans coming from behind their gags. They came within fifteen feet of the gate.

Then ten.

Five.

The breeze shifted, began blowing toward Matt and the rest from the direction of the ATV. Matt got a whiff of something he didn't like. *It could be coming from the ATV...*

The four reached the open gate.

Or not. He sniffed again.

The first two staggered through the gate, followed by the third, followed by the fourth. Bound together, they all approached with shuffling steps.

"Shut it," Kingman hissed.

Walter's fingers clattered over the control panel.

Immediately, the gate began to rattle shut. Everyone on the porch tensed, every muzzle was lifted...But the ATV stayed where it was, its engine thrumming powerfully, its exhaust drifting toward the compound along with the smell of...

"Oh Jesus," Matt said.

A flame flared to life between the ATV headlights. It grew until it encompassed a fiery bolt. Hidden hands slid it into the drawn wire of a crossbow.

Matt threw himself against the chain link, shouting, shouting to the prisoners, "Get down! Get down!"

"The hell are you doing?" Kingman roared, grabbing Matt by the elbow.

Matt shook him off. "Can't you smell it? They're doused in"—the crossbow released with a *fwick*—"gas!"

The flaming bolt flashed through the chain-link fence and hit the nearest scout square in the back. There was an incredible *whoomf*, and he exploded into a twisting, screaming ball of fire. A line of flame shot along the strap connecting him to the nearest prisoner, who immediately *whoomfed* into a second fireball, and so (*whoomf*) ignited the wailing third, who (*whoomf*) lit the shrieking fourth.

"No!" With a strangled cry, Kingman made a lunge for the steps—only to have Matt grab him by the collar and jerk him backward. As soon as he did, splinters erupted from the porch pillar that Kingman had been standing next to only moments before.

"Let me go," Kingman yelled, struggling. "We've got to help them!"

"No fucking way," Matt said, looking out at the four screaming figures, engulfed in flames, that were rolling on the ground. "There's only one way to help them now." He looked meaningfully at Arkady. The clown's painted eyes met Matt's, and in that instant, they understood each other.

"Do it," Matt said.

Arkady lifted the AK-47 to his shoulder, sighted, and squeezed off four chattering bursts.

The screaming ended as abruptly as it had begun. Only now a new sound had taken its place: a familiar, high-pitched, grinding sound.

"The chainsaws again," Walter said hoarsely. "But what're they...?"

Suddenly, the mosquito whining of the saws cut out entirely.

The silence that followed was filled with a slow, splintering crack, then a stuttering groan that grew louder and louder. Matt turned to see a darkness detach itself from a greater darkness: a great pine came crashing down, flattening a section of the electrified double fence in an explosion of sparks.

Immediately, the ATV launched forward, roaring over the downed fence. Behind it, a half dozen other glowing headlights lit up like malevolent eyes, and three more ATVs shot forward to join the first, rolling over the felled tree trunk and snapping off branches as they came.

And in their wake, charging forward with a rebel yell, came dozens of howling soldiers.

"Get back!" Matt yelled. "Get back in the house! *Now!*"

CHAPTER THIRTEEN

They didn't need much encouraging. Kingman grabbed Roma by the arm and pulled her through the doorway, while three militiamen followed. In the meantime, Arkady swung his AK-47 around the corner of the tin sheeting and pulled the trigger. The weapon crackled, and a line of fire stitched across the yard into the first rank of the marauders. Three of them jerked backward with shouts of pain and flipped into the dust.

"You too—inside! You too!" Arkady shoved Matt into the house with his elbow as he reached for another clip.

"All of us," Matt said, and reached for his arm—too late. Arkady jammed his thumb into three of the control panel's buttons, and the metal door immediately started rumbling shut.

"Arkady!" Matt yelled.

"Is being no problem, dawg," the juggalo said, slapping another clip into his semiautomatic. His eyes were fever bright with anticipation, and his painted skeleton teeth grinned. "Clown loco is busting a nut in their melons, no? Word is bond, G."

And the door slammed shut.

Jesus, Matt thought, *who* are *these people?*

Matt tried to pry the door open, but there was no latch and he didn't know how to work the inside control panel.

Outside, he could hear the roar of ATVs and the clatter of bullets puncturing tin.

He ran into the armory. One of the militiamen had taken the bazooka off the wall and was hoisting it onto his shoulder. Another two had ripped the lid off a crate and were pulling out large ordnance to put into it.

"Roma, go upstairs!" As she moved toward the steps, Matt ran up to a plywood-covered window and looked through the muzzle slit.

Even though the halogens were blown out, the night was illuminated by the strobe-like flash of automatic gunfire. Matt saw soldiers swarming the yard chaotically, while in their midst stood Arkady, his painted face roaring with laughter as he wielded an AK in one hand, and—dear God, was that a *meat cleaver?*—in the other. Matt watched in amazement as, whooping with delight, Arkady squeezed off a round to the right, then to the left, then slung the cleaver in a wide arc that put about a foot of distance between a militiaman's chin and his Adam's apple.

A sudden, blinding glare of headlamps: the ATV had pulled up just a few dozen yards away, facing the window. What was Baldy up to? Matt couldn't tell, but he knew how to find out. He squeezed four blind shots out the window slit, then sprinted past the crew that was cursing over how difficult a bazooka was to load. *Might have wanted to practice that once or twice before tonight,* he thought, running up the stairway and catching up to Roma at the landing halfway between the first and second floors. There, as he remembered, was another window. The two of them breathlessly peered through it, into the yard below.

The first thing Matt noticed was that Arkady was gone. He could still hear automatic fire, but now it was coming from the other side of the house. The second thing he noticed was that the blinding glare was indeed from the ATV, which Baldy had parked facing the downstairs armory window. The third thing was that Baldy, too, had invested in a bazooka, but he and his fellow militiaman had apparently put a few hours in at the range learning how to use the fucking thing.

As Matt watched in horror, Baldy steadied the wide tube on his shoulder, peered through the sight, and pulled the trigger. There was a loud *pffft*, and a jag of white smoke shot from the back of the barrel like a misfiring bottle rocket. Then what looked to be a shooting star snapped from the mouth of the gun toward the house.

"Incoming!" Matt shouted to the guys below, then shoved Roma onto the stairs leading up to the second floor and threw his body on top of hers.

The explosion was cosmic.

The force of it nearly burst Matt's eardrums, and the wall of fire that shot up from the first floor scorched his back as it rolled overhead. When it had passed, Matt peeled himself off of Roma and saw that all the wallpaper had ignited. The stairwell had vanished, and Matt and Roma were trapped in a tunnel of fire.

CHAPTER FOURTEEN

Coughing from the smoke, Matt and Roma struggled to their feet, deafened by the explosion, the roaring flames, and the crack and chatter of ammunition cooking in the inferno below. The heat was incredible, was coming at them from every direction.

Without a moment's hesitation, Matt pushed her up the stairs, gritting his teeth as the hair on his arms was singed off and the skin beneath began to burn.

It wasn't much better at the top of the stairway. There, too, the wave of fire that had rolled up from below had ignited the wallpaper and drywall. The carpet smoked, and each entrance they ran past revealed rooms filled with the crawling fog of tear gas or the disco glitter of flying glass.

All but one: the trapdoor to the attic.

Even then, Matt balked. Suddenly, the idea of being cooked alive, or shot, or gassed, seemed almost preferable to reentering that black space where he'd seen the slide show of past atrocities and glimpsed Mr. Dark's visage in a ribbon of green flame...

And yet, when Roma grabbed hold of the retractable ladder and hauled herself up, Matt knew he had no choice.

He followed.

To be in the attic again was both better and much, much worse. It was better because the attic was not on fire (yet), though it was quickly filling with smoke and heating up. It was worse because of what was chained to the bed.

Jasha looked terrible. And not terrible in a geez-this-guy's-got-swine-flu sort of way, but in a geez-this-guy's-about-to-spontaneously-combust way. His pale skin was now a bruised, mottled purple, and his eyes were rolled back into his skull. His hands were clenching and unclenching, and his whole body was soaked in sweat. He writhed in agony, he groaned, he roared.

"Roma, what's wrong with him?"

Roma didn't answer. Rushing to his side, she pulled a key out of her pocket and began fumbling with his cuffs, crying, "Jasha, oh my Jasha!"

In a few seconds, the cuffs were off, and she grabbed his big head and pulled him upright, whispering to him urgently in a language Matt couldn't fathom. She pressed her lips to his, and suddenly, his pupils rolled into place and his breath became more even. Seeing her for the first time, he put his huge mitts gently against her cheeks and pulled her to him in a very unbrotherly kiss.

Matt stared. *What the fuck?*

The attic had two windows, one behind Jasha and one behind Matt. The one behind Matt suddenly flooded with light. The hair on Matt's neck prickled with foreboding. Shoving aside a stack of boxes, he pushed his way to the lit window and looked out.

"Oh my God."

Three stories below, the flood lamps of the Rahowa ATV were tilted upward toward the attic, and Baldy was once again hunching against the tube of his bazooka, eyeing the window through the sight on his scope.

"Roma! Get him—get out the window! Open the window and get him out!"

She didn't question him—the tone of his voice, the look in his eye was enough. In seconds, she had flung the other window open and crawled out. Holding Jasha's hand, she pulled the staggering giant after her, and when his oversized ass got stuck in the window, Matt threw his shoulder against it with all his might. That—and the shockwave of the second bazooka round hitting the other side of the house—did the trick.

Again, the cataclysmic *BOOM*, an unstoppable, onrushing tide of heat and light...And the three of them were flung out of the attic and onto the roof.

Both the angle and length of the Swiss-chalet-style roof were asymmetrical. The south side of the roof slanted at a gentle cant all the way down to within four feet of the ground, beneath which had been raked a big pile of leaves. The north side of the roof cut downward at a vertigo-inducing angle and then simply ended, asymmetrically, fifteen feet above the ground, with nothing between roof and holly bush but ten feet of ramshackle scaffolding that had been wrapped in canvas tarp.

Unfortunately, Matt, Roma, and Jasha had piled out on the *north* side of the roof.

As soon as they were out, Matt heard Roma scream. He grabbed on to Jasha's arm as the big guy started to tumble helplessly down, and—keeping the ax lifted high above so as not to accidentally decapitate his ally—pulled himself *over* Jasha to try to help Roma. He landed hard on his knees and threw himself forward, yelling her name and grabbing for her wrist, her ankle, her hair—anything.

In vain. His fingers brushed hers briefly, he saw her green eyes widen in terror, and then she fell off the roof.

Matt caught himself just in time at the roof's edge, but then Jasha crashed into him from behind, and he followed Roma.

Spinning in free fall, Matt saw a series of snapshot-like images of what happened next. He saw Roma fall five feet, hit with a grunt the wooden planks of the scaffold's top platform, then roll off *that* and slide down ten feet of tarp, landing, finally, face-first in a holly bush.

Which was pretty much what happened to him, but with more cursing.

It hurt. A lot. But his neck still moved, and his back still worked, and he could move his limbs (barely). Matt rolled painfully over just in time to see Jasha—who had been clutching the last row of shingles—fall onto the scaffolding, crash *through* the boards of its top platform, and disappear behind the tarp. Then came a deep, painful *thud* that he could feel in the soles of his feet as he struggled to get vertical.

That had to hurt.

But it didn't kill him: the agonized bellowing from behind the tarp proved that the big Russian wasn't dead, just sicker, more injured, and *madder* than ever.

Matt looked around, dazed, to find Roma, and did. The good news was that, by the flickering light of the flaming house, he could see that, like him, she, too, was alive, was upright, and looked to have survived with nothing worse than bruises and scratches. The *bad* news was that both of her arms were twisted behind her back by the skinny, red-bearded skag whose twin had bought it back at the grocery.

And there were six more guys behind him.

"Well, I'll be goddamned," Red said, flashing his nicotine-stained choppers. "Shake a strange tree and a strange fruit falls! How ya' doin', bitch?"

Roma shrieked as he hoisted her arms up painfully behind her back and then shoved her, facedown, over a big air-conditioning unit that butted up against the tarped scaffolding.

"Who's up for a slice of dark meat, boys?"

A cheer from the rest. Matt reached down for his ax, but just as his fingers reached the handle, a black jackboot kicked it away and a thick arm wrapped around his throat. He was jerked upright, couldn't take a breath.

Matt hoped briefly that Jasha might come out and mop up the bastards, but the bellowing from behind the tarp proved that he was in no shape to come to the rescue. Though the sheer volume of his roaring was enough to catch Red's attention. He jerked his head toward the scaffold and yelled, "Listen up, boys, first one to bring me that fat fuck's head has got dibs on sloppy seconds with *this* one."

Six ear-splitting whoops as the soldiers ripped hatchets and Ka-Bar knives from their belts and tore through the tarp.

"Jasha!" Roma cried. "No!"

Matt jerked forward, but the guy behind him had him in an iron choke hold. Points of light bloomed and faded before Matt's eyes. His vision blurring, he saw Red roughly pin Roma's face to the AC with one hand and pull at her dress with the other. Laughing at Matt's predicament. "Long time no see, bud!" he crowed. "But fair's fair, right? She killed my brother, and I'm gonna kill hers."

Just for the hell of it, Matt spent the last few molecules of oxygen at his disposal croaking out, "He's not her brother."

Red's brow furrowed in confusion as the six men within the scaffold began to shout in panic, and Jasha's roaring deepened and deepened until it reverberated in Matt's chest like a tolling bell.

"The fuck is that?" Confused, Red glanced up at the tarp, then down at the thrashing girl beneath him. "Steady, Brown Sugar." He lifted and banged her face into the AC. Said, "Wanna hear a joke? What's a foreign bitch like you got in common with a well-cooked sirloin? Give up?" Hoisted her dress up above her hips. "You're both pink inside."

Then it happened.

The roaring rose like the rage of a god. It swallowed six separate screams of panic, and then the tarp exploded in a blizzard of shredded canvas, shattered aluminum bars, a hunk of hair, a hand, a head. The entire rickety contraption of the scaffolding flew apart as from its depths charged the dark, shaggy shape of a *giant Kodiak bear.*

CHAPTER FIFTEEN

The beast was a black blur as it lunged forward, roaring, its blunt muzzle cracked open impossibly wide.

Matt couldn't believe his eyes.

The arm around his neck loosened.

Red staggered backward, releasing Roma to gape in shock at the shaggy monster that reared up before him to its full ten-foot height and swung a paw that looked like a catcher's mitt outfitted with three-inch fishhooks.

All five claws caught Red's jaw on the upsweep. His neck and head were instantly replaced by what looked like three feet of black yarn.

Red's body flew nine feet into the air, flipped, and landed in the mud. Militiamen scattered, screaming, as pieces of his face and frontal cortex pitter-pattered down like chunky rain. Then two soldiers turned, lifted their AKs, and burned a clip wildly in the bear's direction.

But it had moved. It was fast—*really* fast—for something so big. It shot forward on trunk-like legs, the hump of its back raised in a black crest, like a razorback's. Its huge head snapped forward, engulfed the head of the first shooter, shook, and flung him—sans head—into the body of the second. When the second guy tried to scramble away on all fours, the bear came even with him and drove a paw into the middle of his body. It sounded like a stepped-on bag of pretzels.

By now, Matt was released entirely. He spun around to see the goateed hick with the black knit cap embroidered with the Confederate flag. It was the same guy who'd used him for target practice with the tactical slingshot outside the grocery. What was his name? Matt couldn't remember. All he knew was that now the guy was much better armed: in each hand he held a gleaming .357 Magnum.

"Hi, Matt," he said, raising both weapons toward Matt's chest. "Bye, Matt!"

And he blew Matt away.

Both slugs hit Matt at the same time. Both felt like simultaneous sledgehammer strikes. Both pounded him off his feet and sent him flying backward.

Matt's vision went black while he was airborne, but he could hear Roma cry out his name, could feel himself skid to a stop in the mud.

I'm dead, he thought. *Again.*

But should a dead man's chest hurt as much as his did? Should a dead man be drawing such painful breaths?

He opened his eyes and saw his Kevlar jacket rising and falling with two big smoking holes in its armor.

Alive!

He rolled over, got his knees under him, tried to rise.

Not happening.

He grabbed a root for support. The smooth wood slipped perfectly into the groove of his palm.

It wasn't a root.

He knew what it was.

BANG-BANG-BANG-BANG.

A roar of fury.

Matt rose and turned. The Confederate (what was his name?) had put four fat slugs into the bear. The beast had twisted around, bellowing, but when it started forward toward the shooter, its leg gave out.

The Confederate walked toward it coolly, weapons raised. But as he came even with Roma, he swung one of the guns around and pressed the muzzle against her forehead.

"Sayonara, you goddamn chimp."

Suddenly, Matt remembered his name.

"Keith! Hey, Keith—*catch*."

Keith turned just in time to hear it whispering toward him, to see it flash through the darkness. His brow briefly wrinkled in confusion to see its outer iron edge glimmer red in the flame light thrown by the burning house.

Then the ax struck him with a *thwack*, exactly where Matt had aimed: square in the center of his Confederate flag. Both of his guns fell to the ground. Keith's body followed, even as his head, like Dixie, seceded.

Things seemed to go in fast-forward for Matt after that—much faster, but also more disconnected. Matt got his ax back and then was rolling on the ground. He was rolling because someone was shooting at him. He got trampled by three people fleeing something. One of those three got too close to the Kodiak and there was a lot of screaming. Matt tripped over a severed leg, which may or may not have belonged to the screaming person. A small ATV rolled past him with a flaming bolt stuck in one tire. No one was driving the ATV, but Arkady was crouched on its hood, swinging his blood-spattered meat cleaver, laughing, his dreads flying. Then part of the house collapsed, sending out a cloud of red sparks that stung like bee stings wherever they landed. Out of nowhere, a militiaman Matt hadn't seen whacked him from behind with a rifle butt. Matt fell, and when he rolled over, he was looking into the muzzle of the rifle. There was a *crack*, and the militiaman's head snapped sideways. He keeled over. Then came Walton, the fauxhawk kid who'd never read a book, holding his smoking gun and pulling Matt to his feet. He was saying something to Matt.

What was he saying? Matt focused on his lips.

"...got the old man cornered! Come on! Come on! Any longer an' it'll be too late!"

And then Matt was running after Walton to help Kingman. He couldn't have said why. In the back of his head was a faint, calm voice saying, *What the hell do you care about Charles Kingman? If these skinhead idiots want to butcher each other, let them.*

And yet, Walton had saved his life. And also, the weird logic of the battlefield dictated that he aid those on his side and fight those who were not. It made no sense, but he did it anyway. It didn't seem to him that he had a choice. He didn't even think about it. He just ran after Walton to help the mad, murderous racist Charles Kingman.

CHAPTER SIXTEEN

Kingman needed a *lot* of help. He was cornered in a part of the yard that sloped down toward a still-standing section of the electric fence. There he stood on a small pile of two-by-fours, blinded by the headlamps of the huge Rahowa ATV that was circling him. Turning slowly, he screamed his defiance at Alastair, who crouched behind the ATV wheel, while another militiaman stood behind him.

Kingman had a gun but no bullets. He seemed unaware of this and punctuated his rant with frequent trigger pulls, which unleashed nothing worse than an anemic *click-click-click*.

The guy behind Alastair was armed too—with the same crossbow that had incinerated Kingman's four scouts earlier. But he had ammo as well. He had a quiver full of pitch-dipped bolts and what looked to be a vintage Zippo lighter. While Alastair circled Kingman, the archer behind him fitted a bolt, lit it, and let it fly.

The flaming bolt whooshed within six inches of Kingman's face, making him fall backward in surprise. It skidded off the top of an oil drum, ricocheted over the fence, and vanished into the darkness. The archer and Alastair both whooped with laughter.

Matt glanced around, hoping for backup. There was none. The house was engulfed in crackling flames and was beginning to lean dangerously. Shadows darted here and there, but they were no one Matt knew. From the other side of the house, he heard a familiar roar. He couldn't see any sign of Arkady or Roma.

They were on their own.

"Follow me!"

Matt followed Walton to a row of oil drums close to the action. Before Matt could stop him, Walton yelled over the top, "Back off, Alastair—or I'll blow your head off!"

"Don't *tell* him—just *do* it," Matt hissed.

"Can't," Walton whispered back. "Out of ammo."

"Oh *fuck*."

Predictably, Alastair and the archer had turned at the sound of Walton's ultimatum. Predictably, the archer slid another bolt into his crossbow, touched the tip to his lighter, and turned it their way.

"Get down!" Walton said. "Get down behind the oil drum."

"Walton," Matt said, gritting his teeth, "just *think* of what you just said."

A beat. Then: "Oh shit."

"Right." Matt looked over the top of the drum just in time to see the archer line up his eye with the crossbow sight. "Run!" And he bolted to the side at the same time that the archer pulled the trigger.

Fwick.

Matt wasn't looking at the drum when it exploded, so he had no idea what happened to Walton. Had the kid jumped away in time? Or had he been cooked in the oily burst of heat that lit up the night and sent Matt sprawling into the mud?

Matt didn't know, and at this rate, it was possible he would never find out. All he had time to think about was how fast the huge ATV with the steel rhino horns shot forward as soon as the oil drum blew, sweeping around the far side (probably to finish off Walton) before heading for him.

By then, of course, he was up and running. He made for the only high ground in sight: the heap of two-by-fours on which Kingman was standing.

He made it to the top, panting, just as the ATV rounded the drums and turned the glare of its headlamps onto him. Squinting into the light, he could see the archer, in silhouette, pulling another bolt from his quiver.

"Well, by God, it's Matthew Cahill!" Kingman slapped his shoulder like they'd just run into each other at a charity golf outing. "Good to see you! What a night! Isn't it glorious, Matt? And to think that *we lived to see it come!*"

"*It?*" Matt said, not understanding. "What's 'it'?"

"Why, the Rahowa, of course! The final standoff between the chosen and the forsaken, the enlightened and the ignorant, the good and the evil! *The Rahowa, Matt—it's finally arrived!*"

Matt's mind blanked at the sheer incomprehensibility of the statement, and he was saved from responding by a soft but audible *fwick*.

Kingman jerked backward with a grunt. He looked stupidly at the flaming bolt sticking out of his left shoulder. Then his gaping mouth closed and his eyes narrowed. He turned toward Matt and said—with an astonishingly steady voice—"Do you know what makes a man a success in this world, Matt?"

Smelling the hair-singeing funk of scorched flesh, Matt said no.

"The will to power." Slowly, Kingman wrapped his right hand around the flaming bolt. "I had it, Matt. Remember that." And with the sound of tearing muscle, he ripped the bolt out of his body. Held it aloft. Waved it at the ATV.

"You'll have to do better than that, you clueless bastard! You're no son of mine! You're no—"

Fwick. WHACK.

Suddenly, a flaming bolt was jutting out of Kingman's forehead like a unicorn horn. He jerked backward, eyes rolling back into his skull. His jaw fell open, and he collapsed onto his back, still clutching the first fiery bolt.

Alastair gunned the ATV. "Hold on!" he yelled to his archer, who gripped the back of his seat. "Cahill? This here's for what you done to our brother-in-arms. Prepare to meet your maker!" And the ATV shot forward.

Matt's first impulse was to run—but he stifled it. Because he'd grown up in the country. He knew ATVs. He knew that this oversized job was a Kawasaki Brute Force and had its tank in the back and a clearance of about fifteen inches— more than enough room for what he intended to do. But he couldn't do it standing on a pile of two-by-fours. On a pile of two-by-fours he'd just get mowed down.

But on the muddy ground? That was a whole different story.

Matt charged the ATV.

As it roared closer, he cleared the woodpile. Gripping his ax in both hands, he took a final look at the gleaming row of steel horns, eyes, fangs, RAHOWA—and then he extended his right leg and fell back on his left, like a batter sliding into home.

It worked. The mud was slick, and he slid smoothly under the ATV as it shot harmlessly above him. As it passed, he thrust upward with the ax with all his strength and heard the blade bite into the undercarriage with a *chink*.

Unable to stop in time, the ATV crashed up and over the woodpile where Matt had been standing only moments before, then made a furious U-turn.

Matt followed it, running back onto the woodpile, looking for the traces of the ATV's passing. He found it: a thin spray of wetness darkening the pine two-by-fours, from where he'd chopped its tank.

"Lock 'n' load," Alastair bellowed, his great white head crevassed with hellish fissures. Behind him, the archer slid another bolt into his crossbow and lit it.

Matt reached down and tried to pull the flaming arrow from Kingman's hand. Amazingly, even in death, his grip was too fierce to pry it free.

"Comin' for you this time, Cahill," Alastair yelled, gunning the ATV forward. "Gonna burn your ass alive!"

"Wanna bet?" Matt put his foot on Kingman's face, grabbed the flaming arrow jutting out of his head, and ripped it free. Then he threw himself to his knees and jammed the fiery bolt into the gas-streaked wood.

The result was immediate.

A hot blue flame flared to life and shot forward, following the spray of the leaking tank down the woodpile and into the mud. The fiery ribbon flashed past the approaching ATV, gaining speed. The archer craned his neck around to watch it sweep behind them, following their tracks in a tight U-turn, and then hungrily rush after the leaking tank, snaking across the mud, getting closer, closer...

The archer dropped his crossbow and slapped Alastair furiously on the shoulder, gesturing behind them. Baldy took one look and then surged, panic-stricken, to his feet. They both crouched to jump free of the vehicle at the very second that the blue ribbon of flame reached the leaking tank.

KA-BOOOOOOOOOOOOOOOOOM!

There were actually two explosions: a smaller and a larger. When the smaller hit, Matt saw the four big ATV wheels shoot off in opposite directions, saw the hood levitate twenty feet in the air, saw the seat eject as if from a nose-diving F-14. He saw a black-and-red ball of fire that consumed vehicle and drivers alike, and then surged outward in every direction in a *second* explosion, twice as loud as the first—one that seemed to wipe out the compound, the slope it sat on, the woods that surrounded it, and the stars that glared at it from above. One that blew Matt backward in an inescapable wave of heat and light, followed by a surging tide of darkness.

CHAPTER SEVENTEEN

His dreams were scattered, overlapping, inchoate. And they melted, as the song goes, like cake in the rain.

Matt blinked. Large wet drops were splashing on his forehead, his cheekbones, his chin. Cool water pooled in his ears and the hollow of his neck. It was not unpleasant.

Breathing in the campfire smell of charred wood, he turned his head stiffly to see the smoldering ruin that had been the compound. Part of it had fallen. Part of it hadn't. All of it had burned. Some of it was still burning, and glowing orange lines of fire squiggled slowly like worms through the blackened, smoking beams of what had once been a decent little lodge.

There were other smells, less pleasant. Like a cookout where the cook left the meat unattended.

Matt painfully got to his feet. He didn't ever remember being this sore. Shuffled a few steps forward and nearly tripped over his own ax. His back ached so badly that it took about two minutes to pick it up. When he was done, he began a slow, halting circuit of the house.

It was still dark, though the eastern tree line was lined in gray and the faintest rim of pink. By the light of the crescent moon and the smoldering house, Matt began counting bodies. By the time he'd circled the compound, he was up to thirty-two, give or take a few partials here and there. He didn't find any sign of Roma, Walton, or Arcady, or the big bear that had been Jasha. He would have assumed that he'd dreamed that part, if not for the state of some of the bodies he passed.

But he did find his bike, and he did find his bag. Not wanting to attract attention, he rolled the bike over the downed fence and quietly walked it through the woods, avoiding the pathway he'd come up on.

Big drops fell from the pine boughs, slowly soaking his hair and clothes. He didn't mind. Burned out, Matt welcomed the rain's cool touch and the light mist that it pulled from the earth as he passed between the red-barked trunks.

Christ. What a fiasco.

So many dead…And for what? What had he learned? Only that Charles Kingman—buried alive (as Matt had been) and haunted afterward (as Matt was)—had tried to fend off the murderous temptations of his shadow-self by willfully descending into a paranoid, arrogant fantasy of superiority and hate, which spread like a contagion fed by poverty, ignorance, and pseudoscience, culminating finally in the ritual holocaust that he had originally sought to avoid.

So, had Matt actually accomplished anything here tonight?

He doubted it. But maybe there was a lesson here somewhere. Now that he saw to what insane depths Kingman's pride had taken him, he would remember that his search for a cure—his hunt for a way to forever purge himself of Mr. Dark's hateful presence—could never come at the expense of another, no matter how tempting the idea might be. That path was a one-way ticket to the hell he'd just stumbled out of, and having visited it once, Matt vowed never to return.

Light-headed, Matt paused to catch his breath, to let his sore body rest a moment. He pressed his singed brow against a pine trunk and welcomed the clean, wet, rough rasp of the bark.

Matt breathed in. Froze.

Suddenly, the air smelled, tasted different. Along with the wet-pine scent, he inhaled the strong odor of wet fur.

Instantly, knew he was not alone.

The hairs on his neck prickling, Matt slowly turned around.

There, between two large tree trunks, silhouetted against the dawn light, was the black hulk of a gigantic bear. It crouched silently on all fours, watching him intently. Standing at its side, equally still, was the cleaver-clutching shadow of a short man with dreads. Astride the shaggy beast was a third and final shadow: slim, with flowing hair that fell over her shoulders, down to her waist.

How was it that, shadowed and featureless as all three were, their eyes glowed gold and green?

Was it just a trick of the light?

"Matthew." Roma's voice, low and assured.

Matt swallowed. His heart pounded in his chest, but not with fear, exactly. It took him a moment to identify the emotion that threatened to overwhelm him. But then it fell into place. It was *awe* he felt. Awe for the three of them. For her especially.

"Matthew?"

He licked his chapped lips. How to address her? She had told him her name was Roma. But clearly there was more to her than met the eye. Much more.

"Who...are you?" he said.

She shifted slightly, so that the dawn light illuminated half of her face. "I am myself. I am the Bride of the Bear." She ran a hand across Jasha's rugged coat.

"Uh-huh." Digested that. "But how did he...did you two...ah..." Overwhelmed, he couldn't formulate a coherent thought. He knew he knew nothing. He knew he needed to know everything. But where to begin?

"Matthew."

"Yes?"

"You have not, I think, been to Kamchatka?"

"No."

"Right." She nodded, and he thought he could detect on her full lips a smile, both sad and strange. "So trust me? You would not understand."

He opened his mouth and closed it. "OK."

She held out her hand. "Approach me," she said.

He did. And as he did, he felt a weird emotion that was halfway between exhilaration and terror. Each step took him closer, until he was even with the great bear's head, looking up at her. The smell of wet fur was overwhelming. It mingled with the scent of black earth, of pine needles, of wet fern—and of her naked body. As he got closer, he could see that the dress she had been wearing had burned off. Her long hair covered her full breasts, and Jasha's shaggy crest covered what lay beneath her belly. But it could not cover the scent of her. *A green scent.*

Roma's outstretched hand stroked the line of his jaw. "Thank you, Matthew, for saving me."

"Sure. Sure, it was nothing."

"It was not nothing to me." She leaned down slowly and pressed her full lips to his brow. Kissed him, softly.

The Kodiak let out a low warning growl that made Matt's stomach flip.

Roma slowly pulled away. Whispered, "Good luck on your journey, Matthew."

At the first touch of her lips, all soreness had drained from his body. At her blessing, a rejuvenating energy had flooded every limb. And yet, he needed more than that. Much more.

"Roma?"

"Yes?"

"I…" He swallowed nervously. "I need more than luck. I need information. And I think…I think that you could help me, if you wanted to."

Dawn light shafted through the trees, illuminating the sheen of her black hair, the swell of one breast, the way her right hand buried itself in her husband's black mane.

"It is dawn, Matthew. Our kind must go. You understand."

"No, actually. No, I don't."

"But you will."

Slowly, Jasha backed up, pressing past a series of wet boughs that fell between Matt and them as they edged back into the darkness.

"Please!" Matt took a step forward, his desperation rising. "I'm haunted too, like Kingman was! I don't want to make the same mistakes! How can I fight Mr. Dark? Give me something. *Anything.*"

Jasha and Roma had already vanished into the encompassing darkness. But the short, dreadlocked clown hesitated beneath an uplifted bough. Turned back toward Matt.

"His weakness, bitch? Is…ah…how do you say? *Wagering.*"

Matt cocked his head, confused. "I'm sorry?"

"He likes to gamble, bitch. To *bet*."

Matt's mind raced. "Who does?"

Arkady gave a skeletal grin, equal parts menace and mischief. "Who do you think, bitch? *Who do you think?*"

And he, too, disappeared in the darkness, leaving Matt standing in the glade to watch the rising sun slowly banish every shadow.

CHAPTER EIGHTEEN

At the foot of the hill, Matt found the road, and it felt good to hear his wheels crackle the gravel and begin putting distance between himself and Kingman's smoking compound.

A few miles along, Matt swerved carefully around something that he at first thought was a dead snake, but on closer inspection, it turned out to be a soggy, discarded black-and-red armband. A hundred yards farther on, he passed a badge embroidered with a white fist, with strands of stitching trailing from it like hair on a corpse. He half expected a brass ring with a big fake garnet to be next, and so he wasn't disappointed when one appeared, glittering in the mud where it'd been thrown.

He cautiously rounded a hairpin curve. There, up ahead, he saw a figure walking along the side of the road. Even before he pulled even with him, Matt recognized the hunched shoulders, the clenched fists, the unruly fauxhawk.

Matt's bike puttered in neutral, and he pulled up alongside Walton.

"Wet day for a walk."

"Wet day for a ride."

He had a point there.

"Looks like you lost some gear back there, Walton."

Walton shook his head, stooped a little more in the wet wind, putting one foot after the other. "I'm done with all that shit. Seems like you gotta be a PhD to understand anything about it. And even if you do, it's just FUBAR." He shot Matt a quick glance. "You know what that means, right?"

"Fucked up beyond all recognition," Matt said.

Nodding. "There ya go. Like I said, I'm done with it all, for good. If I ever hear someone shootin' off about racial this or Aryan that, it'll be too soon."

Matt walked his bike alongside the kid in silence for a while, then decided to ask it. "So where you heading?"

"Town. Bus station. Gonna catch the eleven fifteen."

"To where?"

"Far as I can get from this pissant pocket of the world. Got a hundred and fifteen dollars in my pocket, and I'm gonna spend every dime of it. I hear the Missouri Ozarks got short winters and pretty girls."

Matt nodded. "I've heard that too. If you wanna hop on, I could give you a lift to the station."

"Nah. Only a mile or two more. I wanna walk out of this town on my own steam, if that makes any sense."

"It does," Matt said, feeling some respect for the kid for the first time. And that made him think of something. "Hold up." He stopped, and the kid did too. Matt slid his backpack off the rear seat. Unzipped a pocket and took out his wallet. He extracted a twenty-dollar bill that he kept for emergencies.

"What's that?" Walton said in surprise.

"Bookmark." Matt then took out, from the very bottom of his backpack, a worn paperback. He opened its creased cover and flipped through its dog-eared pages until he got about halfway through. He inserted the twenty between pages, closed it, and handed it to Walton.

Walton looked at it in surprise. Read the title aloud: "*The Executioner #38.*" He looked up, squinting. "What's this?" he asked.

"It's called a book. If you read the words in the order they're written in, Missouri will come a lot sooner. And I've got it on good authority that those Ozark girls admire the bookish types."

Walton snorted. "Let's hope not." He looked over the slim volume. "Still and all, I thank you for it. I'll do my best to read it."

"Good." Matt revved the bike. "Good luck to you, Walton."

"You too, bud."

Matt gave him a final nod, then pulled away. It felt good to feel the engine throb to life. He let out the throttle, heading for the bright country ahead.

THE END

THE DEAD MAN:
FIRE AND ICE

By Jude Hardin

Some say the world will end in fire,
Some say in ice.
From what I've tasted of desire
I hold with those who favor fire.
But if it had to perish twice,
I think I know enough of hate
To say that for destruction ice
Is also great
And would suffice.

Robert Frost, *Fire & Ice*

6:05 a.m.

Pete McCray was in Nitko's security office dumping sugar into a cup of coffee when Kevin Radowski marched in and shot him five times in the chest. McCray dropped to the tile floor, facedown, knocking his ceramic coffee mug and the glass sugar dispenser off the table in the process. The blood oozing from his body mingled with the hot coffee and the sugar granules, creating a ghastly stew that, remarkably, smelled like grape jelly. Kevin finished him off with a shot to the back of the head.

"Have a nice day," Kevin said, tipping his Nitko cap to the fallen officer.

Kevin had grown up in one of the shitty little company houses on the dirt road behind the plant. He'd had a happy childhood, mostly, but on a shelf somewhere in the deepest, darkest recesses of his subconscious cellar stood a row of Mason jars marked *Bathtime with Mama*. All of these jars were filled with splish-splash warmth and joy, with Mr. Bubble and toy boats and a rubber dinosaur named Roscoe.

All of them, that is, except one.

In this one particularly cloudy sample, two-year-old Kevin did something horrible, something vile and disgusting and practically unforgivable.

But he was only two, after all. He thought massaging Mama's back with poo-poo was a good thing. He did it while she rinsed her hair, and she told him it felt *oh so good*. But when she looked in the mirror and discovered what Kevin had actually done to her, she cursed and shouted and violently beat his tender little ass raw with the palm of her hand.

It was the last time he ever took a bath with Mama, and the painful memory was repressed almost immediately.

Despite the nightmares and frequent bouts of constipation related to his grave mistake as a toddler, Kevin Radowski did well in school and managed to project an appearance of normalcy. In tenth grade, he even tried out and made the baseball team. Some of the guys started calling him K-Rad that year, using the great major league infielder Alex Rodriguez—A-Rod—as inspiration.

The nickname stuck.

K-Rad graduated from high school with a B average, but he lacked focus and discipline and flunked out of college after two semesters. That's when he started working for Nitko. That was twelve years ago.

K-Rad had never been arrested, had never been in any trouble with the law, and had obtained a Florida concealed weapons permit with no problem. He owned a pair of Berettas, the M9 model used by the US military and scores of police agencies, and he owned two twenty-round magazines and a silencer and a LaserMax for each pistol. He went to the firing range every chance he got. It was his hobby. It excited him in ways that a woman couldn't.

He grabbed Officer McCray's pistol and cell phone and shoved the items into his backpack. He knew the silenced gunshots from his Berettas would attract very little attention. Nitko was a noisy place, even in the offices. Booms and clanks and whistles and horns, electric motors blending product and pneumatic pumps sucking it through the presses and into packaging machines, forklifts whining and ventilation fans humming, and every other kind of noise pollution imaginable filtered in from the production area all day, every day. And on top of all that, many of the front-office employees listened to music through earbuds while they worked at their computers. An army tank could blast through the front door and they wouldn't know it.

K-Rad closed the security office door, poured himself a cup of coffee, and waited. In a little over an hour, the real fun would begin.

6:10 a.m.

Matthew Cahill rose with the sun, grabbed his ax from his backpack, and walked outside. Behind the double-wide mobile home there were pieces of oak branches and sections of trunk cut into eighteen-inch lengths with a chainsaw. The wood appeared to have been thrown haphazardly from the back of a truck, and someone with a log splitter could have come over and turned it all into stackable firewood in a few hours. The job would take Matt a lot longer, but if he came out early for a while every morning, he should be able to finish in a week. That was the plan.

He positioned the largest piece of trunk roughly in the center of the mess and used it for a chopping block. He hefted a log onto the block, came down hard with his grandfather's razor-sharp ax head, and split the formidable chunk of hardwood into two pieces with a single swing. He split those two pieces in half, grabbed another log, and repeated the process.

It was a hazy, humid, late-summer dawn, and Matt soon worked up a thick lather of sweat. He peeled his shirt off, wiped his face with it, and kept chopping. How Janey had loved to watch him swing that ax. She would stand on the deck with a cup of coffee and watch the splinters and sweat droplets fly, and when he finished, she would often attack him in the bedroom before he had a chance to shower. She would drop to her knees and lick the salty skin on his inner thighs. She drove him crazy when she did that, and what she did next could only be described as magic. Matt would never love another woman the way he loved Janey. He knew in his heart that he would not.

He looked over and saw her standing there with a white ceramic coffee mug, and for an instant, he was back in Deerpark, Washington, and his beloved was still alive. He shook his head, squinted, and focused. It was Shelly Potts, of course, standing there in her pink bathrobe, and this was Copperhead Springs, Florida.

Copperhead Springs had a Walmart and a community college and a single-screen movie theater built in the twenties. The US Army had housed troops there during World War II, and some of the barracks along the river had since been torn down and others converted to condos. There was a tattoo parlor and a barbershop and a two-story motor lodge painted flamingo pink.

Matt had struck up a conversation with Shelly a few nights ago in a bar and grill called the Retro. Matt said he needed work, Shelly said she knew of a temporary opening, and one thing led to another. Shelly seemed to enjoy his company, in and out of bed, knowing he would eventually be moving on. The temporary job she helped him get was at her own place of employment, a hundred-degree metal oven disguised as a chemical plant called Nitko. Today would be his third and final day.

Shelly had a towel wrapped around her head, and her face looked freshly scrubbed.

"Hey, sexy. Come on in and I'll fix you some breakfast."

"Sounds good," Matt said. "I'll just grab a quick shower first."

Shelly laughed. "I was going to suggest that."

Matt bathed and put on a fresh pair of Wranglers and a clean white T-shirt. He walked to the kitchen. A glass of orange juice, six strips of bacon, and a stack of pancakes waited for him at the table.

"Looks great," Matt said. He sat down and slathered the pancakes with butter and squeezed some syrup on them from a plastic bottle. Shelly brought him a hot cup of coffee.

Matt had ridden into Florida on a Greyhound and had seen a billboard advertising Nitko Chemicals just south of Palm Coast on Interstate 95. The smiling man on the sign had ulcers the size of quarters all over his face, shiny rotten boils oozing with green pus.

And that's when he knew that Mr. Dark had set up shop at Nitko. Matt wanted to know why.

So far, he didn't have a clue.

"Eat up," Shelly said. "We need to get going in a few minutes."

Matt took a bite from the pancake stack and washed it down with some coffee. There was something very satisfying about being here with Shelly, yet something disturbing as well. She projected a genuine warmth Matt hadn't experienced in a long time, but occasionally, she would stare into the distance as though entranced by some faraway vision. Matt wanted to know what it was she saw, but every time he brought it up, she changed the subject.

She brewed another pot of coffee and filled a thermos with it. She wore jeans and steel-toed boots and a chambray work shirt. Her dark-brown ponytail dangled from the back of a red Nitko ball cap. She sat at the table across from Matt. "I can't believe it's Wednesday already," she said. "So what are your plans, Mr. Matthew Cahill? You just going to wander around aimlessly forever?"

Matt had been traveling around the country for a while now. For the last few weeks, he'd been sleeping under the stars, bathing at filling-station restrooms, and dining on beans and Spam and bologna sandwiches.

"What makes you think my wandering is aimless?" he said.

"Ah. Let me guess. You're searching for your soul. You're trying to find the true meaning of life."

"Or the true meaning of death," Matt said. He took a bite of bacon.

"Ever think about settling down?"

"Sometimes."

"You might be able to get on permanent at the plant. I know for a fact there's an opening in Waterbase. One of the guys there got fired last week. It's hard work, but the pay sucks."

Matt grinned at Shelly's joke, but the thought of signing on full-time at Nitko made his stomach tighten. Shelly had driven him there Monday morning and had led him up a set of concrete stairs and in through one of the loading dock doors. Sweat beaded on his forehead almost immediately. Huge electric ventilation fans hummed high on the corrugated steel walls, but they didn't move enough air to cool the building much, and they didn't adequately lift the blanket of chemical fumes. Shelly guided him through a labyrinth of industrial shelving stacked twenty feet high with cardboard boxes, five-gallon jugs, and fifty-five-gallon drums. Some of the containers were marked with labels that said FIRE, others with labels that said ICE. Fire and Ice were Nitko's flagship fountain solutions, Shelly had told him. They were top-of-the-line cleaning products for the printing industry, considered to be the gold standard worldwide since the mid-sixties. Fire was acidic and the color and clarity of orange soda, while Ice was alkaline and a shade or two darker than Windex.

In the distance, electric motors whirred and pneumatic pumps pulsed and human beings shouted instructions at one another. Forklifts darted to and fro like confused squirrels, picking up pallets of product here and dropping them off there.

Matt and Shelly made it through the maze to the north side of the building, where there was an employee break room and men's and women's locker rooms and a Kronos electronic time clock. Shelly swiped her badge, and from there, she took Matt to Human Resources and then to the main production area to talk to the foreman. The air was even hotter there, the fumes thicker and the din exponentially louder. The workers' grim expressions spoke volumes. Stories of missed opportunities and unfulfilled dreams, of being stuck in a long and arduous never-ending journey to nowhere.

The conditions were horrible, the pay obscene. Matt felt sorry for Shelly and everyone else who depended on Nitko for a paycheck. Anyone unlucky enough to be born in Copperhead Springs stood a good chance of ending up in that hellhole, and it just wasn't fair. It wasn't fair at all. No, Matt had no intention of working there permanently, but he did want to extend his job as a temp. He needed to find the reason behind that rotting face on the billboard.

He sipped his juice. "I like you a lot," he said, "but I have to be honest with you. I'm just not ready to settle down yet." Matt saw Shelly's hand tighten around her coffee cup.

The muscles flared in her wrist and then relaxed, some battle surrendered without a fight.

"Typical man," Shelly said. "Unable to commit. Come on. Let's go to work."

7:21 a.m.

An administrative assistant who worked in Human Resources stood at the cluster of vending machines outside the security office, trying to decide which brand of soda to buy.

K-Rad stood behind her.

The woman's name was Kelsey Froman. K-Rad had known her since elementary school. She'd been a homely little girl—thick glasses, metal braces that made her breath smell like the lid of a sardine can, hair the color of dirt. Cruel little monsters that they were, the other children nicknamed poor Kelsey Froman "Frog Man," and they bullied her and teased her and reduced her to tears almost every day of fifth grade. She had blossomed at some point, though, and had morphed from an ugly duckling into a beautiful swan. Now she had a great body and a killer smile and contact lenses that brought out the blue in her eyes. Her long brown hair was expensively styled and streaked with highlights the color of bourbon. K-Rad had asked her out for a drink one time, and she had stifled a laugh and made up a lame story about her cousin being in town. Her loss.

Pepsi or Mountain Dew? Which one would it be? Kelsey Froman chose Mountain Dew. K-Rad's favorite! She pressed the button, and her selection clattered to the receiving tray.

When she bent over to retrieve it, K-Rad blasted a hole the size of a silver dollar through the left cheek of her shapely ass. She fell to her hands and knees and retched, like a cat trying to cough up a hair ball. K-Rad lifted the back of her skirt, positioned the Beretta's muzzle between her legs, and fired twice. She fell to the floor and stared blankly at the bottom of the drink machine. K-Rad opened the Mountain Dew and chugged it.

"Have a nice day, Frog Man," he said, and walked on.

7:27 a.m.

A six-foot chain-link fence topped with barbed wire and razor ribbon guarded the perimeter of Nitko's property. Employees were required to scan their badges and enter a password into an electronic keypad to open the double set of gates to the parking area. There was one way in and one way out. It reminded Matt of a prison.

Shelly tooled around the parking lot in her 1995 Ford Taurus station wagon, ignoring the five-mile-per-hour speed limit, her head bobbing to the beat of an AC/DC song on the radio. She finally whipped into an open slot and braked to a stop with an abrupt jerk.

"I have a question," she said. "Why do you bring that ax to work with you?"

Matt had stowed the tool on the floorboard between the front and back seats. He didn't take it inside the plant with him, of course, but he liked having it nearby. "It's my talisman," he said. "My good-luck charm. I don't go anywhere without my ax."

"That's not much of an answer," Shelly said. She went into one of her spells then, staring through the windshield at something beyond the horizon. After a few seconds, Shelly snapped out of it and looked at her watch and said, "Come on, we're going to be late."

The way she drove, Matt thought, it was a wonder they weren't late in more ways than one. He followed her to the loading dock at a trot and then through the maze of shelving to the time clock. Shelly swiped her badge.

"Made it!" she said. "Hot damn, that was close. I'm already on probation for clocking in late too many times. One more this year and I'll get a three-day suspension."

"Maybe you could use a little vacation," Matt said.

"A little vacation," she repeated.

"You know, get away from here for a couple of days," Matt said. "Remind yourself what the rest of the world looks like."

"You going to come with me?"

"Let's do it," he said.

For a moment, her eyes took on that empty, dreamy look, and the hint of a smile appeared on her face. Then a horn blew from somewhere inside the plant and she snapped back to attention.

"That's three days without pay. Can't afford it."

Can't rhymed with *paint*. Matt liked Shelly's Southern accent. He thought it was sexy. But as he got to know Shelly better, he was beginning to hear what lay behind that honey accent. She came across as laid-back and easygoing, but there was a sadness underneath. And why not? He could tell she must have been a knockout as a teenager. She'd probably thought she'd own the world. Now she had a no-future job in a chemical hell and the only good thing in her life was a guy who'd announced he wasn't going to stick around more than a couple of days.

They walked into the break room and put their lunch sacks in the refrigerator.

"I'm going to head on over to the foreman's office," Matt said. "See what he has in store for me today."

"All right, sweetie. See you at lunch."

Shelly headed toward Shipping and Receiving, and Matt toward the area of the plant called Waterbase. It was already at least ninety-five degrees inside the building. By noon it would be a hundred and ten.

Sweat trickled down Matt's back as he made his way to the foreman's office, a portable enclosure the size of a large closet with windows in front that overlooked the production area. From the office, you could see the twin fifty-five-hundred-gallon stainless steel mixing tanks where Fire and Ice were blended, Fire in the left tank and Ice in the right, and a press the size of a '57 Cadillac where they were filtered. You could see the forklift charging stations and the scaffolds and hoses and the pneumatic pumps. Matt knocked on the door, and a voice from within said, "Enter." Matt entered. The air-conditioned space felt like an oasis after a long trek in the desert.

Mr. Hubbs sat at his desk sipping a cup of coffee and reading a memo. Hubbs was middle management, just a tiny notch above the laborers he commanded. He wore jeans and steel-toed shoes and occasionally ventured out to the production area to help the blenders dump bags of chemicals into the tanks. Unlike a lot of the supervisors Matt had worked for, he wasn't afraid to jump into the fray with his subordinates.

Hubbs looked up from his memo. "Good morning, Cahill."

"Good morning, Mr. Hubbs. Just wondering what you wanted me to do today."

"Have a seat. There's something I've been meaning to talk to you about."

Matt sat in the steel-and-vinyl chair beside the desk. "What is it, sir?"

"You're a good worker, Cahill. I pulled some strings with the guys upstairs, and I'd like to offer you full-time employment right here in Waterbase. The starting pay isn't the greatest, but you'll get a raise after your three-month probation period and another one after six months. You'll get health and dental, and all the other benefits Nitko has to offer."

Matt thought about it. He had been making three times as much money at the lumber mill back in Washington, and it didn't involve working in an oven full of noxious fumes. The only future at Nitko was a bleak one. If he worked real hard and kissed plenty of ass, someday he might be able to afford a single-wide trailer and a ten-year-old vehicle from the buy-here/pay-here lot. If, that is, the heat and the chemicals didn't kill him first. No thanks. He had no intentions of working at Nitko forever, but he did need some time to investigate whatever it was that had brought Mr. Dark there. And signing on full-time would allow him to stay in Copperhead Springs a while longer and get to know Shelly better, maybe get to the bottom of her focal episodes. "What other benefits?" Matt said.

"Are you accepting my offer for full-time employment?"

"Yes."

Matt didn't plan on staying, but he wasn't out to dupe anybody, either. He would give Nitko an honest day's work for the duration and then he would give them proper notice when the time came to leave.

"Great!" Hubbs said. "Welcome aboard. I want you to go over to Human Resources, and they'll explain the pay and benefits package in detail."

"Thank you for the opportunity, sir. I'm looking forward to working with you."

Hubbs rose and smiled and shook Matt's hand. Matt left the Waterbase office and headed for Human Resources.

7:58 a.m.

Shelly wrestled a fifty-five-gallon drum full of Fire onto an oak pallet. The guys in production usually palletized the drums, but this one was a stray that had come from the end of a batch, and it had come up a little light on the scales. It would have to be sent back and either topped off to the proper weight or repackaged into smaller containers. She climbed onto her forklift and guided the forks under the load. She had backed up and started to turn around when a voice behind her said, "Hey!"

It was Drew Long, the Shipping and Receiving supervisor. "Meeting in my office in two minutes."

"OK," Shelly said. "You want me to take this drum back over to—"

"Just leave it there. You can get it after the meeting." Shelly eased the pallet to the concrete floor, switched off the electric forklift, and walked to the water fountain. She slurped and swallowed and slurped and swallowed and thought about Matt and the great time they'd had in bed last night. Matt was kind and gentle and attentive to her needs, and he didn't gripe that she insisted on total darkness. Why couldn't she have met someone like him fifteen years ago? Instead, she pissed her youth away with a string of bad boys whose sole good feature was that they pissed off her mother. That seemed fun at the time, less so now that life kept insisting on teaching her that Mom had been right all along.

"What are you, part camel or something?" Drew said. "We have a meeting, remember?"

She wiped her mouth with her hand and followed him to the office. She was wet from sweat, and the sudden drop in temperature gave her a chill. She hoped the meeting wouldn't last long. Drew held them only once a month, but he tended to talk a lot. That's where he got his nickname. "Drew Long-winded." People called him that to his face sometimes. It was good-natured teasing, and he didn't seem to mind. Drew was a nice guy. He was the kind of guy who would say things like *Don't do anything I wouldn't do*, or *One in the hand is worth two in the bush*, or a hundred other corny clichés. Even so, Shelly liked him a lot.

If you counted Drew, there were four full-time employees who worked the first shift in Shipping and Receiving. On very busy days, HR would sometimes send them a temp, but today was not one of those days. Shelly, Hal Miller, and Fred Philips sat on steel folding chairs as Drew wrote topic points on his dry-erase board. There were six topics to be covered. Looked like it was going to be a long one.

She thought again about what Matt had said. A vacation. She hadn't taken a vacation in so long. When she'd just started at the plant, she and a couple of girlfriends used to take long weekends every couple of months and trek off to find some beach where there was nothing but white sand, warm water, and cold margaritas. When she came back, she'd feel fresh and happy and relaxed for weeks.

But her girlfriends got married, and then they got pregnant and they couldn't get away anymore. Then Shelly bought the double-wide, and then the bastards who ran the plant slashed her pay when the market tanked, and now she couldn't even pay her bills on what she made. Staying here was killing her slowly, but taking even a day off would kill her quickly. Someday that might seem like the better option, but that day wasn't here yet.

8:02 a.m.

A short and narrow enclosed walkway connected the production plant to a two-story office suite. From the road, people saw the orange-and-blue Nitko sign and another sign with a smiling guy wearing a hard hat and the shiny mirrored-glass building and the electric gates on wheels. From the road, Nitko looked like a nice, clean, safe, happy place.

Matt punched the code into the push-button lock, opened the door to the walkway, and strolled toward the office suite. When he got to the end of the walkway, he punched the same code into an identical lock and took a left toward Human Resources. Noise from the plant filtered over, and Matt wondered why the building hadn't been better insulated. It all boiled down to money, of course. Why pay more when you can get away with paying less? He figured the execs' offices upstairs had top-notch soundproofing, though. He figured those offices were as quiet as a church.

When he turned the corner by the drink machine, he saw Kelsey Froman lying on the floor with a fat hole in her left buttocks and a gallon of bright-red blood between her legs.

The sight hit him like a gut punch.

He'd seen a lot of death since his own, and it was always a shock.

This was brutal, violent, and…

Evil.

It was what he came here to stop. He looked around. The sign on the door to his left said SECURITY. He banged on it, but nobody answered. He turned the knob and opened the door and saw a man in uniform splayed facedown in a puddle of brown goop.

It was Officer McCray, the day-shift security guard. Matt's pulse pounded in his eardrums. He stepped over the corpse and thought back over the last few days. Why hadn't he seen this coming? What clues had he missed?

He grabbed the phone on the desk. Dead. The shooter, or shooters, must have cut the phone lines. Nitko had a strict policy against bringing cell phones onto the property, something about stray signals having the potential to ignite some of the volatile oils used in the Petrol area. Any employee caught with a mobile phone was subject to immediate termination. Any employee, that is, except the security guards. They carried one in case of emergency. This certainly qualified, Matt thought.

He checked Officer McCray's gun belt and his pockets and found nothing but a can of Mace and a wallet and a set of keys. No phone. He stuffed the Mace into the back pocket of his jeans. He needed to call 911, and he needed to call Shipping and Receiving to warn Shelly. He had no way to do either. He thought about climbing the stairs to the executives' offices. Surely those guys carried cell phones. Then he remembered that all the VPs were at a convention in Miami and the CEO was at a groundbreaking ceremony for a new toll road. The offices upstairs were empty for the day, but maybe the landlines up there were on a different circuit. It was worth a try.

Matt stuck his head out the security office door, looked both ways, and darted for the stairs. He climbed as quietly as he could in the heavy work boots. He bypassed all the vice presidents' doors and went straight for the big guy's.

Matt had done some research on Lester Simmonds, the chief executive officer at Nitko, one night on Shelly's home computer, and Shelly had told him some other things generally unknown to the public. Simmonds had graduated from the University of Florida with a degree in chemical engineering and then with a master's in business administration. His résumé included stints with DuPont, International Paper, and Fuller Glue. He had worked for some lesser known companies, all of which he had ruthlessly whipped into the Fortune 500. Nitko wasn't quite there yet, but Simmonds had been with them for only two years. He'd frozen cost-of-living raises and merit raises, and he'd lowered the shift differentials by 30 percent. The company used to match 401(k) contributions dollar for dollar, and now it did only half that, fifty cents for every dollar.

The production employees quietly referred to Simmonds as the "Old Bastard." They hated him. He was as tight as a tightwad could be, but he was also extremely paranoid. He knew the workers hated him, and for that reason, he kept a personal bodyguard nearby whenever he was out and about. Maybe he was paranoid enough to have a version of the Batphone in his office, a direct line to the police. Matt hoped so.

He tried the knob, but the door was locked. Hell with it. He reared back and kicked the Old Bastard's door right the fuck in. The jamb splintered and pieces of the brass lockset tinkled to the marble floor. Matt hoped the killer wasn't close enough to hear the noise he'd made.

The office was huge and windowless. There was a bank of television screens in front of a cherry desk you could have done the tango on. The screens were black. Matt figured the Old Bastard could monitor every inch of Nitko, inside and out, right here from his office. If Simmonds had been here, the authorities would have been alerted at the first sign of trouble. Simmonds, of course, wouldn't have stuck around to see the outcome. His private helicopter would have taken him from the roof to a place of safety. No way the Old Bastard would have gone down with the ship. He loved himself too much.

Matt searched for a switch to turn on the monitors. There was an electronic keypad mounted on the right side of the desk, and Matt figured the pad controlled everything. He pushed the button that said MONITORS, but nothing happened. The keypad must have been password protected, and Matt had no idea what the password was. So much for that.

There was a multiline telephone next to the keypad. Matt lifted the receiver from its cradle and put it to his ear. He tried every line but couldn't get a dial tone. He was about to try another office, hoping one of the VPs had left a cell phone on a charger or something, when the lights went out.

8:17 a.m.

Drew Long was on topic number five when everything went black. Shelly stayed glued to her chair, thinking the backup generators would kick in any second. They did not, which was very strange. Even stranger was the sound of the loading dock doors closing and locking automatically, as if a ghost had thrown the switch.

"What the hell's going on?" Hal Miller said.

"Everybody stay calm," Drew said. "I'm sure it's just a glitch."

In the event of a catastrophic spill—say, one of the fifty-five-hundred-gallon tanks rupturing or something—all the doors in the plant could be closed by a central switch in the main power closet. The doors had strips of rubber on their bottoms that created an airtight seal, thereby containing the spill until a hazardous materials crew could come in and clean it up. In theory, everyone in the production area was to be evacuated before the doors went down. Once the doors were closed, there was no way in or out until the hazmat team declared an all-clear.

Shelly heard Drew fumbling around at his desk. He pulled a flashlight out of a drawer and switched it on. He picked up the telephone receiver and started punching in numbers and then said, "Shit."

"The phone's not working?" Shelly said.

"It's not," Drew said. "Listen, I want you all to stay here while I go up front to see what's going on."

"How about we *all* go up front to see what's going on?" Fred Philips said.

"No, there's no point in all of us stumbling around in the dark. I'll be back in two shakes. Promise. I only have the one flashlight, but I'll leave it here with you guys. Try not to use up the batteries."

"How are you going to find your way?" Hal asked.

"I know this plant like the back of my hand. Plus, there's a little bit of light filtering in through the ventilation fans. I'll be all right."

Back in two shakes…

Like the back of my hand…

Drew and his clichés.

"We'll be here," Shelly said.

Drew handed her the flashlight. "Shelly's in charge while I'm gone."

"Gee, thanks," Shelly said.

Drew opened the office door and disappeared into the blackness.

8:25 a.m.

Kent Dillard, the maintenance man on duty, never knew what hit him. K-Rad had shot him in the back of the head while he was changing one of the steel-mesh filters in the main power closet. K-Rad had then pulled his night-vision goggles out of his backpack and put them on and had thrown the big red breaker switch that cut the power to the entire plant. He had taken the key ring from Kent's belt and had tried seven different keys before finding the one that fit the emergency lockdown panel. He'd disabled the backup generators earlier, so now the plant was dark and everyone was trapped inside. Perfect.

K-Rad walked to the lab, where Fire and Ice and the other solvents Nitko produced were tested before shipping. There were four people on duty there, a chemist and three technicians. The chemist's name was Ashley Knotts. He didn't know the technicians' names, but he knew they were all men. Ashley was attractive, in a librarian sort of way, with wire-rimmed glasses and hair pulled back in a bun.

When K-Rad opened the door to the laboratory, Ashley and the others were huddled together at one of the counters with a flashlight. They were looking at a trade magazine and laughing about something. Undoubtedly, they were thinking the lights would come back on any minute and the emergency lockdown would be released and everything would go back to normal. K-Rad picked them off one by one, like ducks at a shooting gallery. He worked left to right, Ashley being the last in line. Before shooting her, he said, "Would you mind taking your hair down for me?"

"Please don't kill me," she sobbed. "I have children at home. I'll do anything you want."

"I want you to take your hair down."

She reached behind her head and pulled out the pins holding her hair up, and the long, silky blond locks fell to her shoulders. Her hands were trembling. K-Rad could see everything with the night-vision goggles on.

Tears rolled down her cheeks. "Please, I don't want to die."

"Maybe we can work something out," K-Rad said. "Take your glasses off."

She took her glasses off. She was a very beautiful woman. K-Rad guessed her to be in her early thirties. He aimed and fired and the top of her skull exploded. She fell to the floor, landing on top of one of the techs.

That took care of the front offices. Everyone was dead now. The production area would be trickier, but K-Rad felt up to the challenge. He felt good. He felt strong.

He had picked this day because he knew all the vice presidents were at a convention in Miami and the head honcho was cutting the ribbon at the site for a new toll road. He had worked for Nitko for twelve years, and this was the first time he knew of when all the brass was missing in action on the same day. Boneheads. He had no interest in killing them. By the end of the day, their lives would be ruined. Thinking about it made him smile.

One of the lab techs, the one Ashley Knotts had fallen on top of, started stirring and moaning. K-Rad walked over and finished him off with one to the head.

8:31 a.m.

Matt had to get to Shipping and Receiving and warn Shelly, and everybody else, that there was a killer on the loose. He felt his way down the staircase. When he reached the bottom, he took a right. With one hand touching the wall and the other out in front of him, he blindly made his way to the walkway door. He felt the push-button lock and punched in the code.

Then he heard footsteps. And keys jingling.

Someone was coming his way—fast.

Matt wanted to enter the walkway and make a dash for the production area, but the footsteps were approaching too quickly. He got on his hands and knees and backtracked until he felt the hallway that led to the Human Resources office. He turned the corner and backed in a few feet, and he heard the footsteps coming and the keys jingling, but he didn't see any light. How was the killer walking so fast without a flashlight?

He hunkered down and held his breath. If the killer looked to his right as he walked past the hallway leading to HR, Matt was as good as dead.

8:33 a.m.

Shelly switched the flashlight off to save battery power. She and Fred Philips and Hal Miller sat in complete darkness.

Fred was the junior member of the troupe and had been with Nitko for only a few weeks. "Anything like this ever happen before?" he said.

Like what? Shelly thought. *Like thinking you've hit bottom and then everything goes to shit? Only every day of my life.*

"We have drills sometimes," Shelly said. "But the procedure is to get everyone out of the plant before initiating emergency lockdown. I'm sure you saw the safety videos when you were on orientation."

"I kinda slept through some of those videos," Fred said. "So you think this is a drill?"

"I don't know what it is. I think—"

"It's some sort of test," Hal said. "The Old Bastard is testing us, trying to see who freaks out under pressure. I guarantee you Drew and all the other supervisors are in on it. The best thing we can do is sit here and calmly wait it out."

"I ain't sitting here forever," Fred said. "If Drew ain't back soon, I'm bailing."

"Where you going to go? The whole damn place is sealed up like a Mason jar."

"I'll find my way out of this place somehow."

"We're the Old Bastard's playthings," Hal said. "Can't you see that? He makes over a million dollars a year while we struggle to make ends meet, and now he's going to toy with us like a kid catching fireflies. I guarantee you that's all this is. Think about it. The suits are having a good laugh about now, thinking about us peons sitting around in the dark. I guarantee you—"

"Shh," Shelly said. "Did you guys hear that?"

"Hear what?" Fred said.

"I thought I heard something. Like a door slamming or something. Listen."

Everyone shut up and listened for a minute, but the only sound they heard was the battery-operated clock hanging on Drew Long's office wall. The plant was as void of sound now as it was of light, and a disturbing thought streaked across Shelly's consciousness like a lightning bolt.

The ventilation fans.

With the power off, the fans were off, and that meant the chemical fumes would accumulate unchecked. Eventually the fumes would displace the oxygen, and everyone trapped in the plant would suffocate. Shelly had no idea how long that would take, but her guess was a few hours tops. And even before the fresh air ran out completely, the fumes would start making people sick. They would become weak and vomit and have seizures and suffer agonizing head-to-toe pain. Just thinking about it put a knot in her stomach.

So much for dying slowly instead of dying quickly, she thought. *One last fucking brilliant choice to cap off the life list.*

"I don't hear nothing," Fred said.

"Maybe it was just my imagination. Fred, I think you're right. We can't just sit here and wait forever. If Drew isn't back in a few minutes, I say we try to escape."

"And just how do you suggest we do that?" Hal said.

"The ventilation fans."

"Huh?"

"We could climb up there somehow and take the grates off and then crawl through. Maybe one of you guys could raise me up with a forklift."

"Sounds like a damn good idea to me," Fred said.

"It's forty feet up and then forty feet down on the other side," Hal said. "What are you going to do, take a parachute with you?"

"I don't know. Maybe we can make a rope out of stretch wrap or something."

"Even if all that works, there's still a problem with the idea. Two of us might be able to get out, but the third would be stuck with nobody to operate the forklift. The third wouldn't have any way to get up to the fans."

"Only one of us needs to get out," Shelly said. "Then whoever it is can find a telephone and call for help."

"Hell yeah," Fred said. "There's all kinds of houses and businesses around here. I say we go for it. I'll even volunteer to be the one to crawl through and rappel down the other side."

"What if the power comes back on while you're crawling through?" Hal said. "The fan blades will cut you in half."

"What's the likelihood of that happening? A million to one? Fuck it. I'll take the chance."

"Hal has a point," Shelly said. "I never even thought about the power coming back on. And even if that doesn't happen, which it probably won't, it's still going to be a risky operation. Maybe we better just wait a while and think it over. Maybe there's another way."

"Y'all can sit here and wait if you want to," Fred said. "I'm getting out."

"Just stay put for a few minutes. You can't get up to the fans by yourself, anyway. Drew will probably be back any second. Then we'll see what he thinks."

"Turn that flashlight on for a second," Hal said. "We got trucks coming in later. I want to see what time it is."

Shelly switched the flashlight on and pointed it at the clock. It was...

8:41 a.m.

All this killing had made K-Rad thirsty. He stopped at the drink machine for another Mountain Dew, but of course the machine didn't work with the power off. He thought about trying to break into it, but he didn't have the right tools. He'd brought a pair of bolt cutters in his backpack and, in the wee hours, had used them to cut through the fence, but he needed a pry bar to break into the drink machine and he hadn't thought to bring one. He hadn't anticipated the need for one. *Fuck.* He really wanted another Dew, and he wanted it now, and there was only one way to get it.

8:43 a.m.

The overhead fluorescents blinked to life.

"Ha!" Hal said. "I told you it was just a test. Now let's get back to work."

Shelly squinted against the sudden brightness. "We'll get back to work when Drew comes back and tells us to get back to work," she said.

Drew was happy, Shelly thought. He'd married his high school sweetheart and saved all his money until he could afford that adorable three-bedroom house and plastic flamingos for the lawn. So what if he was boring and people made fun of him? He'd made all the right choices in his life. *So let him make this one—God knows his track record is better than mine.*

Fred opened the office door and looked out. "The lights and the fans are on, but the loading dock doors are still shut. Looks like we're still in lockdown. I'm with Shelly. We should wait for Drew."

"We got two semis coming in at four o'clock and we need to stage the product before they get here. If we don't get a move on—"

"Chill out, Hal," Shelly said. "If they've got us locked down, they can't blame us for not doing the job."

"Bullshit they can't," Hal said.

Shelly let out a bark of a laugh. "Yeah," she said, "but they can blame us for violating protocol if we don't follow safety procedures. So since they're going to fuck us whatever choice we make, let's go with the one that doesn't have us out there breathing fumes."

Hal stood up and walked toward the door. "Go ahead and write me up if you want to. I'm going back to work."

"I will write your ass up," Shelly shouted, but Hal had already slammed the door and walked away.

"What's with him?" Fred said.

"I don't know. Maybe the heat and the fumes got to him."

"Are you really going to write him up?"

"Yeah, because what I really want out of life is to give management an excuse to dock Hal's pay so they can shovel a little more money to the Old Bastard," Shelly said.

She sat down and folded her arms over her chest and stared at the wall. She didn't know how much time had elapsed when Fred said, "Earth to Shelly. Hey, you think Drew's ever coming back?"

She popped out of her trance. "Damn. Since the lights are back on, maybe the phone's working too."

She picked up the receiver, and the room went black again.

8:47 a.m.

While the lights were on, Matt had taken the opportunity to dash through the walkway to the production area. From his position by the Human Resources office, he'd heard the footsteps and jingling keys fade off in another direction and figured it might be his only chance to make a run for it. Now he was out in the warehouse and the power was off again, but a small amount of light seeped in through the ventilation fans. He couldn't have read the biggest letters on an eye chart from two feet away, but it was enough light to keep him from busting his head on a steel shelf or something as he made his way toward Shipping and Receiving.

He passed through the oily fumes emanating from the Petrol area and wondered if anyone back there was still alive. The chemicals in Waterbase were bad enough, but the ones in Petrol could knock you flat on your ass. They had special vents in that area, and with the power off, the fumes were probably building to explosive levels. Matt hoped the employees had gotten out of there before succumbing to the noxious vapors.

He made it to the Fire and Ice tanks and took a right at the big press. From there it was only a short distance to the Shipping and Receiving office. He tried the knob, but the door was locked. He banged on it twice with his fist.

"Drew?"

Matt recognized Shelly's voice. "It's me," he said. "Let me in."

The door opened and Matt walked into the Shipping and Receiving office. Shelly wrapped her arms around him and said, "Damn, am I glad to see you."

"Listen, we've got a serious situation here. There's a guy with a gun shooting people up in the front offices. Kelsey Froman in HR and McCray in the security office are dead. There may be more."

"Oh my God," Shelly said. "We thought it was just a drill or something. Drew's out there somewhere, and so is Hal."

Matt could feel her trembling in his arms now. "Just try to stay calm. We'll figure a way out of this."

"I don't know about y'all," Fred said, "but I'm getting the fuck out of here."

Matt hadn't known there was someone else in the room. "Who's that?"

"That's Fred," Shelly said. "He's only been working here a month or so. Fred, you just stay put, now. If you go out there, you're liable to get your head blown off."

"You think I'm just going to sit here and wait for the motherfucker? Screw that. Let's do what we talked about earlier—raise a forklift up by the vent fans and take the grates off and climb out."

"That's not a bad idea," Matt said. "One of us could climb out, find a phone, and call for help."

He was about to suggest they proceed with the plan when a series of muffled gunshots erupted.

9:01 a.m.

K-Rad had turned the power back on just long enough to buy a can of Mountain Dew. With the lights off again, he'd donned his night-vision goggles and traversed the walkway from the office building to the production area carrying the soda in one hand and a 9mm Beretta in the other. When he rounded the corner by the big tanks, he saw Drew Long, the Shipping and Receiving supervisor, heading toward his office.

K-Rad fired three times.

The plant was like a huge, eerily quiet cathedral now, and the Beretta's silencer muffled the shots but did not squelch them completely. Drew's knees buckled on the third shot, and he dropped to the concrete floor like a sack of wet Dicalite.

Dicalite. Ha! At least K-Rad would never have to mess with that shit again.

Dicalite was a white powder added to batches of Fire and Ice. It came in thirty-pound bags. When wet, the powder formed a sort of putty that gathered on the press panels and aided in filtering the product as it was pumped into fifty-five-gallon drums or five-gallon pails or one-gallon jugs. Once all the product was packaged, the press had to be disassembled and all that moist Dicalite putty had to be scraped off the panels and stuffed into plastic bags for disposal. Up until last Friday, scraping the presses had been part of K-Rad's job.

But last Friday, a few minutes before K-Rad's shift was over, a coworker named Shelly Potts tapped him on the shoulder and said, "Mr. Hubbs wants to see you in his office." K-Rad finished what he was doing, parked his fork-lift, and plugged it into the charger. He hosed the Dicalite off his boots, wiped the sweat from his face with some paper towels, and clomped to the glassed-in foreman's office in Waterbase. Hubbs was sitting at his desk sipping coffee from a Styrofoam cup. An armed security guard—Officer McCray—stood at parade rest a few feet to his right.

"Shelly said you wanted to see me," K-Rad said.

"Sit down, my friend. Can I get you a cup of coffee?"

Friend my ass, K-Rad thought. "No, thanks. What's the guard for?"

"Listen, I'm going to get right to the point. We've decided to let you go."

K-Rad felt a chill wash through him. He wanted to make sure he'd heard correctly.

"You're firing me?" he said.

"I'm sorry. The decision came down from the main office. There's nothing—"

"I've been here twelve years. You're going to can my ass, just like that? Why?"

Officer McCray shifted his stance.

"I think you know why," Mr. Hubbs said.

"I don't have a clue."

"When you were on nights a couple of months ago, one of the loading dock doors was damaged. Someone obviously forgot to lower the forks on their forklift, but nobody ever came forward and confessed. It cost the company a lot of money to fix that door."

"I didn't do that."

"But you were in charge that night."

"So?"

"The bigwigs upstairs figure you either did it yourself or you know who did it. I'm sure you remember the meeting we had about that."

K-Rad felt like jumping across the desk and twisting Mr. Hubbs's head off like a bottle cap. "I didn't wreck the door," he said. "You can't blame me for somebody else's actions."

"Again, the decision came from upstairs. Officer McCray here is going to escort you to your locker and then to the parking lot."

Officer McCray escorted Kevin Radowski to his locker and then to the parking lot. He told K-Rad to have a nice day.

Now everyone's going to have a nice fucking day, K-Rad thought. He sipped his Mountain Dew and walked toward the fallen Drew Long.

Drew was still alive, but his breathing was rapid and shallow. He was on the way out. K-Rad pointed the gun at his skull and cocked the hammer back.

"Why are you doing this?" Drew said.

K-Rad smiled. "A stitch in time saves nine," he said. He pulled the trigger, and Drew stopped breathing.

9:04 a.m.

A minute or so after the initial burst, there was a single gunshot and then silence. Matt felt his way around the dark office until he found a chair. He sat down, and Shelly sat beside him.

"Oh my God," Shelly said.

"What are we going to do now?" Fred said. "We should have gotten the fuck out of here when we had the chance."

Matt stood up and found the doorknob. He twisted the little brass dial to the locked position. "Well, we can't leave the office now. Stepping to the other side of this door would be suicide at this point. Is there a desk in here?"

"I'm sitting at it," Fred said.

"Let's push it up against the door as a barricade. If he can't get in here, he can't shoot us."

Matt felt his way to the desk, and he and Fred pushed it flush against the door.

"We're going to run out of air pretty fast," Shelly said. "The fumes are going to choke us to death."

"All we can do is hope some help comes before that happens," Matt said. "Unless—"

Shelly switched the flashlight on. "Help's not going to come. Help never comes. Unless what, Matt?"

"Unless one of us goes out there and tries to rush the guy."

"You said yourself it would be suicide to step on the other side of that door."

"I know, but it might be our only chance."

"I'll do it," Fred said. "I'll go out there and take the motherfucker down."

"No way. If anybody goes, it's going to be me," Matt said.

"I've only been here a few weeks, Matt, but you've only been here two days. I know the plant better than you do. Way better. I can find my way around in the dark and ambush the guy. Let's move the desk and I'll get on with it."

"You might know the plant better, but I'm stronger. If it comes down to a hand-to-hand combat situation—"

"Look, we can stand here and argue about it all day, or we can do this." Fred reached into his pocket and pulled out a quarter. He flipped it in the air, caught it, and slapped it on the back of his hand. "Heads or tails. Loser has to go to battle."

"Heads," Matt said.

Shelly pointed the flashlight at the coin on the back of Fred's hand. The quarter had landed on heads.

"That settles it," Fred said. "I lost fair and square. Help me move the desk."

Matt sighed. "You sure you want to do this?"

"I'm sure."

"You'll need a weapon. Something..."

"There's a toolbox over by the scales. I'll grab a drum wrench."

"Any idea where to start looking?"

"Not really."

Who would just waltz into the plant and start shooting people? Matt wondered. *What could the killer possibly want? What was his plan?* He thought about the first questions a police detective might ask.

"Do y'all know of anyone in particular who might have a grudge against Nitko?"

"Could be anybody," Fred said. "There's been days—"

"I think I know who the shooter is," Shelly said.

Matt turned to her. "Who?"

"Last Friday a guy named Kevin Radowski got fired. He'd been here a long time, like twelve years or something. He worked in Waterbase, and they blamed him for one of the loading dock doors getting messed up. It was almost quitting time, and the foreman told me to find him and send him to the Waterbase office. He was escorted off the premises. Those fuckers wouldn't even let him finish out the week."

Matt considered that. "If it is Radowski, he'll probably go after Hubbs, the guy who probably fired him."

"I'll go hide somewhere by the Waterbase office, then," Fred said. "Hopefully I'll come back and give y'all some good news in just a little while."

Matt and Fred scooted the desk away from the door, and Fred exited the Shipping and Receiving office. Shelly told him to be careful out there.

As Fred was leaving, a man wearing a tuxedo and holding a martini came in.

9: 27 a.m.

K-Rad figured everyone in Petrol was dead by now, but he wanted to make sure. He opened his backpack and pulled out a gas mask and a helmet equipped with drop-down night-vision binoculars. He removed his regular night-vision goggles, put them in the backpack, and strapped on the cumbersome apparatus. As soon as he got it situated exactly the way he wanted it, he felt the overwhelming urge to take a piss. *Figures,* he thought.

He walked to the locker room. His kidneys were floating from all the Mountain Dew he'd drunk. When he finished urinating, he caught his own reflection in the mirror by the sink. With all the high-tech gadgetry on his head and the flak jacket on his chest, he looked like some sort of machine. That's what he was. A machine. A killing machine. By the end of the day, he would be famous. Everyone in the world would know the name Kevin Radowski. Everyone in the world would know K-Rad.

The door to the Petrol room was protected by a push-button lock, but K-Rad knew the code. He'd worked at Nitko for twelve years. He knew all the codes to all the doors, even the ones he wasn't supposed to have access to.

When the emergency lockdown had been initiated, the employees in Petrol had essentially been trapped in a toxic tomb. Of course, emergency lockdown was never supposed to happen with people still in the plant. Even if it did, and even if the power went out for some reason, emergency generators were supposed to kick in and keep the ventilation fans in Petrol pumping in fresh air.

But K-Rad had disabled the generators at a little after 3:00 that morning.

On the north side of Nitko's property, nearly a quarter mile from the main building, stood an aboveground diesel tank the size of a boxcar. Nitko stored the fuel for use in the emergency generators, outdoor forklifts, and delivery trucks. The tank created a blind spot, and K-Rad had easily sliced his way through the fence with his bolt cutters. He knew from experience that the night shift took a long break at 3:00 a.m., and he knew from experience that the lame-ass roving security guard could always be found snoozing in his pickup at that time. At approximately 3:05, he filled two five-gallon cans with diesel fuel and then walked to the generators and cut the battery cables. Perfect. Oh yes. By the end of the day, everyone in the world would know the name K-Rad.

He looked at his watch: 9:41. Still plenty of time for more fun. He punched in the code and opened the door to Petrol and walked in like he owned the place.

9:42 a.m.

Matt looked over at Shelly. She sat on one of the folding chairs, staring into space, unaware of the man in the tuxedo. Mr. Dark.

"When I go to a show, Matthew, I expect to be entertained," he said. "If I didn't have this martini, I'd be asleep already."

It wasn't just that Shelly didn't notice Mr. Dark. She was totally still, her eyes frozen in mid-blink. Time had stopped.

Mr. Dark turned his back to Matt and stepped in front of Shelly, blocking her from view. "Let's liven things up, shall we?"

And now Matt knew, with horrifying certainty, what was coming next.

Matt tried to shout *leave her alone*, but the words came out sounding as though they had been uttered from the bottom of a swimming pool. The cheap plastic clock on the wall stopped ticking. Matt closed his fists and tried to launch a series of punches to Mr. Dark's kidneys, but it seemed someone had strapped something heavy and cumbersome to his hands. It was like trying to box using bowling balls for gloves. He moved in super-slow motion, grabbing for Mr. Dark's shoulders, but then he was gone, and time suddenly started up again as if the world had been trapped in a cosmic freeze frame.

The flashlight fell from Shelly's hands.

When she reached to pick it up, her ball cap fell from her head and Matt saw a cluster of festering wounds crawling with maggots on her scalp, rancid flesh dripping from her exposed skull to the floor in sickening, wet glops.

Mr. Dark had touched her.

9:47 a.m.

Just as K-Rad had expected, the floor in Petrol was littered with dead bodies. They say suffocation is a rough way to go, and from the expressions on their faces, it looked like they had all died horrible and agonizing deaths. Some of them looked as though they were straining to take a shit, their eyes shut tight and their neck ligaments stressfully flexed. Others seemed to have witnessed some sort of ghastly revelation. Their eyes bulged and their faces were puffy and swollen, as though someone had inflated them with a bicycle pump. It was funny. It made K-Rad laugh. He was about to leave the area when he heard a tiny voice say, "Help me." He followed the sound to a young woman who had collapsed near a stack of wooden crates. How had she survived when all the others had perished? Interesting. Very interesting. She had beaten the odds with the fumes in Petrol, and it seemed a shame to just shoot her. Maybe he could think of something a little more fun.

He walked over to her and crouched down like a baseball catcher.

"What's your name?" he said. The gas mask muffled his voice, and she looked at him uncomprehendingly. "What's your name?" he said again, louder this time.

"Terri. My name's Terri. Are you going to rescue me?"

"Yes. Everything's going to be all right."

"Really? You promise? Oh, thank you. I thought I was going to die in here."

"I hate to tell you this, but none of your coworkers made it. How were you able to survive?"

"Please. I need air. Please help me get out of here."

"OK."

K-Rad holstered the Beretta, lifted the petite young woman, and carried her out of the Petrol room. He carried her all the way to Waterbase and gently set her down on a bed of ammonium nitrate bags behind the big tanks.

"Stay here," he said. "The paramedics will come for you shortly."

"OK."

She closed her eyes and breathed peacefully. Her face had regained a healthier color on the trip from Petrol to Waterbase, and K-Rad wanted to make sure she didn't get up and go anywhere. He opened his backpack and pulled out a roll of duct tape.

10:02 a.m.

Matt's stomach lurched and he staggered back in horror.

Mr. Dark's touch had transformed Shelly from a beautiful young lady to a smiling, rotting jack-o'-lantern from hell.

Whatever darkness Shelly had festering deep inside before, Mr. Dark's touch had brought it raging to the surface.

The evil was eating her alive. And it was Matt's fault.

Because if he had never gotten involved with her and brought Mr. Dark into her life...She wouldn't be about to do something very, very bad.

More people were going to die.

And that, too, would be Matt's fault.

He had to stop her. Fast. And he had to stop K-Rad. The easy way would be to kill her right now.

He thought about it for an instant but knew he couldn't do it, not in cold blood, not when there still might be a chance to save her from her demons.

That split second of hesitation was a mistake.

Shelly sat up and slammed her fist deep into his groin. It was a sucker punch, pure and simple, to the most vulnerable part of his body, and it landed with full impact before he had a chance to react. When he doubled over, Shelly kneed him in the face. Droplets of bright-red blood dripped from his nose and splattered on the tile floor. The world was spinning now, and Matt felt like he was going to vomit. He leaned on the desk, trying to steady himself, and felt something very hard smash into the back of his skull.

10:15 a.m.

Hal Miller had been fooling around with one of the forklifts when K-Rad blew his left kneecap off. K-Rad knew Hal and had even considered him a friend for a while. They drank beer and shot pool together at the Retro sometimes. He almost regretted the fact that he was going to have to kill him now. Almost. But Hal had been working nights with K-Rad a few months ago, and Hal was the one who'd fucked up the loading dock door with his forks raised. If Hal had confessed, K-Rad would have never gotten fired. In essence, it was Hal's fault that all this was even happening. He lay on the concrete floor in the fetal position, holding his ruined knee with his hands and moaning in agony.

"Who are you?" Hal asked, his voice cracking with fear. "Why are you doing this?"

K-Rad was still wearing the gas mask and the drop-down night-vision binoculars. He didn't need the apparatus now that he was out of Petrol, but he thought it looked cool and menacing. He wanted to be wearing it when his picture was broadcast globally on TV and the Internet. He wanted to look like the killing machine that he was. He walked over, sat on the floor, and pressed the barrel of his pistol against Hal's forehead.

"It's me. Kevin Radowski. K-Rad, your old drinking buddy."

"Look, I'm really sorry about—"

"It's a little late for apologies, don't you think? You should have come forward the day you wrecked that door."

"I have a family to support, K. Come on, man. Give me a break."

"I gave you a break by not snitching you out. You repaid me by sitting back and watching me get canned for something I didn't do."

"Let's go to Hubbs's office right now," Hal said. "I'll tell him everything. I swear."

"Oh, I'm going to Hubbs's office, all right. Soon as I blow your fucking brains out."

"Please. Please don't kill me. I'll tell him I wrecked the door. You can get your job back, and I'll be the one to get fired."

"I've already killed a bunch of people, Hal. Call it a hunch, but I doubt they're going to hire me back."

"Oh my God. Who did you kill?"

"Lots of people. Including you."

K-Rad pulled the trigger. The bullet entered through Hal's forehead, tore through his brain, and exited through the back of his skull. It ricocheted off the concrete floor, then the steel plating on the electric forklift, and hit K-Rad dead center in the sternum.

Good thing he was wearing his Kevlar vest.

"Ouch," he said, and proceeded toward Mr. Hubbs's office.

10:17 a.m.

Matt was high in a tree house, and something invisible had pushed his wife, Janey, out the door. She was on the way down, plummeting headfirst like a human missile, arms stretched toward the ground in a futile attempt to lessen the impact.

"Janey!" Matt cried.

He pursed his lips and concentrated, and his physical surroundings blurred to a tunnel of swirling colors. He saw only Janey, sinking slowly now, as if through an enormous vat of molasses, teeth clenched and eyes bulging. A silver ring outlined the tunnel, constricting more and more, like an aperture, until Matt's entire world flashed to a stark and blinding white.

Against this white background came a galloping horse with a knight in full armor, the rider and his mount as black and dull as axle grease. The knight gripped the reins with one hand and a spiked metal ball on a chain with the other. The weapon was a brutal-looking thing, a skull-busting apparatus of the highest caliber, and the knight wielded it like an extra appendage, like something he'd been born with. The knight's name was Pain, and his steed Death, and Matt knew he could not defeat them, no matter how hard he tried. He knew that the only way to save Janey was to make a pact with them, to bow down to them and give them what they wanted.

The horse stopped and reared, chomping at the bit, an expression of extreme agony on its face. The tortured animal snorted and sneezed and bucked and stomped, stirring a sandy white storm in Matt's throbbing head.

When the dust finally settled, Sir Pain raised his flail and spoke: "I will give you the power to save your wife, but with the power comes a responsibility—and a debt."

"I'll do anything," Matt said.

"You must become a soldier in the Dark Army, and you must—"

Another gunshot rang out, and Matt woke with a start. He had the worst headache of his life, and his testicles felt as though someone had parked a truck on them.

"Shelly?" he said.

No reply. She and the flashlight were gone, unless she was hiding in the darkness, but he doubted it.

Another employee had just been murdered, maybe Fred or Shelly, and Matt knew what he had to do. He rose and staggered to the door, exited the Shipping and Receiving office, and headed for Waterbase.

He was still a little dizzy from the blow to the head, and the heat and chemical fumes only made matters worse. He crept behind the massive stainless steel Fire and Ice tanks, peeked through the eighteen-inch space between them, and in the dim light filtering through the ventilation fans saw the silhouette of a figure walking toward the foreman's office. The man wore a heavy vest and a backpack and a helmet. He walked slowly, legs stiff, almost shambling along, like some sort of zombie astronaut. He carried a pistol in his left hand.

All Matt could do was try to ambush the man and take him down without getting shot in the process. He had started to creep along the wall toward the office when he heard a childlike moan. He stopped, crouched down, and duckwalked back behind the tanks. He followed the mewling sounds to an area where bags of dry chemicals were stored and saw a petite young woman squirming on top of one of the stacks. He gently peeled away the duct tape covering her mouth.

"What's your name?" Matt said.

"Terri Bonach. I work in Petrol. The guy who put me here said everything was going to be all right, but then I woke up and I couldn't move or talk. Who are you?"

"Matt Cahill. I'm a temp."

"What's going on? We went into lockdown, and I think everyone in Petrol is dead now. Oh my God. What the hell's going on?"

"Someone came in and started shooting people this morning. The man who left you here was not a rescuer. He was the bad guy. Kevin Radowski. Do you know him?"

"No, but I heard about him. He works in Waterbase. They call him K-Rad. You know, like A-Rod. Makes sense that it's him. I heard he's kind of crazy, and I heard he got fired last week."

"Yeah, that's him."

K-Rad.

An anagram immediately formed in Matt's mind. K-Rad was *dark* spelled backward.

"So why didn't he kill me? I mean, I'm happy he didn't, but—"

"I don't know," Matt said. "But he didn't, and this is probably the safest place for you to be right now."

"Screw that. Get me out of here!"

"Shh. He's going to hear you, and then we'll be dead for sure. I'm going after him now."

"Help!" Terri screamed. She was hysterical. Matt put the duct tape back over her mouth. She would be all right where she was until help arrived. He only hoped that K-Rad—and Shelly—had not heard the shouts.

Because Shelly was around somewhere, and she was every bit as dangerous as K-Rad was.

10:22 a.m.

How in the fuck did that bitch get the tape off her mouth?

K-Rad thought about going back to the tanks and blowing her away. He should have done it before, but the idea of blasting her to mincemeat had been too appealing. He thought about going back, but he was only a few feet from Hubbs's office now. Plus, his legs were hurting like a motherfucker. It was at least a hundred degrees in the production area, and the bulletproof vest and the gas mask and the heavy backpack had K-Rad sweating profusely. He was getting dehydrated. He could feel it. He was light-headed and his legs were cramping. The two Mountain Dews hadn't been enough. He needed more fluids. After he killed Hubbs, he would go to the fountain by the time clock and fill his belly with water. Then he would go to the Retro and fill his belly with beer.

K-Rad was about to kick the office door in when he was blindsided and knocked to the floor. The pistol in his hand skittered away, and a man straddled him and hit him in the face with a drum wrench. K-Rad recognized the man. It was Fred Philips from Shipping and Receiving. *Fool.* The initial blow smashed the right side of the night-vision binoculars, and Fred was about to come down with a second when K-Rad reached into the pocket of his fatigue pants and pulled out a switchblade. Before Fred knew what had happened, K-Rad buried all five inches of the blade in his windpipe. Fred gurgled and spat blood and fell sideways, clutching his throat. It took him about thirty seconds to die.

K-Rad crawled to his pistol a few feet away, picked it up, and checked it for damage. It looked all right. The altercation had given him a surge of adrenaline. His legs didn't hurt anymore. He couldn't see as well with one side of the night-vision binoculars broken, but he could see well enough. He got up and kicked Hubbs's door in. It flew open and showered the office interior with splinters and lock parts. Hubbs was alone, crouched down in a corner like a mouse in a snake's cage.

"Kevin, it was the guys upstairs. I had no choice. I swear, I tried to talk them out of firing you. You were always one of my best workers."

"Hal fucked up the loading dock door. Just so you know."

"Hal did it?"

"Yeah. When we were working nights together."

"Then he'll be dealt with, and you're off the hook."

"He's already been dealt with," K-Rad said. "As for me being off the hook, it's way too late for that."

"We can work something out."

"No, we can't."

"I have some money. I have about twenty thousand dollars in a savings account. I'll give it to you. All of it. We can go to the bank right now."

"What am I going to do with twenty thousand dollars?"

"You could leave the country. You could go to South America. Anywhere. I've heard you can live like a king in the Philippines for five dollars a day."

"Really?"

"Sure. So is it a deal? We can leave right now, and you can have the money in your hands in ten minutes. You can book a flight and—"

10:27 a.m.

"There's only one problem," K-Rad said. "That would involve letting you live."

Matt was outside the office, standing to the side of the broken doorway. Fred was lying on the floor a few feet away with a knife handle sticking out of his throat, and the drum wrench he'd taken for a weapon lay a few inches from his lifeless hand. Surrounded by what seemed like gallons of inky black blood, he looked like a fallen character in a horror movie.

Matt picked up the drum wrench, pulled the knife from Fred's throat, and stood by the broken door to the Waterbase office, listening.

"I want you to just think about my offer for a minute, Kevin. With twenty thousand dollars, you could fly anywhere in the world and start a new life."

"I would be a fugitive. Living in the shadows. Who wants that? I want the spotlight for once. I want the world to remember the name Kevin Radowski for a long, long time. Forever would be nice. I want to be immortal. I'm not going to hide in South America. In a little while, after you're good and dead, I'll be sipping on a cold one at the Retro and thinking about how famous I'm going to be."

"I'm begging you. Please don't do this. You don't have to do this. I have a family."

"All you motherfuckers say the same thing. I have a family...blah, blah, blah. You think your family really gives a shit about you? They'll shed a few tears at the funeral, and a few weeks later they'll cash the life insurance check and fly to Maui and sit on the beach with tall blue drinks in their hands. They'll guzzle twenty-dollar cocktails with the money you busted your balls for. You know, I'm tempted to let you stick around until eleven and see the show. It's going to be fabulous."

"What are you talking about?"

There was a pause, and Matt knew that K-Rad was about to shoot Hubbs.

Matt wanted to rush in and try to do something, to save Hubbs from his doom.

But he knew it would be suicide.

And he needed to stay alive, to beat K-Rad...and stop Shelly from whatever she was going to do.

One life—Hubbs's—would be sacrificed for the many Matt could possibly save later.

It sickened Matt...But it seemed that he had no choice but to let Hubbs die.

Then again, maybe there was another way. Maybe a diversion would do the trick.

He hurled the steel drum wrench as far as he could, and it landed on the concrete floor with a series of loud clanks.

10:33 a.m.

What the fuck?

K-Rad shouted through the demolished door. "Who's out there? Identify yourself, or I'll blow your fucking head off."

He knew the sound. He'd heard it a million times before. It was the unmistakable clank of a drum wrench hitting the concrete. Someone was out there. Someone was fucking with him.

He turned and shot Hubbs four times in the chest. "Sorry, boss."

K-Rad's legs were cramping again, his head swimming. He should have thought to put some Gatorade or something in his backpack. How stupid of him not to. How utterly fucking stupid. He rooted through the drawers of Hubbs's desk, found nothing but junk, pulled the drawers out in anger, and dumped everything on the floor. There was a coffeepot on a little table in the corner, but it was empty. He'd planned to walk to the water fountain after killing Hubbs, but now he was going to be forced to deal with whoever it was outside the office.

There wasn't any Gatorade in his backpack, but there was something that could possibly help him out of this little jam. It was a hand grenade he'd bought from a guy he'd met at a gun show. It had cost him two thousand dollars. Two thousand for one grenade. He'd been saving it for a special occasion, and he reckoned being on the verge of collapse from dehydration was special enough.

It was a Vietnam-era Mk 2, commonly referred to as a pineapple grenade because of the grooves in the cast-iron shell, and it was capable of sending deadly shrapnel in all directions up to two hundred meters. You had to take cover after throwing it, or you were likely to get hit yourself. K-Rad pulled the pin and tossed it out the door, toward the area the clanking sounds had come from.

10:38 a.m.

Something flew out of the Waterbase office and clattered across the concrete floor. Matt didn't know what it was, but his instincts told him he needed to get away from it. As he was diving behind the forklift by Fred's corpse, there was a bright flash and an earsplitting boom. Sparks rocketed in all directions, and a molten chunk of red-hot hell seared its way into Matt's left leg above the ankle. It felt like someone had driven an acid-dipped railroad spike through the fleshy area between his shinbone and Achilles tendon. He rolled onto his back, gripped the wound, felt the viscous warmth of raw flesh. He wanted to shout out in agony, but he knew doing so would be a death sentence. He wiped the stinging sweat from his eyes, peeked around the edge of the forklift, and saw the dark zombie astronaut figure known as K-Rad stagger out of Mr. Hubbs's office and disappear from sight.

Matt tried to stand. He could barely put any weight on the leg now, let alone walk or run. He would have to use the forklift to get around, and the whining noise of the electric motor would allow K-Rad to know his location. Fortunately, K-Rad had headed toward the time clock, and Matt planned on going in the opposite direction, toward the Fire and Ice tanks. He felt around for the switchblade but couldn't find it anywhere. He'd dropped it when the grenade went off, and now it was gone. He belly-crawled into the office and felt around on the floor. He'd heard K-Rad dumping the contents of the desk drawers and thought there might be something among the debris to use as a weapon. He felt a stapler and a box of paper clips and some pens and pencils and Post-it pads and a bunch of other crap you'd expect to find in any well-stocked office. What he wanted, but did not find, was a letter opener or a whiskey bottle or something. He was thinking a gun would be nice when he felt the cold metallic cylinder and, for a split second, thought he'd actually lucked into finding one. He picked it up. It wasn't a gun but a small steel flashlight. He switched it on for a second to make sure it worked and then crawled back out of the office. He climbed onto the forklift, pointed it toward the big tanks, and pegged the throttle.

10:40 a.m.

K-Rad made it to the water fountain, took the mask and helmet and binoculars off, and stood there slurping for more than a minute. The air was unpleasantly thick with fumes from the warehouse area and the Fire and Ice tanks, and the water from the fountain wasn't very cold. It wasn't very cold, but it was still good. It was what he needed. He drank until he could drink no more, and then he put the mask back on and took the walkway to the office building.

There was a way out, of course. Most Nitko employees didn't know about it, but there was a way out. How else could a hazmat team come and go in the case of a catastrophic spill? Of course there was a way out. How could there not be?

He opened the door to the main power closet and used a step stool to reach the steel panel in the ceiling. He loosened the four thumbscrews securing the panel to its frame, pulled it forward until its four tabs were aligned with their corresponding slots, lowered it with his hands, and threw it on the floor. He undid the Velcro straps holding the dropdown ladder in place, lowered the ladder, and climbed through the ceiling to the hatch in the roof. The hatch was wheel operated, like the watertight doors on a ship. K-Rad turned the wheel counterclockwise until the seal broke and the hatch swung open. He climbed out onto the roof. The sun was shockingly bright. He took the half-broken night-vision binoculars off and whizzed them like a Frisbee. He didn't need them anymore. He kept the gas mask, just in case. He shinnied down a drainpipe, ran to his hole in the fence behind the diesel tank, got in his car, and drove away.

10:45 a.m.

Matt drove the forklift as fast as it would go. He'd covered about half the distance to Waterbase when the battery died. The lift rolled to a stop, and Matt got off and started limping toward the tanks. Every step shot blue spears of electric pain up his leg and into his spine. When he got close enough, he saw Shelly forty feet in the air, dangling from one of the water pipes near the ceiling. She was making her way, arm over arm, to one of the ventilation fans.

There was enough light shining through the opening for Matt to see her face, which looked like something exhumed from a graveyard.

Matt hobbled to one of the forklifts plugged in by the wall, unplugged the charging cable, put the lift in reverse, swung around, and knocked four empty drums off an oak pallet with the forks. He picked up the pallet, positioned the lift under where Shelly was hanging, and raised the platform. He wanted to knock her off the pipe and onto the pallet. Then he would lower the fork and deal with her on the ground. He had to stop her from leaving the plant. If she made it outside, there was no telling what she might do.

Except that people would die.

Shelly looked down and saw the pallet rising toward her. She was only a few feet from the fan now, and she sped up her actions.

"You're too late," she said.

The pallet was about two feet from her when she made it to the fan. She held on to the pipe with one hand and yanked the grate off with the other. The grate fell to the floor, and Shelly climbed into the opening. Matt rammed the wooden platform toward the fan, but Shelly was inside the cylindrical housing now and the pallet was too fat to reach her.

"Shelly, I want you to—"

"You want to fuck me as long as it's convenient for you—then you want me to smile and wave good-bye when you're tired of me," Shelly said. "Too bad I don't give a shit what you want. I'm going to do what *I* want for once."

"And what's that?"

"Your ax is in my car," she said. "Maybe I'll try chopping wood. Chopping something, anyway."

She started laughing, an insane cackle Matt hadn't heard before, and then she was gone.

But then he saw Mr. Dark sitting on one of the pipes, his feet dangling over the side, sipping his martini.

"Oh, yes, this is much more fun," Mr. Dark said.

10:48 a.m.

K-Rad drove by his childhood home on the dirt road behind the plant. He stopped and put the car in park. He just wanted to look at his old house for a minute, to see it one last time. School hadn't started yet, and there were three boys in the front yard running gleefully through a sprinkler. They were probably second graders, about seven years old. K-Rad remembered doing the same thing when he was that age. Such a simple thing, but such fun.

The house hadn't changed much since K-Rad was a kid. White clapboard siding, red shingle roof, swing on the front porch. It really wasn't such a bad little house, after all. Lots of fond memories there. Too bad it still belonged to the greedy motherfuckers at Nitko.

"Hey, mister. Take a picture—it'll last longer," one of the boys shouted. The others laughed.

K-Rad put the car in gear and drove on. *Brats.* If they only knew what was going to happen to them at eleven. If they only knew.

10:49 a.m.

Matt thought about trying to navigate the water pipe, as Shelly had, and following her out that way, but the pipe had bowed under her weight and he was fairly certain it would break under his. Mr. Dark smiled down at him.

"You should have killed her when you had the chance." For a moment, Matt feared that the son of a bitch could read his mind.

Because the thought had occurred to him.

Matt had killed before, but only when there was no other choice. When not killing would have meant more deaths. He wasn't a murderer.

Not yet.

The voice in his head was his own...But it sounded eerily close to Mr. Dark's.

Matt got off the forklift, limped behind the tanks, found Terri, and once again removed the duct tape from her mouth.

"Why did you leave me here like this?" she said.

"I didn't want you to walk around with me and maybe get your head blown off."

"Oh. Well, thanks, I guess."

Matt switched on the flashlight from Hubbs's office, put it in his mouth, and started unwrapping the tape binding

Terri's hands. He wanted her to raise him to the vent fan with the forklift so he could go after Shelly.

Then he saw the red glare.

He stopped what he was doing and scooted one of the bags of chemicals out of the way. A cavity had been created underneath it, and in the center of the cavity was a red metal gas can, the kind people use to fill lawn tractors. But this was no ordinary gas can. Two holes had been drilled through the lid, and a pair of electrical wires snaked from the holes to a black metal box the size of a deck of cards. The box was secured to the top of the can with duct tape.

Matt looked at the bags of chemicals stacked from one end of the tanks to the other. He shined the light on one of the bags and saw the words AMMONIUM NITRATE printed in bold black letters.

He didn't know much about chemistry, but he knew that ammonium nitrate was one of the ingredients terrorists used to make bombs. Timothy McVeigh had used 108 fifty-pound bags of the stuff to blow up the Alfred P. Murrah Federal Building in Oklahoma City.

There were easily ten times that many stacked behind the Fire and Ice tanks.

Matt figured the explosion would not only destroy the plant—it would wipe out a couple of square blocks of nearby residences and businesses as well.

You know, I'm tempted to let you stick around until eleven and see the show. It's going to be fabulous.

Matt had wondered what K-Rad was talking about, and now he knew.

"What are you doing?" Terri said. "Untie me!"

Matt frantically unwound the tape from her wrists and then started on her ankles. "I don't want to scare you," he said, "but if we don't move really, really fast, we're going to be blown to smithereens."

"What are you talking about?"

"There's a bomb about eighteen inches to your right." Terri jumped to her feet and almost fell back down. "Oh my God. What are we going to do?"

"I have an idea, but my leg's messed up. So you're going to have to do most of the work."

"Just tell me what to do."

They hurried to the front of the tanks.

"Grab some two-and-a-half-inch hoses off that rack over there," Matt said. "Get three of the twelve-footers. We're going to need a three-way connector and a reducer and a twenty-foot section of one-inch hose."

While Terri ran for the hose rack, Matt positioned a pneumatic pump a few feet from the valves in front of the tanks. By the time he ran an air hose from its reel on the wall and secured it close to the base of the pump, Terri had gathered the supplies and it was...

10:56 a.m.

Matt instructed Terri to connect one of the fat hoses to the valve on the Fire tank and another to the valve on the Ice tank. The loose ends of those two hoses then went to the cross on the three-way connector. One end of the third two-and-a-half-inch hose was connected to the stem of the three-way and the other to the pump's input port. The reducer and the long one-inch hose were connected to the pump's output. Matt fed the smaller hose between the tanks and let it rest on top of the ammonium nitrate bags.

"I want you to open the valves to the tanks when I give the word," Matt said.

The exact formulas for Fire and Ice were a tightly kept corporate secret, but Matt knew the pH of Fire was 1 and that of Ice was 14. Shelly had told him that much before his first day on the job. Fire was an acid, and Ice a base. The solutions were highly caustic, and the blenders and packagers were required to wear special suits and gloves and respirators and goggles while performing their duties. A drop of either on bare skin would cause an instant blister, a splash in the face lifelong disfigurement or even death.

But what would happen if the two skin-scalding liquids were mixed together? If Matt remembered correctly from high school chemistry, they would neutralize each other and essentially become water. That's what he wanted to happen.

Matt looked at his watch. It was thirty-four seconds to the top of the hour—thirty-four seconds until a ball of fire consumed the entire neighborhood.

...33...32...31...

The valves on the tanks were positioned at an angle, and Terri was able to stand between them and reach both levers. Matt jammed the end of the air hose onto the pneumatic pump and said, "Do it!"

Terri opened the valves simultaneously, and within seconds, the mixture of Fire and Ice came spewing from the one-inch hose and started flooding the area behind the tanks.

...5...4...3...2...

11:00 a.m.

K-Rad walked into the Retro and took a stool at the bar.
The place had just opened, and the lunch crowd hadn't
started sifting in yet. K-Rad was the only customer. He'd
stuffed his gas mask and other goodies into his backpack, and he'd left the Kevlar vest and the Berettas in
his car. The bartender, a chick named Tami with full-
sleeve tats on her arms and quarter-inch gauges in her
earlobes, slapped a napkin in front of him and said,
"What's up, K?"

"Not much. Let me get a Shiner Bock, OK?"

"Sure."

She brought the longneck brown bottle and popped the
top with an opener. The television was tuned to an info-
mercial about an herbal supplement called Zark-O. It was
supposed to make you live to be around two hundred years
old or something.

"Can you turn it on Channel Four?" K-Rad said. Channel
4 was one of the local network affiliates, and K-Rad knew
the boneheads on the news team there would have the big
story before it went national. Those motherfuckers thrived
on human misery. They went after it like vultures went after
roadkill.

Tami wiped her hands with a towel. "I heard that stuff
really works."

"Zark-O?"

"Yeah."

"Come on. It's bullshit. Nothing's going to make you live longer. When your time's up, it's up."

"I just heard it makes you feel better. That's all."

"I think I'll stick with alcohol. Can you change the channel for me?"

Tami picked up the remote and switched the channel. "Wouldn't you want to live forever if you could, though?" she said.

"Immortality isn't about how long you're here," K-Rad said. "It's about what you do *while* you're here."

"Wow. That's deep. I still might try the Zark-O. Just to see what it's like."

K-Rad didn't say anything. He looked up at the television, wondering why he hadn't heard the explosion or at least felt the earth shake. Maybe the Retro was too far away from the plant. Anyway, he was sure there would be some breaking news soon.

"Wait a minute," he said. "Are those sirens I hear?"

Tami lowered the volume on the television. "Yep. Must be a fire somewhere."

K-Rad got up and walked outside. In the distance, he saw plumes of black smoke rising from Nitko's direction. *Yes!* Mission accomplished. He smiled and went back inside to finish his beer.

11:03 a.m.

There had been a deafening *BOOM*, followed by a wall of fire rising from behind the tanks. Matt had stood there helplessly, waiting for the flames to consume him, but he and Terri were miraculously still alive. One of the detonators had gone off, and the fuel can it was attached to had exploded, but apparently the blast hadn't been powerful enough to ignite the ammonium nitrate. Matt's plan had worked, at least partially. The Fire and Ice solution had prevented the big bang, but the plastic bags containing the ammonium nitrate were burning now and filling Waterbase with greasy black smoke.

Matt held the one-inch hose and sprayed the Fire and Ice mixture toward the inferno, but the liquid wasn't coming out fast enough or forcefully enough to extinguish the flames. It wasn't coming out fast enough or forcefully enough, and then it stopped coming out completely.

It took Matt a second to figure out what had happened. There was no electricity to power the compressor, so once the pressure in the reserve tank dropped to a certain level, there was no air to drive the pump.

"Let's get out of here," Matt shouted.

He climbed onto the forklift and motioned for Terri to sit on the pallet.

"What are we going to do? How the hell are we going to get out?" she said, coughing and wheezing between sentences.

"I don't know, but we have to get away from this smoke before we die of inhalation. Come on!"

Terri climbed onto the pallet, and Matt did a one-eighty and headed toward the time clock. His eyes were stinging, and his lungs felt as though someone had stuffed oily cotton balls into them. He wished he had thought to grab some respirators from the safety office when he'd been in the front building. At the time, it hadn't even crossed his mind, but they sure would have come in handy now. He drove on, trying to take shallow breaths, one hand guiding the forklift and the other pressing the tail of his shirt against his mouth and aching nose.

He slowed down and carefully turned a corner, intending to take a shortcut between the floor-to-ceiling industrial shelves loaded with Nitko products, and when he turned, Terri went limp, fell to her side, and tumbled off the pallet like a rag doll. The smoke had gotten to her.

Matt stopped the forklift, got off, and knelt beside her. She wasn't breathing.

He felt her neck for a pulse. Nothing.

Matt put his mouth on Terri's, gave her two quick rescue breaths, laced his hands together, and started chest compressions. He performed two full cycles of CPR. As he started a third, she coughed and turned her head to the side and vomited. Terri was alive, but she wasn't going to last long. Matt stood, dizzy and nauseated from the smoke, the heat, the exertion, and the pain in his leg, picked Terri up and cradled her in his arms, and forced himself to put one foot in front of the other.

11:10 a.m.

Shelly held Matt's ax with both hands and stared out at the road leading to Nitko's gate. Before she had left the parking lot, she'd broken a window on Hal's pickup truck and had taken the sawed-off shotgun he kept behind the seat. It was a twelve-gauge pump, a very nice gun, and Hal, being dead and all, certainly wasn't going to need it anymore. After taking the gun and the box of shells in the glove compartment, she'd left Nitko's property and had backed her car into a patch of woods, out of sight, thinking she would ambush Matt when he tried to come after her.

She'd shoot his ass and then cut his head off with his own ax.

Because she had a feeling he was the one guy who might be able to stop her from what she had to do.

And she couldn't have that, could she? Thinking about it made her giggle.

K-Rad had the right idea. He was the Man Who Stood Up. The Man Who Would Not Take It Anymore. Shelly had let the pricks steal her life away, day by day, dollar by dollar. She was going to take it back. Screw dying fast versus dying slowly. If she had to go, she was going to take a bunch of those fuckers with her.

She watched the smoke rising from the production building and wondered if Matt was even still alive. She would give him a few more minutes, and then she would go have some fun elsewhere.

But where? A fragment of song from her childhood popped into her mind, something about starting at the very beginning, a very good place to start.

Good idea, she thought. *Get them young before they can turn into the kind of miserable fucks who'd stolen her life away.*

In her mind, she mapped out the route to the day care center down the road.

11:12 a.m.

In a little while, after you're good and dead, I'll be sipping on a cold one at the Retro and thinking about how famous I'm going to be.

Matt was no longer worried about getting shot. He figured K-Rad had already left the building.

Of course he was gone. Why would he have stuck around to get blown up?

Matt carried Terri through the walkway to the office suite. The air was better up there, but only slightly. Smoke and fumes had started to seep through from the production area, and with no ventilation and all the doors sealed tight, it was like trying to breathe mud.

There were dead bodies everywhere.

Matt opened the door to the safety office, set Terri on the floor, and found respirators for them both. He put Terri's on first and then donned his own. It was an immediate improvement, and after a couple of minutes, Terri sat up and said, "Now what?"

"Follow me," Matt said.

He could have taken car keys from any of the corpses, but he knew what kind of car Officer McCray drove. It was a 1966 GTO convertible, maroon with patches of gray primer and a white top. Matt had noticed it in the parking lot his first day on the job, and Shelly had told him whom it belonged to.

Matt led Terri to the security office, reached into McCray's pocket, and snatched the keys.

"How are we going to get out of the building?" Terri said.

"There has to be a way out. Firefighters and rescue personnel and hazmat teams are able to gain access during lockdown situations, so there has to be a way. I would imagine it's wherever the breaker box and all that kind of stuff is."

"The main power closet," Terri said. "I know where it is. I used to date a guy in Maintenance."

"Let's go."

They made it to the power closet, saw the drop-down ladder and the hatch, and two minutes later were on the roof. They took the respirators off and tossed them aside.

"Amazing how you take things like fresh air and sunshine for granted," Terri said.

"Yeah." Matt walked to the edge of the flat roof. His leg still hurt, but the pain wasn't nearly as bad as it had been previously. The wound had already started to heal, another part of the enigma his life had become since the avalanche. "You think you're able to climb down this drainpipe?"

"I'll give it a shot."

Matt went first so if Terri fell while climbing down, he could catch her. He used his powerful arms to shinny down the pipe, guarding the bum leg the best he could. Terri did fine, and in a couple of minutes, they were in the GTO, heading for the gate.

"Where are we going?" Terri said.

"The Retro. I want you to climb in back and get on the floorboard. I have a feeling K-Rad's killing spree isn't over."

Terri started sobbing. "I just want to go home."

"I'll get you home," Matt said. "I promise."

He urgently needed to find Shelly too, but he had no idea where to start looking.

Worse came to worst, he'd have to wait...and follow the trail of bodies.

11:15 a.m.

Shelly watched McCray's '66 GTO take a right out of Nitko's driveway.

Matt was driving, and some bitch was riding shotgun. Was he fucking her too?

Had he been all along?

Fuck it. The day care could wait.

Shelly started her car and followed the GTO.

11:16 a.m.

Tami had left an ice pick on the bar near the garnish tray. K-Rad picked it up and put it in his pocket. He sucked the last few foamy ounces from his Shiner Bock longneck and walked outside to once again admire his handiwork. He looked southeast, and the horizon in that direction was now completely shrouded in a haze the color of pencil lead. What fun! Thousands of people were dead now, all because of K-Rad and his perfect plan. This was just too cool, and there was even more amusement yet to come.

K-Rad wanted to be arrested, the sooner the better, so why wait for the authorities to put two and two together and figure out he was the one responsible for the Nitko explosion? Why not just open fire on the lunch patrons at the Retro and expedite the whole process?

The idea had come to him halfway into his second beer. The Berettas were in the car, and he still had plenty of ammunition. No point in all those bullets going to waste. He would drink another beer or two, until the joint was good and crowded, and then he would go at it with a pistol in each hand. He would jump behind the bar and kill Tami first and, from that position, would start picking off customers. Someone would use a cell phone to call the police, and when the cops got there, K-Rad would walk out with his hands in the air and surrender peacefully. *Perfect.*

On their way to the Retro's entrance, a young couple stopped where K-Rad was standing. College students, K-Rad thought, taking a break between classes. The guy had a goatee and diamond studs in both ears.

"Hear anything about the fire?" the young man said, gesturing toward the smoke with his thumb. He was sucking on a cigarette, trying to consume as much of it as he could before going inside. His girlfriend stood beside him with her arms folded, obviously impatient with his vice.

"Nothing yet," K-Rad said. "I've been sitting at the bar watching the news. I'm sure they'll get to it eventually."

"Tyler, can we please go in now? I'm starving." The college chick had a tight knit shirt on and very short cutoff jeans. Daisy Dukes, they called them, after a character in a largely forgotten television show from a largely forgotten decade. She had a pretty face and a nice body.

"Let me finish my cigarette, babe," Tyler said.

"You need to quit that vile habit. You smoke and then you want to kiss on me. It's like kissing an ashtray."

"A sexy ashtray."

"That makes no sense at all."

"Go on in and get us a table. I'll be along in a minute." She stalked away without saying another word. Once she was safely inside, Tyler turned to K-Rad and said, "Women."

"She's very attractive," K-Rad said.

"Yeah, and she's right. I really do need to quit smoking."

"You guys in college?"

"Yeah, CH State, but I'm planning on transferring to the University of Florida when I get my associate's degree."

"Sounds like a good plan."

Tyler dropped his cigarette on the pavement and crushed it with the toe of his sandal. "I better get on in there before she starts freaking," he said.

K-Rad pulled the ice pick from his pocket, gripped it tightly, and jammed it into the side of Tyler's throat. Blood pulsed skyward, as though being shot from a squirt gun. *Must have punctured an artery*, K-Rad thought. Tyler fell to the sidewalk, twitched a few times, and then lay still.

"Now she's *really* going to start freaking," K-Rad said. He dragged Tyler's limp body behind a stand of ornamental shrubs and walked toward his car to get the Berettas.

11:20 a.m.

Terri climbed into the back of the GTO and got down on the floorboard, as Matt had instructed. Matt switched on the radio and turned it to the news channel, just in case Shelly was unleashing whatever hell she had in mind. If a bulletin came on about an ax murderer loose in a school or a department store or something, at least Matt would know where to go.

And what he had to do.

Because every person she hurt...or killed...was on him.

For bringing Mr. Dark into her life.

And for letting her walk out of the factory.

Matt listened to the radio program, but the only story being broadcast at the moment was from an economist, something about the possibility of interest rates going up. The usual boring crap.

"I need to pee," Terri said.

"What?"

"I gotta go. Really bad."

They were currently on a stretch of two-lane blacktop lined with pine trees on both sides. The closest bathroom was at the Retro, still several miles away, and Matt wanted Terri to stay in the car when they got there.

"There's nowhere to go," Matt said. "You're just going to have to hold it. Or pee your pants."

"I can't hold it much longer, and I'm *not* going to pee my pants. Pull over to the side of the road and let me out. It'll only take a minute."

Matt cursed under his breath. He eased to the shoulder, braked to a stop, and put the car in neutral.

11:22 a.m.

Why the hell are they stopping here? Shelly wondered. Then she saw the petite young woman climbing out of the passenger's side door. *He's going to do it to her right there in the trees. Can't even wait to get back to her place.* She should have known he was just like all the rest of the assholes she'd been with.

Matt had his eyes on the bitch and paid no attention as Shelly sped by. No worries about him seeing and recognizing her car. Shelly knew where Matt and his little chickadee were headed.

The only thing out this way was the Retro.

The Retro. *Hmm.* The day care could wait. She'd take out the parents first—then there would be no one to get in her way. It was close to lunchtime, and they'd all be heading to the Retro.

Heads will roll!

She laughed out loud.

11:23 a.m.

Matt didn't see the driver of the car as it passed...But he recognized it from the Nitko parking lot.

And there was nobody alive at Nitko to drive it. Except one person.

Matt jammed the transmission into first gear and burned rubber back onto the highway. Terri was safer here than where he was going.

11:31 a.m.

Shelly pulled into the Retro's lot, found a parking place, and killed the engine. She popped the hatch and reached into the cargo area and removed the long and slender nylon pouch from one of the two tailgating chairs she kept back there. She slid Matt's ax and the sawed-off shotgun into the pouch, walked inside, and made a bee-line to the ladies' room. It was a large restroom, very nice, with eight stalls and a triple granite-top vanity. There was a young woman, college age, standing at the mirror touching up her makeup.

"How's it going?" Shelly said.

"Great, except my stupid boyfriend would rather stand outside and smoke cigarettes than come in here with me."

"Men."

"Yeah, tell me about it. Hey, what's in the pouch?"

Shelly pulled the ax out and in a single swift motion buried the blade in the young woman's skull. The sound of the sharpened steel breaking through bone and tearing into brain tissue made Shelly burst into laughter. Or maybe she was crying—she couldn't really tell. She dragged the body across the marble floor to the stall farthest from the door, positioned it on the toilet, and closed the door.

There were still seven stalls to go!

11:34 a.m.

K-Rad was on his way back inside when an old Pontiac GTO screeched to a stop at the sidewalk. A man got out of the car and limped toward him. The man looked like a nightmare, his clothes black with soot and his face and left shoe crusted with blood.

K-Rad assessed the filthy man. "What the—"

As K-Rad was saying *the*, the man clouted him with an uppercut to the chin. The impact caused K-Rad to bite his tongue, his incisors slicing down hard and completely severing the tip of the highly vascular and highly innervated organ. Blood gushed from his mouth, and he started dancing around trying to stop the flow with his hand. The pain radiated through his jaw and to the bones in his ears.

"Fuck!" he said. "You made me bite my fucking tongue off." *Uck! Ew ade ee ite i ucking ung off.*

The man came forward with his fist cocked. Who the fuck was this idiot? K-Rad knew it wasn't someone from the plant, because everyone there was dead now. Anyone who had avoided being shot had surely died from the explosion. Nobody could have survived that.

The man punched swift and hard, but K-Rad somehow managed to dodge the blow.

Matt could see boils on K-Rad's face oozing with thick pus the color and consistency of custard, and slimy brown earthworms crawled in and out of his eye sockets like living strands of lo mein. K-Rad ran out into the parking lot, bright-red blood dripping down his rotting chin. Matt followed, limping as fast as he could, but K-Rad darted behind a minivan and Matt lost sight of him. Sirens wailed in the distance as more firefighters and rescue personnel headed to Nitko. Matt hobbled forward a few steps, looked between some cars for K-Rad, but didn't see him anywhere.

A muffled gunshot crackled, and a bullet whistled past Matt's left ear. K-Rad stood forty feet away with his elbows propped on the roof of a light-blue compact automobile, a Camry or a Sentra or one of the other generic sedans from overseas. He fired a second time and a third, and both those rounds missed their mark, but the fourth time K-Rad pulled the trigger, Matt felt a sizzling-hot bolus of lead burrow deep into his left shoulder. The shock and pain from the bullet's impact, along with everything else that had happened over the past few hours, caused Matt to have a momentary lapse of consciousness. He fell dizzily to the pavement and lay flat on his back, clutching the fresh wound with his right hand.

K-Rad walked over with the pistol and aimed it straight at Matt's face. "I don't know who you are, but you just fucked with the wrong motherfucker, motherfucker."

Matt stared Radowski down, resigned to his fate now but unwilling to beg or whimper or flinch, unwilling to give this poor excuse for a human being the satisfaction of seeing him sweat.

"Fuck you," Matt said.

K-Rad laughed. He pulled the trigger, but the gun did not fire. While he was reaching into his backpack and pulling a second identical pistol out and jacking a round into the chamber, Matt felt something uncomfortable pressing against his right buttocks.

Then he remembered.

He reached into the back pocket of his jeans. An instant before K-Rad took aim again, Matt sprayed the entire contents of the Mace canister at his unprotected face. Radowski squealed and cussed and clawed at his eyes. Matt scissored his legs with K-Rad's and sent the gunman tumbling facedown onto the pavement.

Matt rose to a sitting position, grabbed K-Rad by the hair, and smashed his face into the hot blacktop. He picked up the pistol, rose and steadied himself, and limped toward the entrance.

11:37 a.m.

From the ladies' restroom, Shelly heard women screaming and dishes breaking and pieces of silverware clanging metallically to the floor. A man shouted, "Oh my God, he's got a gun."

Shelly didn't know what the hell was going on, but she was missing all the excitement and that wasn't cool. Fuck a bunch of waiting around for these bitches to come in and potty. Time to kick things up a notch.

She pulled the Remington twelve-gauge pump from the pouch and stuffed some extra shells into her pockets. She pumped one into the chamber and walked out with the barrel leading the way.

The worst table in a restaurant is always the one nearest the restrooms. There are people constantly walking by, on their way to piss or shit or hock a loogie, and in the worst establishments you can even hear the toilets flushing. Not very appetizing. Plus, the hallway to the restroom is usually near the door to the kitchen, so you have servers and busboys scurrying back and forth with trays of hot food or plastic bins of dirty dishes, and the chef is always shouting at someone for screwing something up. The worst table in a restaurant is always the one nearest the restrooms, and at the Retro, it was a four-top nestled between the lobster tank and a life-sized statue of Elvis. Shelly turned the corner and saw the unlucky party, an elderly couple on one side of the table and a much younger couple on the other. Next to the younger woman there was a little girl, probably between the ages of one and two, strapped into a wooden high chair. The baby was screaming for all she was worth, and all four of the adults had their elbows on the table and their hands laced together and their eyes closed. They were praying. Shelly aimed the gun and pulled the trigger, and chunks of Grandma and Grandpa splattered all over Elvis's chubby face. It looked like someone had thrown a plate of spaghetti and meatballs at him. The young couple's expressions had quickly turned from worry to terror, and they backed toward the wall and held their palms out in a defensive gesture as Shelly turned the gun on them and their baby.

"Stop!"

Shelly looked toward the front entrance. It was Matt Cahill, and he was pointing a pistol right at her.

11:45 a.m.

Decaying flesh hung from Shelly's face in strips, as though someone had fed rotten liver through a paper shredder. Her teeth were thick and yellow, her inflamed eyeballs bobbing around in their sockets like hard-boiled eggs in some sort of ghastly stew. Matt had seen her car in the parking lot when he drove in, so he'd known she was here at the Retro, but he had no clue as to how she'd managed to get hold of a gun. A sawed-off shotgun, no less, a goddamn portable cannon. She had already slaughtered an elderly man and woman, and she was about to do the same to a young couple and their toddler.

"Let them go, Shelly," Matt shouted. "They never did anything to you."

Matt was still dizzy. Sweat trickled down his face in streams, and his heart raced, but jacked on adrenaline, he felt no pain from the shrapnel wound in his left leg or the slug embedded in his left shoulder. He felt nothing but an intense rage at all the bloodshed this horrible day had brought and an intense sorrow for what he was going to have to do now.

He lined the pistol's sites at Shelly's chest, trying his best to focus.

"Drop your gun," she said, pointing the shotgun directly at the baby's head. "Or I shoot the baby."

It was a stalemate. If Matt pulled the trigger, Shelly would die, but so would the baby.

"Why the baby?" Matt asked.

"Why not?" she said. "Aren't they adorable? That's all the bitches at the plant ever talk about. Let them talk about this."

Matt saw her finger tense on the trigger. "What's the baby's name?" He turned to the terrified mother. "Tell me." In a quivering voice, the young woman said, "Kylie. Her name is Kylie."

"You hear that, Shelly? Her name is Kylie. Why would you possibly—"

"Shut up," Shelly said. "Or shoot me. I'd be doing this kid a favor."

"A favor?"

Shelly gestured to the horrified mother. "Look at her, sopping up the beer. A couple years from now, she'll be too drunk to notice when her man starts feeling up little Kylie. Or she'll notice and not even give a shit. Hell, maybe she'll even pimp her out for drug money."

"Or maybe her mother will love her and she'll grow up to live a happy life," Matt said.

"No such thing," Shelly said.

Suddenly, blue lights started flashing against the restaurant's window shades. Shelly saw them too.

The cops had arrived, but Matt knew they wouldn't storm in right away. They would secure the area, try to negotiate a surrender, and eventually send in a SWAT team. By that time, little Kylie and no telling how many others would perish.

One way or another, it would be over soon.

"I know you drift off sometimes," Matt said. "When the pain becomes too much. Where do you go?"

Shelly turned and faced Matt. The expression on her gruesome face seemed to soften, and her voice sounded like it belonged to a little girl.

"High school. Isn't that fucking pathetic? Everybody in the world hated high school, and it's all I've got to look back on...I was almost head cheerleader, you know. I was..." She paused and then shouted, "*Fuck you!*"

She gritted her teeth and scrunched her brow, and as she started to turn back toward the child in the high chair, Matt squeezed the trigger three times in quick succession. Shelly spun and fell backward, and the shotgun blasted a hole in the ceiling as she crashed into the lobster tank. The glass shattered, and a hundred gallons of murky green water flooded the floor.

The liberated creatures did not crawl on Shelly, or even toward her. They crawled away from her, as though she and they were opposite poles of a magnet.

The restaurant patrons, many of whom had climbed under tables or had taken other defensive positions, seemed to breathe a collective sigh of relief.

Someone began clapping.

It was Mr. Dark, sitting at a table, wearing a lobster bib, waiting for his meal.

"Nicely done," Mr. Dark said. "Shame you couldn't do it before."

"I'm not a murderer," Matt said.

"No, no, you're not," the baby's mother said, clutching her baby now and sobbing. "You saved us. Thank God, you saved us."

Matt looked at her, wanting to believe she was right. But the bodies on the floor said otherwise.

When he turned back around, Mr. Dark was gone.

Epilogue

A pair of police detectives grilled Matt as he lay on a gurney in the emergency room awaiting treatment. He told them everything he knew about the slayings at Nitko and at the Retro.

But he didn't really have to convince them.

By the time he got to the hospital, they'd found Terri Bonach, and she backed up his story. And there was the mother, who credited him with saving her child.

And Kevin Radowski was still alive, somewhere in the same hospital, under heavy guard.

They said that Matt had probably saved thousands of lives.

But it was the few who he didn't—and especially Shelly— that he couldn't stop thinking about.

If only he'd killed her the instant Mr. Dark had touched her...

But he hadn't had the guts. Or the heart.

Shelly was broken long before he'd met her, but no more than the millions of other people who were living lives they hated. The anger and bitterness were just small parts of her. There was joy in her too. He'd seen it. He'd felt it. Maybe if she'd lived long enough, she could have figured out how to let the good feelings overwhelm the bad. Or maybe not. But that was just life.

Then Mr. Dark had touched her, and the bitterness and anger were all that were left.

Matt had kept hoping until the last minute that he could save her from what Mr. Dark had done with his touch. But he could never save her from what her life had done to her—and what she had done to herself. The seeds had been planted long ago. Mr. Dark just showed up for the harvest.

So now Radowski was alive and Shelly was in a body bag. Matt figured the prosecution would seek the death penalty, but even if they were successful, no telling how many years K-Rad would spend on death row filing appeals. Books would be written, movies would be made, and curious women would make him their pen pal. Three hots and a cot, and worldwide fame. That was probably what he had wanted all along, and that was probably what he was going to get.

It wasn't fair that K-Rad had survived and Shelly had not. Score one for Mr. Dark.

The plant may not have blown up, but K-Rad was still alive, someone other psychopaths could look to for bloody inspiration.

Matt asked the detectives about his ax.

The cops told him it had been used to kill a woman in the bathroom.

Matt asked for it back, which shocked the cops.

"It belonged to my grandfather," he told them. "It's very important to me."

The cops figured that since the perp was dead and there wouldn't be a trial, they wouldn't have to hold on to it.

They were going against department regulations bigtime, but they owed him something for stopping the bomb.

So they washed the blood off of the ax and gave it to him in a gym bag so nobody would see it.

He asked for one more thing.

He wanted his name out of the papers. He wanted no credit whatsoever for what he had done.

Or not done.

They were OK with that too.

Matt spent several hours in the emergency room but refused to be admitted to the hospital. Hospitals were not good places for him. He healed too fast, which inevitably raised questions he didn't want raised.

An on-call surgeon removed the bullet from Matt's shoulder and the shrapnel from his leg. Once he was sewn up, cleaned, and bandaged, Matt dressed in a set of surgical scrubs he found on a linen cart, took the staff-only elevator to the basement, and walked out of the service entrance of the hospital before the media arrived.

Gym bag in hand, he slipped through the parking lot and up the ramp to the highway. A mile or so later, he came to a sign that said *95 South to St. Augustine.* He stuck his thumb out.

He didn't know where he was going, but he was in no hurry to get there.

Because he knew one thing for certain. Death would be waiting.

THE DEAD MAN:
CARNIVAL OF DEATH

By Bill Crider

CHAPTER ONE

Sue Jean Eckerd moped down the midway of Cap'n Bob's Stardust Carnival. The flashing red, green, and blue lights didn't cheer her up, nor did the smells of cotton candy, corn dogs, caramel apples, and deep-fried Snickers bars delight her. The music of the carousel and the other rides might as well have been white noise as far as Sue Jean was concerned. She was too pissed off at Madison Carroll to care about any of those things.

She'd come to the carnival with her BFF, but Madison had dumped her within ten minutes for the dubious charms of that pimple-faced dickwad Freddie Pierce, who had nothing going for him at all other than the fact that his father was a zillionaire. But then, Madison had always been shallow. Horse faced too, though Sue Jean would never tell her that.

Besides Madison's deeply hurtful betrayal, there was that goofy fortune-teller. Sue Jean knew better than to have some old hag read her palm, but when Madison dumped her, it seemed somehow like the thing to do.

The inside of the tent smelled funny, and the old biddy at the table with the crystal ball did too. Or maybe the smell came from the incense that glowed in a bowl on a little stand nearby. Sue Jean didn't like incense. There wasn't much light in the tent, either, and the whole thing was totally creepy.

Sue Jean started to leave, but she'd already handed over her five dollars, so she thought she'd make the best of it.

The woman, Madame Zora it said on the sign outside the tent, looked into Sue Jean's eyes, and Sue Jean saw that she wasn't entirely ancient, but she must have been over thirty for sure. The robes and the shawl she wore over her head hid a lot of her features, but Sue Jean knew an old person when she saw one.

Madame Zora took Sue Jean's hand and studied her palm. She hadn't looked for more than two seconds before she jerked her head back as if somebody had hit her on her pointy chin. She dropped Sue Jean's hand and let her arms fall away from the table.

Sue Jean thought Madame Zora might have had a stroke or a heart attack, since that was the kind of thing that happened to old people, but there wasn't anything Sue Jean could do about it. She'd heard about what to do on some TV show, or maybe it was in some class at school, but it didn't matter. She hadn't listened. She remembered that if somebody was having a seizure, you were supposed to keep them from swallowing their tongue, but there was no way she was going to touch that old woman's mouth.

Luckily, however, Madame Zora wasn't having a stroke or a seizure. The fortune-teller's head snapped back up and she stared at Sue Jean like she had two heads or a gigantic zit.

"Go home!" was what Madame Zora had said. "You should leave the carnival grounds right now! Don't stay here any longer. It's too dangerous for you tonight."

She looked as scary as Sue Jean's Algebra II teacher on test day, and Sue Jean didn't stick around to hear any more.

Even if it meant losing her five dollars, she was getting out of that tent.

She left in a big hurry and thought she'd better have a snow cone, one of the red ones, to calm herself down. Then she might leave the carnival, but she didn't think there was any real rush. The old woman was just some kind of crazy crank who liked to scare kids—that was all. She was probably jealous of anybody who wasn't some old crone like she was.

So Sue Jean ignored the warning and bought her snow cone and thought about Madison and Freddie "the Puke" Pierce and hoped somebody was barfing corn dogs on them from on top of the Ferris wheel. Maybe she'd walk down that way and see.

The Ferris wheel was at the end of the midway, down near the carousel, and Sue Jean didn't quite get there. Earl Compton stepped out from between a couple of the tents and said, "Hey, Sue Jean."

If there was anybody creepier than Freddie "the Zit" Pierce, it was Earl Compton, and his old man wasn't even rich. Earl had bulging eyes, big ears, a big nose, and big hands. Sue Jean knew what they said about guys with big noses and long fingers, but she didn't want to find out the truth of it from some goober like Earl Compton.

So she ignored him.

As she walked past, she heard laughter, which meant that Harry Thomas and George Simpson were with Earl. No surprise. Those two were always around where Earl was, and if Sue Jean didn't know better, she'd have thought they were all gaywads out for a circle jerk, except there wasn't any way they could make a circle with just the three of them. Maybe they'd have a triangle jerk.

"I guess you didn't hear me," Earl said. He came out after her and grabbed her arm.

Sue Jean dropped her snow cone, and it made a red splash on the hard-packed ground at her feet. A little of it even got on her shoe. She jerked her arm away. "Look what you made me do, you asshole. What's the matter with you?"

"Nothing you can't fix," Earl said, and he grabbed her arm again.

Sue Jean tried to get away, but this time he held on. His long fingers crushed her upper arm, and he dragged her backward. He got a hand over her mouth before she could cry out and dragged her away from the tents and the lights.

Harry and George followed along and giggled like maniacs. When Earl dropped her on the ground, they fell on her. Harry slapped a grubby hand over her lips, and he and George started tearing at her clothes.

Sue Jean kicked and clawed and scratched, but it didn't bother them. They ripped off her shirt and shucked her out of her jeans.

"Thong!" George yelled, sticking his grubby fingers under the stretchy band and trying to pull it off.

Earl, who had stood by watching, said, "That's enough."

George and Harry turned to look at him. A little drool from the corner of Harry's mouth dripped on Sue Jean's stomach as she twisted away and made a grab for her shirt. Earl kicked her hand away before she could reach it.

"My turn now," Earl said, and he unzipped his pants and pulled out his dick.

Sue Jean saw that what people had said was sure enough true, at least in Earl's case.

"Get out of the way," Earl told Harry and George, and they did.

As soon as Harry's hand came away from her mouth, Sue Jean screamed.

Earl laughed. "Yell all you want to. It won't help a bit."

"Not a damn bit!" George said, just before Earl hit her.

CHAPTER TWO

Matthew Cahill walked down the midway. It was a little after ten, and the carnival was still going strong, though black clouds were gathering and lightning threaded the sky to the occasional rumble of thunder off to the north.

If it began to rain, the crowds would be gone soon enough, but for now, everyone seemed happy to stick around. The carnies hawked their wares and their games in hoarse voices. The lights flashed red, green, and blue. The music played clunky melodies over old speakers that had all the fidelity of a tin can. The rides at the end of the midway turned and clanked and whined.

Matt walked by the ringtoss booth, where Jerry Talley tried to lure two marks with promises of an easy win; past the high striker, where a high school jock was about to try one more time to prove to his girlfriend how strong he was; past the milk-bottle toss, where a teenager was arguing that there was no way he hadn't knocked that last bottle down.

Matt grinned. He knew the mark couldn't win that argument. Tony Allen wasn't about to part with one of his big teddy bears or even one of the smaller ones this late in the evening. He might let the kid have a cricket clicker or some other five-cent prize, but the big prizes went early in the evening to a shill who'd carry them around so they could be seen by a lot of marks who couldn't win one if they threw the softballs at the bottles a million times.

Walking on toward the rides at the end of the midway, Matt passed Madame Zora's tent. It was dark and the flap was closed. Matt wondered what had happened. Madame Zora never closed early. As long as there was a dollar to make, she'd be there, waiting for someone to cross her palm with the long green.

Matt had heard some disturbing rumors from a couple of the other carnies about Madame Zora lately, and he'd been planning to have a talk with her. He wondered if what he'd heard about her visions had any part in making her close before all the suckers had been cleaned out.

Well, it wasn't Matt's problem. He was part of the security force for Cap'n Bob's Stardust Carnival, and his job was to prevent trouble. He'd been working for a while now, and so far, the biggest problem he'd had was breaking up a fight between two of the carnies who'd been slugging it out over who had the right to the charms of Madame Zora. Maybe one of them had gotten lucky and was with her right now in one of the trailers behind the rides at the end of the midway.

If that was the worst he had to deal with, Matt thought, life would be good. He'd seen enough blood and death and suffering for a lifetime. For several lifetimes.

While working with the carnival, he didn't stay in one place for more than three or four days and got to travel around the country in the company of people he liked, people who enjoyed their privacy and respected his. It was a way for Matt to look for Mr. Dark without always being the only stranger in town.

Matt hadn't seen Mr. Dark for a while, but he had a feeling that trouble was already on the way. It was nothing definite, nothing more than a tingling between his shoulder blades, as if someone might be watching him, or the way some people knew that there was a storm coming by the smell of rain in the air.

As a member of the carnival's security team, Matt couldn't carry an ax or any other weapon. He had to blend in with the crowd. So like the others, he wore a sap cap. It looked like an ordinary baseball cap, but it had a weight sewn in the back. Grab it by the bill, and it made an effective sap, or so Matt had been told. He hadn't had to use it yet.

He reached up to touch the bill of the cap, and that was when he heard the scream.

CHAPTER THREE

Sue Jean knew it was all her own fault that she was in this mess. Madame Zora had told her plain as day to go home, and that's what she should've done. But she'd had to have that snow cone, and now these three goobers were going to rape her.

She screamed again.

This time Earl didn't hit her. He stood up and twitched his head at Harry and George, and they fell on her like a load of lard. Harry put his mouth over hers while George slobbered all over her tits. Earl zipped up and looked toward the carnival.

The moon was hidden behind the thickening clouds, and with the carnival lights at his back, Matt Cahill couldn't see anything other than the dark silhouette of a man standing in the field near the trailers where the carnies stayed during the day.

While Matt wasn't expecting trouble, he knew that the man hadn't been the one who'd screamed. Someone else had to be close by.

A damp breeze moved across the field and bent the tops of the few weeds that grew there. The man didn't move, so Matt headed in his direction.

When Matt got within twenty yards, the man still hadn't moved. Matt wondered if there was something wrong with him.

"Hey," Matt said. "Is there a problem here?"

The man moved then, walking in Matt's direction. Matt could see that he was holding something in his hand. A knife. Now that the man was closer, Matt saw that he wasn't really a man at all, just a kid. A big kid, to be sure, but still a kid.

"Problem?" the kid said, giving Matt a little grin. "What makes you think there's a problem?"

Matt wished the light were better, but as far as he could tell, there were no maggots squirming around in the kid's eyes, no lesions opening in his skin. No smell of death rolled off him.

"Someone screamed," Matt said, looking beyond the kid. He saw a heap of something twisting around on the ground. "Let's go see what's over there."

The kid lost the grin, and he didn't look around to see what Matt was talking about. "Nothing's over there."

He was cocky and seemed unafraid, but Matt didn't find that strange. After all, he had a knife and Matt didn't.

"I'll just check it out for myself, if you don't mind," Matt said, moving to the side so he could go around the kid without getting too close to the knife. "Just doing my job."

The kid wasn't going to let Matt get away with that. He moved fast, but Matt was faster. He whipped off the cap and slapped it against the kid's wrist as the knife sliced upward. The kid yelled and the knife went spinning away.

Matt didn't see where it landed, but the kid must have, because he took four running steps and reached down for something. By the time he reached it, Matt had caught up. Matt planted a foot on the kid's ass and shoved. The kid did a somersault, came to his feet, and turned around so fast that Matt had trouble believing it. That was one agile kid. He came at Matt, holding the knife low, angling it upward.

Matt swung the cap again, but this time the kid was ready for him. Instead of trying to avoid the cap, the kid went for it with the knife. He stuck the blade into the cloth and snatched the cap out of Matt's hand. With a flick of his wrist, he sent the cap spinning away. It landed twenty yards beyond the kid, near the squirming mass that Matt had seen earlier. Except that it wasn't just a squirming mass.

It was a pile of bodies. The one on the bottom was a girl, and as Matt glanced that way, she got an arm and a hand free. She took hold of the ear of one of the boys on top of her and gave it a hard yank. She must have tried to pull it right off his head, and she came close to succeeding. He squealed like a hog being castrated with a rusty knife and rolled away from her. She beat her fist on the other one's face.

Matt had no time to see any more. He had the kid with the knife to worry about, and the kid was coming right at him.

Matt wished for his ax, and he felt something cold and hard touch his hand. A tent stake. It wasn't his ax, but it would do. He didn't stop to think who might be behind him to help out. It didn't matter.

Matt's fingers closed around the stake just as the kid slashed with the knife. Matt slipped to the side and brought the stake down on the kid's wrist. The stake worked a lot better than the sap cap.

The kid's wrist cracked like pond ice, and he howled as he sank to his knees. Matt kicked him in the face, not too hard, and the kid flipped over backward.

Matt looked around to see who'd handed him the tent stake. No one was there. He'd thought it might have been one of the other security guys—Ken, maybe, or Fred. It wouldn't have been like them to run away, however.

Matt didn't let it bother him. He could figure it out later. He stuck the stake in his back pocket and ran to help the girl.

She didn't need him. The boy whose ear she'd almost removed was lying on his side in the fetal position, whimpering. The sap cap had landed near the girl, and she'd somehow gotten hold of it. She swung it back and forth, whacking the other boy across the face. Blood flew from his nose and smashed lips as Matt watched.

Matt took hold of the boy's shirt and pulled him away from her before she brain-damaged him. The boy was as limp as boiled pasta. Matt tossed him aside.

"I'll take my cap," he said, putting out his hand.

The girl dropped it and covered her breasts with her arm. "I need to get dressed."

Matt nodded and picked up his cap. There were splotches of blood on it, so he stuck it in the pocket with the tent stake and turned his back so the girl could cover up while he thought about what he was going to do. One thing Cap'n Bob had insisted when he hired Matt was that the cops should never be called.

"We handle our own problems," the cap'n had said.

He was a portly man with a seemingly sincere smile that invited trust. For some reason, Matt didn't find it effective.

There was something about the cap'n that bothered him, but not enough to keep him from taking the job.

"The cops are not our friends," Cap'n Bob had continued. "We take care of our troubles on our own and in our own way. We don't want anybody meddling in our business. Especially cops."

That was fine by Matt. The carnies were a little strange, most of them, but certainly no more strange than Matt himself. Like Matt, a lot of them had secrets, and they knew how to keep them. In fact, Matt hadn't even told Cap'n Bob his real name. He'd said he was Matt Axton and that he'd like to be paid in cash. Cap'n Bob had no problem with that.

Some secrets were easier to keep than others, however. Attempted rape was serious business, and Matt didn't like the idea of letting the three kids off the hook.

"You can turn around now."

Matt turned and saw that the girl had put on her pants and shirt. She looked about fifteen, but she was probably older—seventeen or eighteen, maybe. Matt had trouble judging the age of anybody under thirty.

"What's your name?" he asked.

"Sue Jean. I want to get out of here."

Matt looked at the three young men who'd attacked her. The one whose ear she'd almost removed was still lying curled up on his side, but he'd stopped whining. The one who'd been whacked across the face with the sap cap was making snuffling sounds as he tried to crawl away. The one with the cracked wrist sat cradling his arm and glaring at Matt.

Three teenage punks who'd thought they could get away with something, Matt thought. He still didn't see any signs of corruption on them. He also didn't see any sign of whoever had handed him the tent stake. Where the hell had he gone? There wasn't anyplace to go. No time to worry about it. Right now Matt had other problems.

"You think we should call an ambulance?" Matt asked. "Or the cops?"

"I don't care who you call, but I'm not staying here," Sue Jean told him. "I need to get away from this place. That old woman told me to. I should've listened to her. Then this wouldn't have happened."

"What old woman?"

"That fortune-teller, whatever her name is. She told me to leave, but I had to have a snow cone."

Maybe those rumors Matt had heard were true, but he couldn't keep from grinning. Madame Zora wouldn't appreciate being called an old woman.

Sue Jean started walking.

"Hold on," Matt said. "Don't you want to press charges against these three?"

Sue Jean didn't slow down. "I don't care about them. They didn't hurt me."

Matt started after her. If she didn't care, maybe he shouldn't care. Cap'n Bob almost certainly wouldn't, not as long as the culprits had suffered some damage. Which they had. Matt still thought he should try.

When he caught up with Sue Jean, he said, "Do you know who those guys are?"

"Assholes."

"Yeah, I figured that out for myself. But I meant aside from that."

"I know who they are. Just some guys from school. What difference does it make?"

Matt thought it over. OK, maybe it didn't matter. The kids weren't hurt badly, except for the one with the knife, who probably had a broken wrist. Well, it would heal. They'd get over what had happened, and they could find their own way home. He was sure they could come up with some clever way to explain their injuries rather than telling anybody they'd been trying to rape one of their classmates. And Cap'n Bob didn't want the cops coming around. Matt didn't want them any more than the cap'n did.

But the whole thing bothered him. So he tried again. "They wanted to hurt you. They might try to hurt someone else."

Sue Jean gave a short laugh. "Them? They're drunk, or they wouldn't have bothered me. I think they learned an important lesson."

Matt hadn't smelled any liquor, but maybe the girl was right about the lesson. They'd sure gotten their asses kicked.

As he and Sue Jean got back to the midway, Matt turned back to look for them. He didn't see them anywhere.

He also didn't see the lollipop wrapper that the breeze blew across the bent tops of some weeds. It caught for a moment on the jagged edge of a leaf and then slipped away to move on.

CHAPTER FOUR

Madame Zora's real name was Gloria Farley, and she was scared witless. She'd been scared before, but never like this, not even when she'd been arrested that time in a little northern Mississippi town for shoplifting. She'd been eighteen years old and two days away from the home she'd fled the day after her stepfather had come into her bedroom for the first time.

She wouldn't have tried shoplifting if she'd known of any other way to get free food at the supermarket, but she didn't think they'd give it to her. She was trying to slip out with a couple of cans of tuna and five candy bars when they grabbed her. The candy bars had probably been a bad idea. Not much nutrition in a candy bar.

She'd thought that if she cried enough and acted younger than her age, she wouldn't go to jail, but Mississippi was tough on shoplifters, at least in that part of the state, and she went to the pokey, all right. It turned out that the chief of police wasn't a whole lot different from her stepfather when it came to methods of interrupting sleep, and after she got out of jail a couple of days later because the supermarket manager decided not to press charges, she promised herself she'd never go back in.

Not long after that, she met a woman named Frances Devore, a woman who was old and getting frail but who still had an active and inquiring mind. She and Gloria had both been in a public library in another little town in Mississippi, which, in spite of what some people thought, did indeed have a literate population.

Gloria was there because it was warm and had comfortable chairs. Frances was there to read the magazines and be around people for a change instead of being cooped up in her house. She'd struck up a conversation with Gloria that had begun with her asking why Gloria wasn't in school. Gloria had told her the truth, more or less, glad to have a sympathetic listener, and Frances got interested.

She was looking for somebody who'd help her out a little bit, keep house for her, do her shopping, drive her to the doctor, and fix a few meals.

"I could give you a roof over your head and your own room," she said, "and I'll keep you out of trouble."

It sounded like a good deal to Gloria, who went home with Frances and stayed for six years, until the old lady died. Frances had an eclectic library of her own and didn't mind if Gloria read the books that were there. In fact, she encouraged it. Frances didn't have a TV, so when Gloria wasn't doing her chores, she read. She read novels and biographies and self-help books, books about Greek and Norse mythology, Shakespeare. She'd discovered that she loved to read. Whenever a book interested her, she picked it up and read it, and she was interested in a lot of things.

One day, Frances saw Gloria with a book on palmistry and said, "You could learn to read palms in about five minutes."

"It's all a fraud," Gloria said.

Frances sniffed. "Of course it is, or at least the kind in that book is. But palmistry's real enough, if you have the gift. Some people really can see a person's future in those lines."

"Ha," Gloria said, but she read the book, studied the charts, learned about the shapes of hands, and memorized all the lines and what they meant. After a while, she tried out her new skills on Frances.

"Not bad," Frances said when Gloria had finished. "You almost had me believing you a time or two. You have a way of sounding convincing."

"I don't have the gift, though," Gloria said.

"No, you don't, and that's a good thing. People shouldn't know the future. It never holds anything good, not even for a pretty young girl like you, and especially not for an old woman like me."

"That's not very encouraging."

"Wasn't meant to be. You should know by now that life gives everybody a hard row to hoe. And then you die."

Gloria thought about her stepfather and about that police chief. Life hadn't been so hard for them, as far as she knew, but maybe they were dead. It was pleasant to think so. She hoped they'd been run over by a bus or a train or some other form of heavy transportation and flattened out like roadkill. Serve the bastards right.

Gloria was with Frances for another year or so after that conversation, and although she read many other books during that time, she kept coming back to the one about palmistry. She had it pretty much memorized by the time Frances died.

In her last illness, Frances told Gloria the future, and as she'd promised, it wasn't pretty.

"My cousins never gave a damn about me before, but they'll show up because they think I have money. I don't, but they don't know that and wouldn't believe it if I told them so. They'll run you off first thing, no doubt about it. I have a will, but all I really have is this house, so I've left that to them. Maybe they'll be satisfied. I wish I could do something to help you, but all I can do is give you the money that's in the metal box under the sink. It's not much. I wish it were. You've been a big help to me, Gloria, so you take it and don't tell anybody."

Sure enough, Frances's prophecy came true. The relatives who'd never had anything to do with Frances while she was alive appeared and started squabbling right away. They kicked Gloria out of the house and told her that if she made trouble, they'd call the cops. They told her it would be a really good idea if she left town.

Gloria had already had enough of cops, so she left town, but she left knowing a lot more than she had when she'd moved in with Frances.

Gloria found a little over three hundred dollars in the box, and she put it in her purse. Tell anybody? Fat chance. It was all she had when the cousins kicked her out. They didn't even let her stay for the funeral.

The three hundred dollars lasted Gloria for a month, and just as she thought she might have to resort to stealing again, she happened upon Cap'n Bob's Stardust Carnival. She saw the ads taped to telephone poles in a little town she was passing through and realized that a carnival might be just what she was looking for. What better setting for a skilled palm reader? OK, maybe not skilled, exactly, but good enough. Even Frances had said so.

Gloria wandered around a bit, enjoying the crowds, the music, and the atmosphere. Not bad at all. She asked a barker how to find the boss, and he told her to look for a portly man wearing a ringmaster's outfit. He wouldn't be easy to miss.

Gloria found him in about five minutes near the tent of the Seven Dwarfs. He had a big smile that looked only a little fake, and she told him she was looking for a place to ply her trade.

"And what might that be?" he asked, never losing the smile.

"I'm a palm reader."

"You any good?"

Gloria was tempted to pad her résumé but thought it might not be wise. She said, "Pretty good."

"Follow me," Cap'n Bob said. He led her to a big trailer in the back of the lot, opened the door, and motioned her inside.

Gloria had a momentary flashback to her experience with the cop, but she could handle herself better now. If the cap'n gave her any trouble, he'd be sorry.

Cap'n Bob didn't try anything funny, however. When they were inside, he put out a hand and said, "Show me."

Gloria took his hand, pretended to study it, and gave him some of the usual baloney about his life line and his heart line, explaining what each one meant and elaborating on the shape and length of his.

"You'll do," the cap'n said, taking back his hand. "Do you have a costume?"

"I can come up with something."

The cap'n seemed satisfied with that answer, and he explained the percentage of the take he'd get for allowing her to work the carnival.

"That's to pay for your booth space and my traveling expenses," he said. "You can rent a spot in one of my trailers or buy your own."

"I'll rent a spot for now."

"I'll put you in a trailer with one of the other performers. When do you want to start?"

"Tonight would be fine."

"I'll set it up," the cap'n said, and Gloria had been with the carnival ever since. It was a good enough life, better than a lot she could think of, and she'd grown to feel as if the carnival was her home and the carnies her family. She didn't mind the traveling, and she felt safe and happy most of the time.

Not anymore. Not since things had started happening to her, things she didn't understand at all.

She'd developed a good line as Madame Zora. She could string most people along for ten or fifteen minutes with no trouble at all, feeding them a line of bull that they seemed eager to hear and believe. If it made them happy, what was the harm? She didn't believe any of it herself, and there was no harm in that, either.

No harm in any of it, until a few weeks ago. Just about the time when that new security man had started to work. Matt Axton, he called himself, but Gloria knew better.

He'd arrived, and that was when things had started to happen. Gloria had started to see things, real things, not just lines in hands, but things that were going to happen. She *knew* they were going to happen.

At first it was nothing much, like she knew a man was going to stumble when he left her tent, or she knew a woman was going to forget her purse. Little things that wouldn't seem to mean much, maybe, but they gave Gloria a little bit of a hollow feeling inside.

After that, a man came in, and after looking at his hand, she knew that he'd lost his grandfather's pocket watch. More than that, she knew exactly where it was. When she told him, he couldn't believe it, but he rushed out of the tent to go home to look. Gloria knew he'd find it. She should've felt good about that, excited that she seemed to have the gift after all. But she wasn't excited. She was scared. Something had happened. She'd changed, and she didn't know why.

She remembered one particular day when a tall man walked into her tent. A woman was with him, and they were both smiling, happy to be together, having a fine time at the carnival.

"Hey," the man said. "You must be Madame Zora."

"Yes, I am she," Gloria said. Among the other things she'd learned from Frances, she'd picked up a few rules of good grammar. "Please be seated."

The man looked at the woman, and they both laughed. "Can you do us both at once?" the man asked.

Gloria didn't smile. The hollow feeling was back, and it was worse. "Not for the single price."

The couple laughed again, and the man said, "Didn't expect you to." He pulled a ten-dollar bill from his wallet and handed it to her.

Gloria tucked the money away inside her robes. The hollowness had been replaced with something like despair. She wished the man and woman would go away, but she knew they wouldn't.

"Tell his fortune first," the woman said, and the man held out his hand.

Gloria was reluctant to take it, but she didn't see any way to avoid it. When she touched it, her stomach twisted. Her pain must have showed on her face, because the woman said, quite concerned, "Is something wrong?"

Gloria tried a smile that she knew must be ghastly. *No, not with me. It's him. He has cancer. He doesn't know it yet, but he does. A tumor of the brain. No cure. He'll be dead in six months.*

"Please," the woman said. "Can we help?"

Gloria straightened her face, put on what she hoped was a genuine smile, and said, "I am fine. And so are you two. I see nothing but happiness ahead. Look here at these lines..."

She traced the lines in the man's hand, then those in the woman's, giving them a cheerful lie about their lives. They were laughing again when they left her tent. They'd be happy for a while longer. It was all she could do for them.

When they were gone, Gloria slumped in her chair. Tonight had been the worst so far. She knew the girl—what had her name been?—was going to be attacked. Raped. She could see the faces of her attackers.

So she'd warned the girl, told her to go away from the carnival, knowing all the time that she wouldn't go, knowing that something bad was going to happen.

And knowing that Matt Axton would be involved.

Knowing that Matt Axton wasn't even his real name.

Knowing that, whoever he was, he was surrounded by darkness and that someone surrounded by an even deeper darkness was near the carnival too.

Knowing that things were going to happen, terrible things.

Even worse, not knowing what they were but certain there was nothing at all she could do about them.

So she shut the tent, went to her trailer, located the bottle of Ezra Brooks that she kept in a cabinet for special occasions, and opened it up.

She'd hardly finished her first drink when she heard a crash of thunder. Seconds later, rain started to patter down on the roof of the trailer.

Then all hell broke loose outside, and to her horror, as soon as she heard the commotion, Gloria was sure she knew exactly what the trouble was.

CHAPTER FIVE

Matt decided that he couldn't let Sue Jean just walk away from what had happened. The wind came in gusts across the field, and lightning flashed through a cloud. Thunder followed. The rides would be shutting down because of the danger of lightning strikes, and people would begin leaving.

Matt turned back from the field to look for Sue Jean, but she was already lost in the crowds. He walked almost the length of the midway, but he couldn't find her. He might have continued to look, but he saw that one of the other security guys, Ken, was having a problem at the ringtoss booth.

Ken wasn't a big guy, but he was wiry and had a mean, squinty look. Most of the marks backed down from him without much of an argument, but not this one, a man of about thirty wearing a shirt with the sleeves pushed up to show off his muscles and his tats. He seemed convinced that the ringtoss was rigged.

Which it was, of course, though not so much that it was entirely impossible to win. Just *almost* impossible.

The mark was several inches taller than Ken, and he leaned over him, yelling in his face. A woman stood a few feet away, looking frightened. Matt figured she was with the mark.

"Ain't no way that ring fits over those blocks! I'm taking a prize for my wife and leaving now, and don't you try to stop me."

Matt didn't think a sap cap would do any good against the guy, so he reached back for the tent stake. It was gone.

What the hell?

Well, at least he still had the sap cap, even if it was a bit bloodstained. He pulled it from his pocket and put it on.

"What's the problem, Ken?" he asked, walking up to the two men.

Ken looked happy to see Matt. "Seems this gentleman has a complaint about the game. Says he's going to take a prize, even if he didn't win it."

"Damn right I am," the mark said.

Matt looked at him. He had black, unruly hair that stuck out from beneath a Saints cap, little piggy eyes sunk deep in their sockets, and a thin blade of a mouth. No signs of corruption, no odor of the grave, just a normal ugly guy, except for the anger that distorted his features.

"My game's on the square," Jerry Talley said from inside the ringtoss booth. "I explained the game and showed him how it was done."

Matt knew that Jerry demonstrated to everybody who came by how the wooden ring fit over the varnished wooden blocks. Usually the marks didn't notice that the ring he demonstrated with wasn't necessarily exactly like the ones he handed over when the money changed hands. The ones he gave them would still fit, but it wasn't easy to make them do it.

"Look-a here," Jerry said, dropping the ring he held over a block. "Works just fine. What we got here is a sore loser."

THE DEAD MAN: CARNIVAL OF DEATH

The mark backed away from Ken and Matt. "I'm sore, all right. You're not gonna fuck with me like this."

Some of the crowd stopped to watch what was going on, and the mark grinned at them. Matt thought he might trash the ringtoss booth. Matt couldn't let that happen under any circumstances, much less with people watching. And the parents wouldn't like it if their kids heard too much cussing.

The man's wife was getting embarrassed. "Don't talk like that, Buford, honey," she said. She was small with blonde hair cut short and close to her head. She wore tight jeans and a man's white shirt with the sleeves rolled to her elbows. "Let's us go home before it starts to rain."

"Don't tell me how to talk," Buford the mark said. "And rain or not, I'm not letting anybody cheat me."

"Look, Jerry," Matt said, "why don't you give this man a teddy bear if that will make him feel better. We don't want him to go home unhappy."

It wasn't carnival policy to give an unhappy customer anything, but in this case, even Jerry could see the wisdom of it. He took hold of one of the big teddy bears dangling from a string and gave it a pull. The bear came loose and dropped down. Jerry gave it a wistful look and handed it across the counter to the mark.

Buford took the bear. "You think you can buy me off with a fucking bear?"

"Nobody's trying to buy you off," Matt told him, keeping his voice level. "You have what you wanted. Give the bear to your wife and go on home."

"Fuck you," Buford said. "Fuck her too, and fuck this bear."

He took hold of the bear's head and tore it from its body. Holding the head in his hand, he dropped the body of the bear and stomped it a couple of times.

"Mama," a little boy said, "that man killed the bear!"

Buford laughed and spit on the bear carcass. Then he tossed the head to his wife.

"Hold that while I take care of business," he said. He smiled at Ken and Matt, showing off a gold tooth.

Something was in the air that evening besides rain, Matt thought. First the attempted rape and now this goober going nuts on them. It was time to put a stop to things.

"I'll take the high road," Matt said to Ken. "One...two...three..."

As soon as Matt reached *three*, Ken threw himself at Buford's legs. The man tried to jump backward, but he didn't react fast enough. Ken hit him below the shins, taking his feet out from under him. As Buford tumbled forward, he put out his arms to break his fall. Matt grabbed the left arm and twisted it up behind the man's back as he hit the ground. Matt landed on top of him and shoved the arm up as high as he could. Buford groaned.

Ken was already on his feet, shooing the crowd away. "You all go on home now. This little squabble is over."

Matt wrenched the man's arm one more time and looked at the boy who'd been upset by the bear's decapitation. "We'll see to it that the bear gets a decent burial and that his head's taken good care of."

That got a few chuckles, and most of the people drifted away. As they did, Matt got to his feet, bringing Buford with him by keeping a grip on his arm and pulling him along. Buford tensed a bit as if he might fight back, so Matt cranked his arm a notch higher.

"Jesus Christ," Buford said. "You'll break my arm."

"Yes, Buford, I will," Matt said, "unless you apologize to my friend in the booth and then go home."

"Apologize?"

"That's right." Matt cranked the arm again.

"Fuck! All right, I'm sorry. I'm sorry about the bear too."

He sounded about as sincere as a whore saying *I love you*, but it would have to do. Matt let him go.

"Let's get out of here, Marcy," Buford said. He walked away without waiting for her response.

The woman looked at Matt. "Buford's never done anything like that before," she said, and handed Matt the bear's head before following the mark. Matt pitched the head to Jerry, who contemplated it as if it were Yorick's skull.

"You might want to be a little easier on the customers," Matt said. "Let 'em win now and then."

Jerry tossed the bear's head aside. "Hell, he could've won. He had the easy rings."

"It's been a funny night," Ken said as rain began to spatter down on them. "Not ha-ha funny, either."

Matt knew what he meant. The crowd was much smaller now, and everybody was leaving the carnival. Thunder rolled across the sky like bowling balls.

"Could be a bad storm," Ken said.

Matt was about to comment when he heard yelling. He turned and saw eight or ten men running toward them through the crowd, their arms flailing, their mouths stretched, and their eyes wide with panic.

"The snakes!" someone screamed. "They're killing her!"

"Snakes. Why'd it have to be snakes?" Ken asked nobody in particular.

Matt was already running toward the sideshow tents.

CHAPTER SIX

The Burmese rock python isn't exactly a cuddly beast, but it's popular with snake fanciers who want a pet that's both easy to care for and often shocking to casual visitors, as big snakes sometimes are. It's also attractive in its own way, with brown-and-black patterns on its skin. Even people who don't like the snakes at all are known to buy footwear and other leather goods made from the skin of a python.

While Burmese rock pythons are not native to the United States, they're quite adaptable serpents, as anyone familiar with the Florida Everglades knows. The snakes have become a nuisance there because some Floridians who bought them for pets became uncomfortable with them when they started to grow, as pythons tend to do. Their uncomfortable owners released them into the steamy Florida swampland, where they thrived. They grew to monstrous proportions and reproduced with unseemly abandon. As a result, they've become a danger to wildlife of all kinds, including alligators, formerly the rulers of the swamps and now just snake fodder. The pythons have even inspired bad made-for-television movies starring nearly forgotten pop stars.

Aside from these admittedly unpleasant drawbacks, Burmese rock pythons are nevertheless favorites of carnival sideshow snake handlers, most of whom dote on their serpent companions and treat them as valued thespic partners.

After all, while not exactly affectionate, the pythons generally behave well onstage, and they return human affection as best they can in their reptilian way, which is to say they hardly ever kill their owners as long as they're treated with kindness and respect.

Which was how Serena of the Serpents (real name, Louise Parker) had always treated Clem and Clementine (their real names), the two Burmese rock pythons that performed with her. It wasn't much of a performance, to tell the truth. Mostly, Serena moved lazily in time to some snaky music played over a crackly speaker system, striking an occasional semi-erotic pose while Clem and Clementine slithered around her scantily clad body.

Serena had been doing the act for six years, and Clem and Clementine had been with her the entire time. They often seemed as bored by the act as Serena was, wanting nothing more than to be able to quit slithering and get back to their cages, where they'd occasionally get a tasty snack of a nice juicy rat—or two rats, actually, one for each of them, since Clem and Clementine didn't really grasp the concept of sharing.

They could grasp the rats, though, crushing them before ingesting and digesting them. The snakes didn't need to eat often, as long as the rats were of generous size, and certainly they'd never entertained the idea of crushing Serena and ingesting her, as far as anyone knew.

Until tonight. The thunder and lightning outside didn't bother the snakes, but Serena knew the carnival would be shutting down soon and she was about to end the act. Her audience consisted of exactly ten people, all of them men who were there more for Serena's scantily clad body than for the snakes, if the truth be known, although not one of them gave any evidence of wishing the act to go on any longer.

So the tall, unnaturally blonde Serena gave one last little bump, preliminary to a final halfhearted grind. As she did, the snakes reacted as if galvanized, constricting with amazing suddenness. Clem was, at that time, wrapped partially around Serena's bare white midriff, while Clementine was entwined around her left leg. The sudden reaction of the snakes caught Serena off guard, and she fell to the stage.

The fall didn't disturb the snakes in the least. Clem continued to crush her midsection, while Clementine unwound herself from the leg, coiled so that her mouth was near Serena's head, and opened her mouth alarmingly wide.

Serena screamed and the audience leapt to its feet, not to cheer and certainly not to make any attempt to rescue her. At first they watched in horror, and then all of them turned at almost the same instant, which happened to be the instant Clementine opened her mouth. The audience ran from the tent in panic. At the sight of them in full flight, other people panicked too, even if they weren't sure why, but Matt managed to make his way through them without getting knocked down and trampled.

He knew where the trouble was because Clem and Clementine were the only snakes in the carnival. Serena hadn't had any trouble with them since Matt had arrived, but so many unsettling things had been happening that Matt figured anything was possible.

Rain washed over the garish paintings outside Serena's tent, and the snakes in the pictures almost seemed to move under the sliding water.

When Matt entered the tent, he was stunned to see that the pythons had turned on Serena, attacking her savagely. One of them was even trying to get the top of her head in its mouth.

"God a'mighty," Ken said.

Matt didn't think God entered into it.

Thunder crashed overhead and rain pounded the canvas tent roof.

"What're we gonna do?" Ken asked. He had to speak up to be heard over the sound of the pouring rain.

"See if you can pull them off," Matt told him. "I'll be right back."

Ken didn't move, but Matt couldn't afford to stick around any longer. He left the tent and made a run for the trailer that he shared with Ken. He was soaked when he reached the trailer. He flung open the door, went dripping to his bed, and dragged the duffel bag from beneath it. He unzipped the bag and took hold of the handle of the ax.

The smooth wood felt natural in his grip. It almost tingled, as if the handle and his hand had been formed for each other in some cosmic scheme.

Matt didn't stop to contemplate the cosmic scheme of things. He went back out with the ax and sloshed toward Serena's tent.

Ken was still inside, not having moved, and no one else had come to help.

"Where are the other guys?" Matt asked.

"Damn if I know," Ken said. He sounded dazed. "Crowd control?"

Matt rushed to the stage. Serena's mouth gaped open in a soundless scream. Matt didn't know if she was alive or dead.

He also didn't know which snake to attack first, the one crushing Serena's midsection or the one trying to inhale her head. He decided on the crusher.

The snake seemed as thick as some of the trees that Matt had once chopped down with his ax, and its skin seemed to glisten in the dimly lit tent. Matt aimed for the space in back of the head. It was near Serena's body, but not so near that Matt thought he might miss and hurt her.

The ax came down and sliced through the snake cleanly, easily, dividing the head from the body. Blood sprayed. The head hit the floor with a dull thunk. The coils around Serena's body didn't loosen, however. If anything, they seemed to constrict a bit more.

Matt was about to drop the ax and try to release Serena when someone appeared beside him. He thought at first it was Ken, but a second glance told him that it wasn't.

It was Madame Zora. She was as wet from the rain as Matt, though she didn't have blood on her as he did.

"Get the other one," she said. "I'll see what I can do here."

Matt didn't question her sudden appearance. He moved behind Serena, one foot slipping in the blood of the first snake. The second one was going to be more of a problem, considering that it now had a good bit of Serena's head in its mouth.

It didn't really matter, though. Separate the head from the body and the serpent died. Matt raised the ax and struck.

This time the reaction was different. The head remained attached to Serena's head, but the body flopped and thudded wildly about the stage, spraying blood everywhere—on Matt, on the stage, on the sides of the tent. It jerked and floundered off the stage and landed on the dirt in front of the stage. The flow of blood stopped, and it lay there twitching.

Matt ignored it and dropped the ax. He knelt down and got one hand on the top of the snake's distended mouth and another on the bottom. He exerted all his strength as he tried to pry apart the powerful jaws.

As he struggled with the snake's head, he watched Madame Zora try to get the other snake uncoiled. She was having more luck than Matt was, and the coils had definitely loosened.

Matt's knees slipped on the bloody stage. He skidded backward, but he kept his grip on the snake's jaws and continued to keep the pressure on them. He felt them relax somewhat and strained with all he had. Something in the jaws cracked, and the snake's head came away so swiftly that Matt fell forward. As he did so, he threw the head away from him. It landed on a chair in the first row, bounced, and hit the dirt.

Madame Zora finished uncoiling the other snake and started to give Serena CPR. Matt got back to his knees and watched. It didn't take long. Serena coughed and started to breathe. Madame Zora helped her sit up, and just as she did, Cap'n Bob and the other two security men, Fred and Lonnie, came into the tent. Rainwater dripped from their drenched clothes. They stopped beside Ken, who still stood exactly where he'd stopped when he'd come in earlier.

"Holy shit," Fred said.

"You can say that again," Lonnie told him.

"Holy shit," Fred said.

Rain drummed on the tent and wind whipped the sides. The men had to yell over the tumult.

"Cut out the goddamned comedy," Cap'n Bob said. His wet uniform stuck to him now in a way that was hardly flattering. "What the hell happened here?" he asked.

"Snakes," Ken said. "Why'd it have to be snakes?"

Cap'n Bob ignored him. "Tell me what happened, Axton."

Matt stood up and wiped his bloody hands on his soaked pants. "I don't know. Ken and I came in, and the snakes were trying to kill Serena."

"What about you, Madame Zora?"

Madame Zora sat by Serena, her arm around her shoulders. "I heard the shouting and came to see if I could help."

"Serena?"

Serena's voice was strained. Matt could hardly hear her above the sounds of the wind and the rain. "Clem and Clementine went crazy. That's all I know. Now they're dead." She started to cry.

"You can get some new snakes," the cap'n said. "I'll even pay for them."

"It won't be the same," Serena said between sobs.

Matt picked up his ax and got off the stage. He sat in a chair and slumped forward. Something was happening here, and not just in this tent. The attempted rape, the berserk man at the ringtoss booth, the tent stake that had appeared and disappeared, and now this. Could it be Mr. Dark at work? Matt didn't see how. The signs weren't there.

Mr. Dark always had a goal, and Matt couldn't see what it could be in this case.

"Did anybody call the cops?" Cap'n Bob asked.

"None of us did," Lonnie said. "I don't know about the rubes."

"They were too busy running," Fred said. "Every one of them was hoping somebody else would make the call because all they wanted to do was get off the grounds before those snakes got after them." He took a look at the remains of Clem and Clementine. "Not that there's any danger of that."

"So no cops?" Cap'n Bob said.

Fred shook his head. "I don't think so. People will just be happy they got in their cars or to their homes before the rain."

The cap'n seemed satisfied. "Good. Let's get this mess cleaned up."

Matt thought he'd done his share already, so he got up to go back to the trailer to do his own cleaning up. Nobody tried to stop him.

Madame Zora caught up with him at the entrance to the tent. Like Matt, she was covered in blood.

"You and I need to have a talk," she said when she reached his side.

She didn't sound happy about it, and Matt turned his head to look at her.

"Why?" he asked.

"Because I know who you are."

The words were like a blow to the heart. Matt glanced toward the others, but none of them appeared to have heard her.

"I don't know what you mean," he said.

Gloria looked at his ax. "Axton. Pretty funny. But it's really Cahill."

"How do you know?"

"Never mind how. I just do. There's more. I know you can see things others can't."

Matt started to sweat. "Tell me."

"Not now. Come to my trailer when you get cleaned up. We can talk there."

Matt thought it over and decided he didn't really think he had much of a choice.

"Half an hour," he said. "Maybe the rain will have stopped by then."

Gloria nodded. "I'll be waiting."

CHAPTER SEVEN

The rain was still coming down, but lightly now. It was more like a fine mist that hung in the air. The thunder was a dim sound in the distance, and the occasional lightning flash was too far away to give any light to the carnival grounds. Matt wiped the mud that had accumulated on his shoes on the side of the steps leading to the door of Madame Zora's trailer. Then he knocked.

"Just a second," Madame Zora said from inside, and then Matt heard the unlocking of the door.

"Come on in," Madame Zora said, and Matt entered the trailer. It was much nicer than the one he shared with Ken, but then, the fortune-teller had been with the carnival for a long time and had earned enough to have something a little upscale. Not that it was fancy. It was just bigger, cleaner, and better furnished than most of the others. There were even a couple of comfortable chairs in the small living area, along with a forty-two-inch flat-screen TV and a bookcase overflowing with paperbacks. The place smelled of apples and whiskey. Not a bad combination.

"You watch a lot of TV?" Matt said, just to get the conversation started.

"Not to speak of, but I have a satellite dish, and I can pick up just about anything I care to watch." She paused.

"Not that there's much to watch. You know the old joke. Five hundred channels and nothing worth looking at."

Matt nodded. He sat in one of the chairs and Madame Zora sat in the other. She had changed from her faux gypsy outfit into jeans and a men's blue work shirt. Her dark hair, still wet from her shower, hung down to her shoulders. Her eyes were as dark as her hair.

"You want something to drink?" she asked Matt.

"What do you have?" Matt asked, though he thought he knew the answer.

"Ezra Brooks."

He'd expected something a little more refined, but that was close enough.

"Not exactly sippin' whiskey," Matt said.

"It gets the job done."

"Yeah. Sure, I'd like a drink."

The little kitchen was only a couple of steps away. Madame Zora poured a stiff drink in one glass and a smaller one in another. She handed the stiff one to Matt.

"You're not a drinker?" he said.

"I've had a couple already." Gloria raised her glass. "To better days."

"Better days," Matt said, and took a drink. The raw whiskey burned its way down to his stomach, where there was a small explosion. Warmth spread over him like a thin blanket.

"Look," he said after a couple of seconds, "I don't know what your real name is, but I'm pretty sure it's not Madame Zora."

"Gloria," she said.

"It almost rhymes."

"That wasn't the intention. I think I saw it in a book somewhere."

Matt took another drink and found that the whiskey was almost gone. It hadn't affected him other than the first rush of warmth. "You mentioned that you knew my real name."

"Matthew Cahill," Gloria said. "And you're dead."

Matt held up a hand to stop her. "All right, fine. You know who I am. I don't want to hear all that. You could get it from Google."

"I don't think Google could tell me about the things you see, the rot in people's souls."

Matt felt a chill.

"How did you know that?"

Gloria took a sip of her drink. "I just knew. I don't know what's happened to me. It's strange. It's scary. I could never really tell fortunes before, but now, all of a sudden, I...know things."

That pretty much confirmed the rumors Matt had heard about her. The talk among the carnies was that she'd been telling some real fortunes for a good while now. It had them spooked a little. Matt didn't doubt it was true. He'd experienced too much to question the possibility.

Under the current circumstances, her newly acquired ability just added to the weirdness of the other things that had happened that night. What he needed to know was whether whatever had suddenly given her the power to see the future was connected with Mr. Dark. And if it wasn't, was there anything she could tell him about Mr. Dark or about his own future?

Matt looked at Gloria again. She was probably in her early thirties, but her skin was smooth and clear. She wore no makeup now, and she really didn't need it. She usually hid herself beneath the gypsy garb of robes and scarves but had no reason to hide that Matt could see. She was an attractive woman with no sign of the corruption that would have told him she was somehow associated with Mr. Dark.

Matt knocked back the rest of his drink and asked Gloria what else she knew about him.

"That's all. I'd tell you if there were more." She finished her own drink. "You don't have to worry about me telling anybody who you are. There are plenty of people here who don't want anybody talking about their pasts."

"Do you know their stories or just mine?"

"I've heard a few of their stories, but I don't know how true they are. Their stories don't matter, anyhow. They're not part of what's happening. I'm sure about yours, though." She frowned. "Do you want another drink?"

Matt looked into his empty glass. "No, I think I've had enough. You don't know anything about a…darkness that's associated with me?"

Something showed in her eyes. Fear? Matt couldn't tell.

"This knowing, this sensitivity of mine, started when you came," she said. "I don't know why or how, but you have something to do with it."

"But you don't know what it is?"

"I don't know anything more than I've told you," she said, turning the whiskey glass in her hands.

"You might be able to find out," Matt said. "That's why you asked me to come here, isn't it?"

"I…I don't know. I have a…feeling that I'm supposed to do something, but I'm not sure I want to do it."

Matt didn't blame her. The strangeness of the night would have been enough to make anybody uncertain.

"You showed up at Serena's tent just in time," Matt said. "I don't think it was because you heard the shouting."

"I did hear something, but there was more to it than that."

"Another feeling?"

"You're making fun of me now."

"I'm the last person in the world who'd make fun of something like that," Matt told her. "Believe me."

She looked into his eyes. "I believe you."

"You handled yourself very well in that tent. Better than Ken did."

"Some people have a problem with snakes. I don't."

"Maybe it was the blood he had a problem with."

"That doesn't bother me, either."

"You're awfully tough, aren't you," Matt said.

"Not really. It's just that I've learned to face things when I have to. And that's what I should be doing now." She put her glass on the floor by her chair. "There's no use putting it off any longer. Give me your hand."

Matt hesitated. "If you don't want to do this…"

"It's not what I want that matters. This is something I have to do. You understand?"

He did. It was why he left his home, ax in hand, and went out searching for Mr. Dark, hoping to stop the evil that he spread.

And if there was something she could tell him, answers to the questions that had plagued him since his resurrection, he wanted to know it. Good or bad, it didn't matter. He wanted to know it.

Matt knew this might be a trick, that she could be some willing, or unwilling, puppet of Mr. Dark's, but he had to take the chance.

He leaned forward in his chair, set his glass down on the floor as she had done, and put out his hand.

Madame Zora—Gloria—closed her eyes and sighed. Matt waited, his hand extended. Gloria opened her eyes after what seemed like quite a long time and said, "I can't promise you anything."

"I don't want promises," Matt said. "I just want to know."

"Knowing can be dangerous."

"Yeah. I've found that out."

"I can't promise you the truth, either."

Matt pushed his hand forward. "Just have a look. After you tell me, we can worry about what's truth and what's lies."

"All right." Gloria closed her eyes again and took his hand.

When Gloria touched his fingers, it was as if a mild electric shock went through him, all the way down to his toes. If Gloria felt anything, however, she gave no indication. She held his hand in hers and stared down at it for several seconds.

Then she dropped it, slumped forward, and fell onto her side on the floor.

Damn, Matt thought. *That can't be good.*

He raised Gloria up and got her back into her chair. She was breathing heavily and her face was flushed, but otherwise, she seemed OK. He would have liked to think that she'd just had too much to drink, but he knew that wasn't the problem. He rubbed her wrists, then put a hand on her shoulder and shook her.

She stiffened, opened her eyes, and took a deep breath.

"You want to tell me about it?" Matt asked.

"Not really." Her voice shook. "I need another drink."

Matt took her glass and stepped into the kitchen, where the bottle of Ezra Brooks still stood by the sink.

"A little or a lot?" he said.

"A little. I'll be fine. I was just caught by surprise."

Matt poured the drink and handed it to her. She was a bit shaky, but she took the glass with both hands and took a sip.

"What was the surprise?" Matt asked.

Gloria took another sip and looked at him with something like pity. "You're wrapped in darkness. It's like another person that you carry with you."

"I know all about the darkness," Matt said. "I even know his name. What I'd like to do is get rid of him."

"I'm not sure you can. He...*it* is too much a part of you." She trembled. Matt knew she must be frightened by what was happening, though she was trying not to show it. She had guts—he'd give her that. "Have you ever heard of Loki?"

Matt shook his head.

"Loki was one of the Norse gods," she said. "He was a trickster, a shape-shifter, a father of monsters. He loved disorder and chaos. It was like a game to him."

"That sounds a lot like someone I know," Matt said. "I call him Mr. Dark."

"I'm not saying that it's Loki you're dealing with. Just someone similar, someone who's powerful and who likes to play games. I guess Mr. Dark is as good a name as any."

Whoever he is, he told me we'd have fun. He said that at the very beginning, but I don't want to play his games. What's fun for him isn't good for anybody else.

Games. Matt remembered the way the stake had appeared when he needed it and then disappeared afterward. The carnival was all just part of a game Mr. Dark was playing with him.

"Is Mr. Dark responsible for what happened tonight?" Matt asked.

"I think so," she said. "But he's hiding himself from me. There was more to see, but I could see only as much as he wanted me to."

"I don't get it," Matt said.

"Neither do I, but I know I'm a part of it now, whether I want to be or not," she said. "And it terrifies me."

"I know how you feel," Matt said.

But it was much more than that. He felt a sense of kinship and relief that almost overwhelmed him.

Finally there was someone who understood, who saw— or at least sensed—what he did.

He wasn't alone anymore.

CHAPTER EIGHT

When Sue Jean woke up the next morning, she didn't feel well. She couldn't quite decide what was wrong. It wasn't quite a headache, and it wasn't quite a stomachache, but it was something sort of in between.

She thought about what had happened the night before. That didn't make her feel any better. She and the carnie guy had given those turds something to remember her by, but somehow that didn't seem satisfactory now. She wished she'd been able to do more to them, hurt them worse, maybe do some permanent damage. Jail wasn't the answer, though. She was sure of that.

It was Saturday, so she didn't have to go out if she didn't want to. Her parents didn't care. They were probably working in the yard, pulling weeds or planting flowers or poisoning ants or something. She couldn't figure out why anybody would want to do any of those things, but it was fine with her if they wanted to, just so they left her alone and didn't try to make her help them. Maybe if they got really lucky they'd win the "Yard of the Month" award and get their picture in the paper. What a thrill that would be.

Sue Jean lay in bed until around noon, listening to tunes on her iPod and wishing she felt better. After she finally got out of bed, she cleaned herself up and put on makeup, noticing, as she often did, how much prettier she was than her former BFF, Madison, that horse-faced bitch. She supposed that Madison and Freddie had survived their night together at the carnival, since her mother hadn't come in and told her about anybody meeting with a horrible accident.

Too bad. The more she thought about the two of them falling off the Ferris wheel or getting crushed between a couple of the bumper cars, the better she felt. That was strange, but it was true. She imagined them being impaled on spikes, and that made her feel better still. She didn't know why. Evil thoughts had never affected her that way before, but then, she'd never felt bad in quite the same way that she had earlier. Now she seemed to be feeling just fine.

She went down to the kitchen, where she heard the lawn mower and the gasoline edger roaring in the backyard. She looked out the big bay window and saw her mother, wearing goggles and green gardening gloves. She guided the edger along the bottom edge of the wooden fence that separated their backyard from the Kingstons'.

Her parents felt nothing but contempt for the Kingstons, who hired a crew to come by once a week and do their lawn and weed the flower beds. On her parents' scale of values, people who didn't do their own lawn care ranked some-where below the homeless.

Sue Jean had thought she was hungry, but she wasn't. She couldn't think of anything she wanted to eat. She went into the den, turned on the TV, and flopped down on the couch. There wasn't anything she wanted to watch. NASCAR, for God's sake. She scratched her forehead. She had all kinds of little itches under her skin, but she still felt great. Hating on Madison and Freddie had done wonders for her.

She was a little sleepy, though. Her parents would be in the yard for hours, and then they'd probably power-wash the driveway, so Sue Jean pulled a couch pillow under her head and drifted off.

Her parents woke her up arguing in the kitchen. It was well past noon, and they were all worked up over whether it was time to plant the petunias or whether they should wait until next week. Sue Jean wished they'd shut up, but they could go on for hours about things like that.

She got off the couch and looked around. What the hell, she didn't have to stay there and listen to them. She had a better idea. A much better idea. She pulled her cell phone out of the pocket of her jeans and called Madison.

"Want to go back to the carnival?" she asked when Madison answered.

"Well," Madison said after a second's hesitation, "Freddie's supposed to meet me there."

"I won't be in the way," Sue Jean said. "I promise. I just want to see you for a while. Then you and Freddie can have all the fun you want to."

"Well, OK. I'll meet you out front."

Sue Jean was smiling when she ended the call.

Earl had felt funny all day—not sick, exactly, but not right, either. It wasn't his wrist. For some reason, his wrist didn't hurt at all. He'd thought it was broken, but today it felt just fine. He'd taken a couple of aspirin, but that was all. He didn't know aspirin had healing qualities, but maybe it did. It wasn't like he was a doctor or anything.

In spite of the fact that his wrist was OK, he'd been pissed off all day. Pissed off at that whore Sue Jean, who probably put out for every guy at school but didn't want him and his homies even to have a sniff of it. And pissed off at that asshole from the carnival who'd interrupted them.

Earl didn't like being pissed off, and it was time he did something about it. His old man worked on Saturdays, and neither he nor his father had seen Earl's mother in years. She went off one night with some guy at a bar and never came back. It didn't bother Earl, and it didn't seem to have bothered his old man, either.

Earl went into his father's bedroom and looked in the sock drawer of the wardrobe. He pushed the socks aside and found the pistol. He'd first found it a couple of years ago when he was snooping around for condoms, not that he'd have any use for one, considering his record with the opposite sex. That was another thing that pissed him off.

The pistol was an old .38 revolver. Earl picked it up. It was surprisingly heavy, and it was loaded. Earl didn't know much about guns, but he'd seen plenty of movies. All you had to do was point the pistol and pull the trigger.

He stuck the .38 in his back pocket. It felt right back there. Like he should carry it with him always. He made sure his shirttail hung down far enough to cover it. It did. He was feeling really good now. He thought he should take aspirin more often.

It was time to call Harry and George and see if they wanted to have a little fun. Well, it was going to be a lot more fun for him than it was for them, the assholes. They'd blamed him for what had happened with Sue Jean, and they'd whined about it for blocks after they'd left the carnival. They'd be sorry about that. Earl grinned just thinking about how sorry they were going to be.

Buford Dorman was pissed off too. The bastards at the ring-toss booth had treated him like shit, and they'd made him look like a fool. If he hadn't been outnumbered, he'd have shown that smartass who'd twisted his arm a thing or two.

And then there was Marcy. She should've supported him. Kicked one of those fuckers in the balls or something. That was the least she could do for him. She was his wife, after all. Instead, she'd let them bully him and make him look bad. And he didn't even get the fucking bear. OK, he'd gotten it, but he'd been so angry that he'd ripped it apart. Same thing.

Buford opened the closet in the bedroom. His deer rifle was in the back, behind his shirts, and there was a box of ammo on the floor. He pushed aside some shirts and bent down to pick up the box of .30-30 cartridges. He tossed it on the bed and got out the rifle. He hadn't been hunting for a few years, so the rifle was a little dusty, but he'd cleaned it before he'd put it away. It would be fine.

He filled his pockets with cartridges from the box on the bed and then loaded the rifle.

"Marcy," he called, "come in here for a second."

Serena of the Serpents still couldn't believe that Clem and Clementine were dead. She was thirty-one years old, unmarried, and unlikely ever to marry, considering that she was of the sapphic persuasion and the kind of marriage that might have interested her was currently, if unjustly, illegal in most states. Clem and Clementine had been like the children she'd never have, and while she could replace them, what person in her right mind would want to replace her children? Clem and Clementine had had their own slithery personalities and were as distinct to Serena as any two human children could be, and no replacement could ever replicate their cute little ways.

The thought of the coldhearted way that the security guy had killed her darlings chapped Serena's ass. Sure, he'd used the excuse that he'd had to kill them to save her, but that didn't mean anything to Serena. She didn't know why her babies had turned on her. The thunderstorm? The pounding of the rain on the tent? It didn't matter. Not now. Now they were dead, and somebody had to pay for that.

Who had to pay? For some reason, that didn't matter, either. It would be just fine if the security guy...what was his name, anyway? Matt? Serena thought that was right. Matt. She'd like to see him flattened. Flat Matt. It would be just fine if he paid the price, would make her feel good all over, but that Madame Zora, the fake gypsy, was in on it too. She should get hers. And even Cap'n Bob. He was there, ordering people around and yelling about her babies. He should pay if anybody did. But if she couldn't get to any of them, she'd just find someone else.

Like Gloria, Serena had her own trailer, and it had a tidy little kitchen. In one of the drawers of the tidy little kitchen there was a foot-long butcher knife. Serena kept it sharp because she liked to have everything in good order. She had a nice sharpening steel, and she went into her tidy little kitchen, took the steel and the knife out of the knife drawer, and began to draw the knife blade slowly up and down the steel, honing the edge to a fine sharpness. She liked the sound of steel on steel almost as much as she was going to like the sound of the screams she'd be hearing later on.

The carnival opened at noon on Saturday, and Matt was uneasy and watchful as he moved among the crowds. The sun was bright, the sky was blue, the humidity was low, and the air was cool. A perfect day. The people laughed, joked, played the games, took in the shows, and ate cotton candy and corn dogs. They didn't mind the little bit of mud from last night's rain. They didn't have a care, or if they had one, they'd left it at home when they came to the carnival. The cheerful music from the rides at the end of the midway matched their mood.

Matt's talk with Gloria had left him feeling worried and uneasy. The dreams he'd had later that night after he'd finally fallen asleep had only made things worse. He couldn't remember them, but he'd awakened feeling sad, empty, and apprehensive. He was sure that Mr. Dark had been involved in all the strange things that had happened, but he didn't know how or why.

Maybe everything would be all right after all. Maybe Mr. Dark had done all that he'd intended to do.

Matt almost laughed at his moment of hopeless optimism. He hadn't seen the physical signs of decay on anyone yet, but he knew that Mr. Dark was around and that he wasn't finished.

Because nobody had died yet.

But maybe now, between his sight and Gloria's, he finally had an advantage over Mr. Dark...and could actually stop whatever it was from happening.

As Matt neared Gloria's tent, he saw that she hadn't opened for business. He didn't know if that was bad or good. A dozen or so people stood outside the tent, milling around, talking among themselves. Matt heard enough to know that they were wondering when the fortune-teller would show up or if something had happened to her, but they weren't worried. They just wanted to have their palms read because they'd heard that the gypsy was the real thing, someone who could really see into the future. They smiled and talked and waited, their moods light.

Everybody was having a fine time at Cap'n Bob's Stardust Carnival.

Gloria didn't want to be Madame Zora anymore. She wanted to go somewhere far away and forget all about telling fortunes, true ones or false ones or any fortunes at all.

That wouldn't do, however. She knew there was no escaping whatever was to come. She swathed herself in her skirt and blouse and robes and scarves and left her trailer and books behind, wondering if she'd ever see them again. She couldn't see her own future at all.

Maybe she didn't have one.

She could see something about Matt, though, and while it wasn't clear to her, she knew that she had to tell him something and that he wasn't going to like it. Beyond that, she had no idea what might happen, other than that it was going to be bad. Very bad, indeed.

CHAPTER NINE

Sue Jean met Madison at the entrance of the carnival. Sue Jean sniffed.

"You're wearing your mother's perfume," she said.

Madison blushed. "I thought Freddie might like it."

"Oh, I'm sure he will." Sue Jean smiled. "Is he meeting you inside?"

"At the ringtoss. He's going to win me a bear."

"Great! You deserve it. There's something I want to show you before we go in, though."

"What is it?"

"It's a surprise," Sue Jean said, taking Madison's hand. "Come on."

At first she thought Madison might pull away, but Sue Jean gave her a big smile and clasped her fingers with a friendly squeeze. Madison smiled too and came right along.

"What's the surprise?" she asked again.

"You'll see. You'll never believe it."

About a block from the carnival was a big open field that served as a parking lot. Sue Jean led Madison into it. Except for the parked cars, the field was deserted. The ground was muddy from the previous night's rain, and there were ruts in the mud. Sue Jean and Madison threaded their way along, trying to stay on the grass and avoid puddles and mud.

"You stand right here," Sue Jean said, dropping Madison's hand. "It's too muddy for you. I'll go get the surprise."

"It's a car!" Madison said. "Your dad got you that new car you've been wanting!"

"You guessed it," Sue Jean said. "I can't wait for you to see it."

Madison waited while Sue Jean went off to get the car, which wasn't new at all, just the old family sedan, a gray Camry that was four years old. Sue Jean started it up, pulled it out of the parking space, and headed for Madison. When she got so close that Madison couldn't get out of the way, she gunned it. The car slewed and mud flew from beneath the front tires.

The look on Madison's face was priceless. Surprise, shock, fear...It was wonderful. The sound the car made when it smashed into Madison was even better.

Madison's body disappeared under the front of the car. Sue Jean kept right on going, having disconnected the airbag earlier. She didn't even realize she knew how to do that. It just came to her.

At the entrance to the lot, Sue Jean turned around and located another parking spot. After she'd parked, she walked by what was left of Madison. Her body was mashed down in the mud, and her horsey old face was greatly improved by the way the car's front end had rearranged her features.

Sue Jean giggled with happiness. She could hardly wait to meet Freddie at the ringtoss booth.

Buford looked down at Marcy, lying there on their bedroom floor. She hadn't bled much. Buford was a little disappointed.

You'd think that with a hole that big through her chest, she'd have bled a lot more. Oh well, you couldn't have everything. He took a deep breath and enjoyed the satisfying smell of gun smoke.

He thought about dressing Marcy out, the way he'd have dressed out a deer, but he didn't really have time for that. He had other things to take care of, namely those bastards at the carnival. He hadn't looked forward to anything this much in years.

He put on his Saints cap and gave it a tug to settle it on his head. He picked up his rifle, gave Marcy one last look, blew her a kiss, and left by the kitchen door.

Earl picked up Harry and George at their houses in his old Ford pickup. George was a mess. His lips were puffy and his nose looked a little askew, as if someone had moved it to one side and hadn't moved it back. He talked funny too, like he had a cold.

"I think my fuckin' nose is broke," he said. "You said Sue Jean was begging for it. You said it'd be easy."

"Shut up," Earl said.

Harry was in a little better shape. His ear was puffy and red, but it was still firmly attached to his head. "Don't be such a pussy, George," he said.

George slapped his ear, and Harry howled.

Idiots, Earl thought. He drove them to a little convenience store near the edge of town. They knew the guy who worked the late-afternoon shift there, and he'd always sell them a six-pack if they slipped him a buck or two extra.

"I'm paying today," Earl said when he stopped at the side of the store. He handed Harry some bills. Couldn't send George, not the way he looked. "Don't get that fucking Old Milwaukee."

"Yeah," George said. "I don't know how you can stand that stuff. Get a good beer. Like Miller Lite."

Harry sneered. "Miller Lite?" Harry fancied himself a comedian, and he made a farting noise, which for him was the height of humor. "That stuff tastes like piss."

"You should know," Earl said. "Just go get the beer."

Harry went into the store and came back with a six-pack of Budweiser.

"Will this do?" he asked, tossing a can in George's lap.

"It'll do," Earl said. "Let's go drink us a couple for lunch."

"Can't we just drink it on the way to the carnival?" George asked.

Earl shook his head. "Can't risk it. We might get stopped."

"I'm going to start mine anyway," George said. He took a can and snapped it open.

"Shit," Earl said.

He headed out of town and turned off on the first country road he came to, a gravel-topped lane that didn't lead anywhere of consequence. After he'd gone about half a mile, he pulled off on the shoulder and pointed to a clump of bushes.

"Let's go drink over there. Nobody can see us from the road."

The others bitched a second or two, but they went. When they were sitting on the ground slurping from their cans, Earl said, "You two still blame me for last night, don't you?"

Harry touched his ear. It was red and swollen. "It was your idea."

Earl got up and stood behind Harry. He pulled out the pistol. It had been digging into his back the whole time he drove, and he was relieved to have it in his hand.

"Look what I have," he said, holding it up for George and Harry to admire.

"Where'd you get that?" Harry said, turning to look.

"At the gettin' place," Earl said. "Drink your beer."

Harry didn't need any encouragement. He turned back to his drinking.

"Is it loaded?" George asked.

"Hell, I don't know," Earl said. "Let's find out."

He shot Harry in the back of the head. Harry's skull came apart in a haze of blood, bone, and greasy hair, a lot of which spattered on George, who dropped his beer and screamed.

"Shit! Shit! Shit!"

Earl didn't approve of screaming, so he shot George right in the center of his forehead. The bullet didn't make much of a hole going in, but it took a nice-sized chunk out of the back of George's head.

"Whose fault was that, asshole?" Earl said.

He picked up the beer cans. He'd drink the beers and recycle the cans. A friend of the environment, that's what he was. As for Harry and George, well, they were biodegradable. They'd make good fertilizer for the bushes if nobody found them, or they'd be good food for some scavenger or other. Earl didn't really give a shit.

Serena had never liked Ken, and he'd been there in the tent when her darlings had died. He'd done nothing to stop the killing, so he was just as guilty as the rest of them.

He was also the first person she saw when she came out of her trailer. She wore jeans and a long-sleeved plaid shirt. The knife was hidden in the right-hand sleeve.

"Hello, Ken," she said.

She knew just the kind of voice to use on him. He was a man, after all, and men were stupid. They'd fall for anything, even a come-on from a woman that everybody in the carnival knew didn't like men in the least.

"Hi," Ken said. "I was just coming to check on you. Cap'n Bob wanted to know if you were doing OK and if there was anything he could do for you."

"He did?" Serena smiled. "How thoughtful of him."

"Yeah," Ken said. "The cap'n's a thoughtful guy."

"Let's talk about that, Ken, shall we?"

"Uh...sure. Why not?" Ken looked back toward the midway. "Seems peaceful enough. Things don't start hoppin' until sundown."

"That's right," Serena said. "Why don't we step right over here and chat awhile."

She led the way between two of the trailers. One of them belonged to the Seven Dwarfs, though there were actually only four of them. They doubled the parts. The other belonged to a couple of freaks, the Alligator Boy and his mother, the World's Strongest Woman. They'd be busy in their tents and wouldn't bother anybody.

Once they were sheltered between the trailers, Serena stood close to Ken and said, "You were telling me how thoughtful Cap'n Bob is."

"Yeah. Right. He's always looking out for us, y'know?"

"I suppose that's one way of seeing things." Serena paused and gave Ken a piercing look. "Can he bring back my babies?"

"Babies? You mean the snakes? No. No, he can't do that. But he said to tell you he has a line on a couple of pythons just like Clem and Clementine. A little younger, but just the right age for you to train. You'll be back onstage in no time."

"I don't think so," Serena said.

"But—"

"No buts. And no snakes are *just like* Clem and Clementine."

"Well, I'm sure the cap'n didn't mean anything bad when he said that. He doesn't know much about snakes, I guess."

"I'm tired of talking to you," Serena said, and she let the knife drop down from her sleeve into her hand.

Ken saw it. "Wha—" was all he could say before the knife slit his shirt and slid into his stomach and ripped upward though his skin and muscle as if it were slicing through a loaf of bread.

Serena pulled out the knife, stepped away, and looked at him. Blood ran down the knife blade and dripped on the ground.

"Y…you…," Ken said, or tried to say as he attempted to hold in his intestines with both hands.

"Can't you finish a fucking sentence?"

"I…I…sh…shit." Ken sank to his knees.

"You surely did," Serena said. "Or maybe that's just your guts. It stinks, whatever it is. I'll be leaving you now."

Serena walked around behind him and kicked him forward onto his face.

"There aren't any other snakes that are *anything at all* like Clem and Clementine," she said, not that Ken gave a damn about that or about anything else, being pretty much dead by then.

Serena wiped the knife blade on the leg of her jeans and left him there.

CHAPTER TEN

Matt continued his patrol of the carnival grounds. He was passing the Ferris wheel when he saw Gloria heading in his direction. Matt smiled. She wore her gypsy duds. The show must go on. He stopped smiling when he saw the look of fear in her eyes.

"Something very bad is about to happen," she said.

"What is it?"

"I don't know," she said. "But it's already begun. It can't be stopped."

But Matt knew better than that. In his own way, he saw the future too, every time he looked into the decaying face of someone eaten alive by evil.

"That's what he wants you to think," Matt said.

He brushed past Gloria and headed for his trailer. Gloria reached out to touch him, but he ignored her. When he got to the trailer, he looked back. She was right behind him. Matt went inside. Gloria followed. He didn't try to stop her.

Matt pulled his duffel bag from under the bed.

And took out his ax.

Whatever game Mr. Dark was playing was entering another phase. Matt felt like a checker that was being pushed across the board from one square to the next.

He'd had that feeling before.

He hated it.

"Go back to your trailer," he said. "You don't want to be a part of this."

"You're right, I don't, but I am whether I like it or not. Hiding from it isn't going to change anything."

"OK, but it's going to be ugly."

"I know," she said.

They walked out together, Matt holding the ax at his side. He didn't care who saw the ax. It was more important to him to have it handy and ready.

They had gone only a few steps when they heard dogs growling and snarling. Snapping teeth clicked together.

"What's that?" Gloria asked.

The ruckus was coming from somewhere between the nearby trailers. Matt moved cautiously in the direction of the sound, his ax raised, Gloria safely behind him.

He rounded the edge of a trailer and stopped cold.

Three mongrels were tearing at something that had been a man. They'd ripped away most of its stomach, and bits of flesh lay on the ground. The dogs were chewing busily. One of them stopped and turned to look at Matt, its snout bloody, its teeth bared, its eyes blazing.

"Ken," Gloria said at Matt's shoulder. "That's Ken."

The dog started toward them, and Matt turned around, taking Gloria's hand. "It's not Ken now. Come on."

Gloria let herself be led away, but she said, "We can't just leave him."

"We can't help him, and the dogs won't let us move him."

Gloria gasped. She stopped and bent over.

"Are you going to be sick?" Matt asked.

"I'll be all right," Gloria said after a couple of deep breaths and looked back at the trailers. The dogs were out of sight, but they could still be heard as they worked at the body. "Should we call the police?"

Matt shook his head. "If anything, bringing men with guns into this could make things worse."

More checkers for Mr. Dark.

They walked on in silence, Gloria holding his free hand. They went past the Ferris wheel and the carousel with their happy crowds and their merry tunes that were so out of place with what they'd just seen. Matt thought about warning everyone he saw to leave the carnival, but what good would it do? Everyone was as much a piece on the checkerboard as Matt himself. What Matt had to do was change the rules of the game.

And then it hit him.

Perhaps he already had. Just by coming here.

Matt's arrival had awakened some latent gift in Gloria, and now, in her own way, she saw the darkness that he did.

He'd gained an ally.

And a new weapon against Mr. Dark.

And even though she was frightened, she'd shown that she had the courage to act when needed.

Matt felt a small surge of hope.

The two of them headed down the midway. Matt noticed a crowd growing around the ringtoss booth. As they got closer, he heard shouting.

From a distance, Matt could see someone standing at the edge of the booth, yelling at Jerry.

It was Buford, the mark from the previous night.

Today Buford wore a long overcoat, though the day was warm. His face was red, and the veins stood out in his neck. The people nearby seemed fascinated, but they gave him plenty of room. Matt didn't blame them. He headed into the crowd just as Buford opened his coat, took out his rifle, and blasted open Jerry's stomach.

The crowd broke into a panic, nearly trampling Matt and Gloria in their hurry to get away. For some of them it was too late. Buford started picking them off. The sound of the rifle shots was almost deafening. A woman fell, then another man. People screamed. Most ran, but some stood rooted in place, shocked into paralysis.

Mr. Dark had made his move.

CHAPTER ELEVEN

Buford whirled around and fired again, missing this time. Matt could see that he wasn't aiming at any particular target. He was just making random shots, not caring who lived or died.

"Stay here," Matt told Gloria. He hefted his ax and advanced on Buford.

Matt and Gloria were so focused on Buford that neither one of them saw Serena standing at the edge of the crowd.

If Matt had seen her, he wouldn't have recognized her. She looked like a cadaver that had been in the sun for a while, her bubbling, putrid flesh dripping from her moist bones.

Just as Matt made his move on the shooter, Serena stepped up to a dark-haired woman who'd been frozen in place by the horror of the shootings. Serena took hold of her hair, pulled back her head, and slit both carotid arteries in her throat with one smooth stroke of the butcher's knife. A fan of blood arced out, splashing over two men standing near, and they suddenly discovered that they could move after all.

Serena let the woman fall and went looking for her next victim.

And saw Gloria, the bitch who had helped kill her babies.

Buford saw Matt coming and fired off a shot that singed Matt's ear as it buzzed by. Before Buford could pull the trigger again, Matt feinted to the left.

Buford tracked him with the rifle, and Matt dodged back to the right. Going in low, he punched Buford in the stomach with the head of the ax. Buford doubled over but kept hold of the rifle.

Matt stepped back and swung the ax with one hand. The blade severed bone and sinew, slicing cleanly through Buford's wrist. The hand didn't lose its grip on the rifle, however. Hand and rifle dropped together, the index finger still poked through the trigger guard. Blood pumped out of the stump of Buford's arm, but he either didn't notice or didn't care. He came at Matt, spitting and screaming.

Matt hit him in the temple with the flat of the ax, and he fell to the ground, blood still squirting from the end of his arm. Maggots seethed out of his nose, his mouth, and his ears and spread over his entire body.

Matt ignored the fallen man and was turning to look for Gloria when...

The world stopped.

No music.

No screaming.

The people became as lifeless as mannequins.

Except for Matthew Cahill, who could still move, though it was as if the air had become Jell-O.

And one person who moved with no trouble at all.

A man dressed in a tuxedo and eating an enormous wad of cotton candy.

"I love the carnival," Mr. Dark said. "So many games to choose from. Are you having fun?"

"I'm sick of the killing," Matt said.

Mr. Dark picked at his cotton candy, dropping bits in his mouth. "Well, if you aren't enjoying yourself, then you should go."

"And let you finish whatever you've started? I don't think so."

"It'd be no fun without you, Matt. Oh, look what's happened. My fingers are all sticky." He held up the fingers he'd been using to eat the cotton candy. They were sticky with sugar. "And so are yours."

Matt looked at his hands. They were spattered with blood.

Suddenly, the world came alive, like the play button had been hit on a paused video.

Matt looked up and Mr. Dark was gone.

But not the blood on Matt's hands. It must have been Buford's. He wiped them on his shirt and turned to look for Gloria.

And that's when he saw her, wide-eyed with fear.

Serena embraced Gloria from behind and held a butcher knife to her throat. Gloria stood helplessly, Buford's rifle and severed hand at her feet. Serena's face was now just a skull with some clumps of flesh sticking to the bone, her eyeballs like curdled milk.

It was not a pretty picture.

"You killed my babies," Serena said to Matt. "Now I'll kill one of yours."

Matt took a step toward her. There was no way he could stop her if she decided to slit Gloria's throat.

"Wouldn't it be better to kill me instead?" Matt said.

"You're next," she said, glaring at him.

It was in that instant, when Serena's attention was briefly focused on Matt, that Gloria acted. She jabbed Serena in the ribs with her elbow, and Serena jerked her arm away, slicing Gloria's throat, but only skin deep.

Gloria brought her foot down on Serena's instep, causing Serena to yell and drop her arms. When she did that, Gloria pushed away, turned, and threw a pretty fair right cross, catching Serena on the side of her jaw. What little flesh was left on Serena's skull flew off the bone, and her eyeballs splashed out of their sockets.

Serena stumbled back. Gloria picked up the rifle and shook it so that the dismembered hand with the finger through the trigger guard fell to the ground. Gloria put her own finger on the trigger and pulled it four or five times. The bullets tore into Serena and made her dance like a puppet. The knife fell from her hand as she jerked crazily and then fell.

The noise of the shots increased the panic of the crowd. People fled to the exit. Nobody stopped to see what was going on. Everyone just wanted to get out.

Gloria threw the rifle away from her as if it were tainted. She turned to Matt. "Look out!" she cried. "Behind you!"

Matt whirled around to see Jerry jump over the counter of his booth and start toward him, his intestines spilling out of his blown-open midsection. Jerry was holding a tent stake in one hand. Matt wondered if it was the same one that had disappeared from his pocket. Probably. That was the kind of thing Mr. Dark would have considered amusing.

"Jerry," Matt said, "you don't have to do this."

Jerry smiled and a couple of his teeth fell out. He took the stake by the tip and threw it at Matt like a knife.

Matt swatted it aside with the ax. It clanged against the blade and dropped to the ground. Matt got a fresh grip on the ax handle and moved in. Jerry didn't even try to defend himself as Matt brought the ax down and split his head. Grayish goo spilled out, and Jerry tumbled forward.

Gloria gagged, and Matt took her arm. Blood trickled down her neck onto her robes. She took a handkerchief from a pocket and held it to her throat to stop the bleeding.

"I told you it would be bad," he said.

"I knew it would be," Gloria said. "I just didn't know how bad."

"It might just be getting started," Matt said.

"It is," she said. "When Serena had her arm around me, I saw something. I saw the Ferris wheel."

"What about it?" Matt asked.

"People are going to die."

CHAPTER TWELVE

Sue Jean and Earl met at the entrance to the carnival just as the first fleeing patrons were leaving.

"Hey, Earl," Sue Jean said, ignoring the screams and panic around them. She found that she had nothing against Earl after all. "How's it hangin'?"

"Better than last night," Earl said, who wasn't pissed off at her anymore. "You ready to have some fun?"

"That's what I'm here for, but it better be the right kind of fun."

"Oh, it is," Earl said with a grin. "It is." He showed her the pistol. "See what I mean?"

"A pistol? Is that all?"

"It's enough," Earl said. "Watch this."

He fired the pistol at a man who was running along with a child in his arms. The bullet hit the man in the knee. He screamed, dropped the child, and fell to the ground, clutching his knee. Blood seeped between his fingers.

Sue Jean shrugged. "Is that all?"

"No way," Earl said. "I think we can really fuck this place up. You gonna come along or not?"

"Why not?" Sue Jean said, and they strolled through the crowd as if it didn't exist. Earl reached out and took Sue

Jean's hand. She smiled at him. "You really think we can do some damage?"

"You just wait," Earl said. "You'll see."

The carnival was so noisy, full of music and bells and shrieks and pops, and the crowd so large and dense, that the bloodbath at the ringtoss and the shooting at the entry had gone largely unheard and unnoticed. The shots had been drowned out and the horrified screams blended into those from the rides. Word of the shootings and deaths had yet to sweep through attendees, but the panic was certainly spreading and soon it would be pandemonium.

Matt and Gloria were heading toward the back of the park, where the Ferris wheel and most of the other rides were, when he saw Sue Jean and Earl, thirty yards away, passing through the crowd like two salmon swimming upstream.

Even from a distance, Matt could see the swarm of blowflies following them.

They were walking dead.

He pointed them out to Gloria. "See those two?"

"Yes," she said. "They're death."

And moving toward the rides.

He headed after them and Gloria followed. But it wasn't easy. People eager to get to the rides themselves bumped them, shoved them, and cursed them for trying to get ahead.

Nobody seemed to notice Matt's ax or the blood that was dripping from the blade onto the dirt.

Earl and Sue Jean reached the rides. The carousel music was "In the Good Old Summertime," and people were smiling and having a good time, completely unaware of what was happening at the other end of the carnival.

The Ferris wheel creaked in its circle, the cars swaying, some more than others as the occupants tried to scare each other.

Small airplanes swung out from their center pole at the ends of strong chains, each plane holding a couple of happy kids.

Earl felt power surge through him, as if he were hooked up to the big generator that sent electricity to the rides. He felt taller than the Ferris wheel and wondered if he would just burst right out of his clothes. He looked at Sue Jean to see if she'd noticed the change.

She hadn't. "This isn't fun. I'm bored."

"You won't be bored long," Earl said. "I told you we were gonna fuck this place up. I won't even need my pistol."

To prove he wasn't lying, he extended his arm and pointed at the airplanes. As the crowd watched, the planes began to gain speed. Slowly at first, but then faster and faster until they were spinning so rapidly that they were almost a blur. The cheerful sound of the carousel was drowned out by the screaming of children and their parents, along with the whine of the chains cutting the air and the squealing of the big generator.

Sue Jean hugged Earl and laughed. He felt better than when he'd shot Harry and George.

"I told you you wouldn't be bored," he said.

"Do more," Sue Jean said. "Do more."

Earl wasn't sure at first that he could, but power welled up inside him and he pointed to the carousel, which, like the airplanes, began to pick up speed. More screams as children clung to the horses' necks and to the poles that ran through them. A man ran to get his child off the horse, but the carousel was going too fast. He managed to jump on, but the whirling carousel flung him right back off. He skidded across the ground and lay still.

Sue Jean clapped her hands. Earl sure knew how to show a girl a good time.

"Do the bumper cars!"

Earl did the bumper cars, which began whizzing around the ring entirely out of the control of the young drivers. They banged into each other with such force that their front ends were flattened.

Sue Jean laughed, but her laughter died almost at once.

"Nobody's killed," she said. "Why isn't anybody killed?"

"You want somebody killed?"

"All of them," Sue Jean said. "All of them."

"Pick a ride," he said, being generous and eager to show off his newfound powers.

"The Ferris wheel," Sue Jean said. "Do the Ferris wheel."

"Not a good idea," Matt said, yelling to be heard above the panicking crowd, the zinging chains, the howl of the straining generator, and the screams of the riders, as he advanced on the couple.

Sue Jean and Earl didn't seem surprised by his appearance. Matt saw the decay in their faces as they turned to him. Earl brought up the pistol and leveled it at Gloria, who was coming up behind Matt.

"The asshole from last night," Earl said.

Sue Jean giggled and poked Earl in the ribs with her finger.

Earl grinned and said to Matt, "Things are different now. You'd better stop where you are. I'll shoot your girlfriend if you don't."

Matt didn't doubt that Earl would do it. He stopped. He hoped that someone in the milling crowd would jump Earl and take the pistol. Nobody did.

"After I kill her," Earl said, "I think I'll tear loose that Ferris wheel and let it roll through the midway."

"Do it," Sue Jean said. "Do it."

"Goddamn right," Earl said, but he was distracted by the airplane ride, where the noise had increased even more as the planes began to whirl ever faster, the chains stretched out almost parallel to the ground.

One of the chains snapped with a metallic twang as the links separated. The plane flew. Not like a real plane. Its wings were too stubby for that, but it had plenty of speed. It buzzed over the heads of the terrified crowd and slammed into the carousel like a bomb. Pieces of horses and poles exploded outward.

"Look, look!" Sue Jean said, clapping her hands. "Now do the Ferris wheel!"

Earl smiled, and the Ferris wheel began to turn faster. The screams of the riders were drowned out by the creaking of the wheel, the roar of the airplanes, the whir of the carousel, the high-pitched whine of the generator, and the screams of everyone else.

Matt didn't want to kill Sue Jean and Earl. But they were as good as dead already, puppets of Mr. Dark now. They'd lost any humanity they'd once possessed.

Earl's attention turned from the Ferris wheel back to Matt and Gloria. It was as if he knew that Matt was about to make a move. If he did, he wasn't bothered. Instead of killing Gloria, he started to fire his pistol at random into the crowd.

Matt charged forward. He felt rather than saw Gloria move too. He didn't know what she was up to, and he didn't have time to worry about it.

Earl had saved one bullet for him, but as his finger tightened on the trigger, Matt swung the ax in a short arc and knocked the pistol from his hand.

Earl smiled and raised his arms. The Ferris wheel spun so fast that it was almost a blur. Still smiling, Earl lowered his arms and started to say something to Matt.

Whatever it might have been, he didn't get it out. Matt swung the ax again and took Earl's head right off his shoulders.

The head bounced across the ground and stopped near the carousel. Because of the confusion and destruction there, no one even noticed it.

Earl's torso fell forward and lay still. Matt looked around for Sue Jean.

She was struggling across the muddy ground, reaching for the pistol. Her progress was slowed by the fact that Gloria was on her back, pulling her head up by the hair.

It was a convenient pose, and Matt didn't waste it. Sue Jean looked up as Matt reached her. He swung the ax like a baseball bat, hitting her in the center of her forehead with the butt. Her forehead caved in like cardboard, shoving splinters of bone into her brain.

Gloria jumped aside and stood up, a horrified look on her face as she brushed brain matter off her robes.

Matt kept right on going. Earl's death hadn't changed anything as far as the rides were concerned. They still spun wildly out of control, and Matt had to stop them. All four were connected to one large generator, which was now howling with the strain. Matt's plan was to cut the cables.

The cables were as thick as Matt's arm, but he knew his ax would cut them, dull though it might be when the job was done.

He chopped through the first cable. Sparks flew and the carousel music died. The smell of burning insulation filled the air. The second stroke stopped the Ferris wheel, the third stopped the airplanes, and the fourth took care of the bumper cars. Most people rushed to rescue their children and to help with the injured. A few yelled into their cell phones.

Matt threw the switch on the generator, and the noise level decreased further.

It was over.

He looked at Gloria for confirmation of what he was feeling and she nodded. He trusted her senses.

Matt could now hear the sirens of police cars in the distance, drawing near. He wasn't inclined to stick around and see what happened when the police arrived. There would be too much explaining to do, too many corpses.

He took her hand and headed for the trailers.

CHAPTER THIRTEEN

When they got inside his trailer, he closed the door and grabbed his duffel bag.

"What are you doing?" she asked.

"Changing out of these bloody clothes, getting what little I've got, and leaving," he said, and stripped off his shirt.

"You saved the carnival, Matt, and countless lives. You're a hero. You don't have to run."

"You don't get it," he said, tossing the bloody shirt and putting on a new one from his duffel bag. "When I'm around, people die. And they don't die easy. If I stay, this is only the beginning. There will be more death. It's better if I leave and draw Mr. Dark away from here before that happens."

"What if he *wants* you to leave?"

Matt looked at her and thought about what Mr. Dark had said to him in that short, frozen moment.

It'd be no fun without you, Matt.

He hadn't had time to stop and think about it before.

But now…He got the message.

It was Matt being there that had brought the carnage upon the carnival.

And Mr. Dark was offering to go if Matt would too.

A truce, of sorts.

But why?

"Because of what you being here has brought out in me," Gloria said as if reading his thoughts. Then again, she probably was. "Maybe this gift of mine scares him."

"It's not a gift," Matt said. "It's a curse."

It was now painfully clear to Matt that Mr. Dark had set out to destroy the carnival and kill as many people as he could...just to show Matt what it would cost him to stay with Gloria, to continue to imbue her with powers with his presence.

He'd given Matt a vision of the future.

And it was soaked with blood.

And it would be Matt's fault.

Oh, look what's happened. My fingers are all sticky...and so are yours.

"If you stay, between your sight and mine, you'd be twice as powerful against him," Gloria said. "Together, we might be able to beat him."

"Or I can go," Matt said, "and perhaps your visions will go away too."

He could save her from his fight, from his fate.

And Mr. Dark gets what he wants...

"Or I can go with you," she said, but without much conviction.

But Matt had made his decision, not one based on winning or losing.

"What you saw today, what you experienced, I've gone through before. Again and again. I've killed so many people I've lost count. I carry that with me every day." Matt wiped the blood off his blade with his dirty shirt and shoved the ax into his bag. "*That's* the curse. I wouldn't wish that on anyone."

"It's my choice," she said.

"No, it's not," Matt said and gave her a kiss on the cheek. "I'm sorry I brought this horror into your life. I hope now that it's gone for good. Take care of yourself."

He picked up the bag and walked out the door. She stood in the doorway of his trailer and looked after him.

And as he walked away, she felt the darkness lifting and she whispered her gratitude to him for leaving her behind.

Matt stuck to the side streets and, over the next few hours, made his way to the edge of town. There was a truck stop just inside the town limits, but he walked on past and down the moonlit two-lane highway. He wasn't looking for company or even for a ride.

But he felt a presence beside him nonetheless.

"I'm going to beat you," Matt said, staring at the seemingly endless ribbon of road ahead.

"How are you going to do that if you fold your hand before all the cards are dealt?" Mr. Dark asked.

"By changing the rules of the game."

Mr. Dark laughed. "You don't even know what game you're playing."

"So tell me," Matt said.

But he didn't get an answer.

He knew he wouldn't get it from Mr. Dark. But it was out there, somewhere.

And he would find it.

ABOUT THE AUTHORS

Lee Goldberg is a two-time Edgar Award–nominated author and TV producer. His many books include *The Walk*, *Watch Me Die*, and the bestselling *Monk* series of original mystery novels. His TV writing and producing credits include *SeaQuest*, *Diagnosis Murder*, *Monk*, and *The Glades*. He's also worked as a consultant for networks and studios throughout Europe, Canada, and Sweden and has served on the Board of the Mystery Writers of America.

William Rabkin is a two-time Edgar Award nominee who writes the *Psych* series of novels and is the author of *Writing the Pilot*. He has consulted for studios in Canada, Germany, and Spain on television series production and teaches screenwriting at UCLA Extension. He is also an adjunct professor at the UC Riverside's low-residency master's program.

James Daniels is a labor organization attorney who performed Shakespeare in London, received a Grammy nomination for his audio book narration, and wrote the hardboiled noir mystery *Ghost Bride*. He and his family live in the Midwest.

Jude Hardin holds a BA in English from the University of Louisville and currently works as a registered nurse in a major urban medical center in North Florida. When he's not pounding away at the computer keyboard, Hardin can be found pounding away on his drums, playing tennis, reading, or down at the pond fishing with his son.

Bill Crider was born in Mexia, Texas. He attended the University of Texas at Austin, where he received a PhD in English. After teaching in public schools and at the college level for many years, he retired to write full time. The author of over seventy-five novels and an equal number of short stories, Bill is credited by Dead Man creators Lee Goldberg and William Rabkin as a major influence on their series.